D0857623

*The Divine Comedy of
Ariadne and Jupiter*

SHERE HITE

The Divine Comedy of
ARIADNE AND JUPITER

*The Amazing and Spectacular Adventures of
Ariadne and Her Dog Jupiter
in Heaven and on Earth*

PETER OWEN
London & Chester Springs PA

With the exception of historical figures, all characters in *The Divine Comedy of Ariadne and Jupiter* are entirely fictitious.

PETER OWEN PUBLISHERS
73 Kenway Road London SW5 0RE

Peter Owen books are distributed in the USA by
Dufour Editions Inc. Chester Springs PA19425 – 0449

This edition first published in Great Britain 1994
© Shere Hite 1994

A catalogue record for this book is available from the British Library

ISBN 0 – 7206 – 0917 – 8

Printed in Great Britain by Biddles of Guildford and King's Lynn

Contents

★

vii

Cast of Characters

Principals

Ariadne
Jupiter
Cleopatra
Friedrich
Kate
Assorted Media Personalities

Cameo Appearances

Harry Truman	Clara Schumann
Marx	Wanda Landowska
Lenin	Martin Luther King
Gertrude Stein	Marilyn Monroe
Voltaire	John F. Kennedy
Dante	Herr Herrhausen
Virgil	Alexis de Tocqueville
Mme de Pompadour	Eva Braun and Hitler
Fala, FDR's dog	Thomas Paine
George Orwell	Pope Pius IX (Pio Nono)
Arsinöe, Frederic the	Andy Warhol
Great's dog	Alfred Hitchcock
Rosa Luxemburg	Carole Lombard
Queen Catherine the	Isis
Great of Russia	Athena
Sappho	Hypatia
Sergei Prokofiev	Assorted Others

Prologue

They were drifting through the atmosphere, floating towards Earth, looking with curiosity at the bright, luminous colours – blue all around, a warm golden haze coming from above, and green grass, flowers and birds of all colours stretching out below them.

Ariadne and Jupiter were singing together as they drifted along, a song they had invented about the beauty of the white spots on Jupiter's furry arms, his lovely, blond, palomino fur.

Suddenly, Jupiter exclaimed, 'Look, Ariadne!'

'Oh, how beautiful! Let's see what's down there!'

They landed with a plop on the soft green grass.

Ariadne and Jupiter played for a while, running here and there. Jupiter spied a particularly large butterfly with brilliant orange wings tinged with elegant velvet black markings, which was flying rapidly across the field, always with a new and fascinatingly irregular pattern. Jupiter loved to race, and he and the butterfly wore each other out, dashing to a small tulip tree, going round it and coming back again.

Ariadne watched Jupiter as he raced, his ears flying in the breeze. She loved it when he turned his head, looking back at her, smiling, his brown eyes dancing, his pink tongue flopping jauntily out of the corner of his mouth. He had the most charming way of prancing round in different tempos – a brisk walk, a rapid trot, or he could dash crazily, full speed ahead, all caution thrown to the winds. For spectacular moments, he would leap several feet up into the air, turn somersaults with wild abandon, all the while yelping, gypsy-style! He was the most graceful, elegant and witty dog that ever existed.

After a while, Jupiter flopped down panting and happy next to Ariadne on the grass. There they reclined, enjoying the cool breezes and light blue sky. Ariadne tilted her head so that the warmth of the late afternoon sun caressed her pale delicate face and glinted off the soft curls on her head like a burnished golden halo. She ran her hand contentedly over Jupiter's warm fur. They decided that Earth was a rather lovely place.

However, so spellbound were they that they didn't notice the evening quickly approaching. Together, they watched the magnificent display of ever-changing colours, culminating in a glowing golden orb which sank slowly into the pink, blue and salmon horizon – their first Earth sunset.

Just as they were thinking it was about time to go home, they began to feel sleepy. But since they had never 'slept' before, they didn't know what this new feeling was. They didn't understand that 'Sleep' is a state of consciousness peculiar to the inhabitants of Earth, and that now it was affecting them too. Or that this Sleep, for them, would be the Transformation that led to something they had not yet experienced – Life on Earth.

Looking at each other with puzzled expressions, they lay down side by side, nestling together, their eyes slowly closing. They fell asleep there on the soft green grass, underneath a little bush. Twilight fell.

The next morning, when they awoke, they looked at each other in dismay: 'Oh, no! Now we've done it! We're late! They're sure to have noticed we're gone by now! What shall we do?'

They thought back to yesterday morning. It had been such a bright sunny day, the sun spilling its creamy rays across the heavens. Everyone had been gathering to watch the giant baseball game in Heaven. Ariadne and Jupiter were playing nearby, tossing a Frisbee back and forth. But somehow they had been feeling strangely restless. Sure, they could go to the game, but to tell the truth, they were a little bored; they wanted to do something *different*.

Lacking her usual concentration, Ariadne only noticed the Frisbee Jupiter sent her way as it whizzed past her, too late to catch. As she raced to pick it up, she nearly ran into Her Majesty Catherine, Empress of All the Russias (looking quite Great that day). Although normally wary of reporters, Catherine was strolling arm in arm with Dorothy Parker, who was interviewing her for a special newspaper article.

'Love on Earth?' Catherine confided to Dorothy, 'Ah, it was superb. The feelings were very intense. But the men . . . the men! It seemed they didn't understand a thing sometimes. . . . So disappointing, my dear!'

Ariadne wasn't interested in these things yet, so she didn't even bother to listen to Dorothy's reply. Talk, talk, talk, she thought. I want to have an adventure!

Jupiter must have read her mind. 'I've got an idea! Let's go flying! We could take off while no one is looking and be back before they miss us!' His tail was wagging excitedly.

'They told us not to; we're not old enough, we don't have any experience. But . . .' she looked at him mischievously. . . .

'I can fly and I'm strong enough for both of us! Come on, I'll take you.'

Ariadne looked thrilled. 'Let's go!'

Off they went, Ariadne's cheek against Jupiter's warm neck, the wind in their faces, looking forward together and smiling with excitement as they flew off into the UNKNOWN!

And now, here they were.

'Well-l-l,' said Ariadne, playfully, 'now that we're here . . . shouldn't we at least look around?' Her clear blue eyes sparkled mischievously. 'We're already late. What difference will it make to be a little bit later?'

Jupiter grinned his super devil-may-care grin. 'Yeah, since we're already in trouble, why not?' He turned a cartwheel in the air.

And this was the beginning of a long adventure. . . .

First Day on Earth

★

So they took off, flying low around the planet, checking it out. Beyond the countryside, beyond the beautiful green fields, they saw people, millions of people, some practising sports, some driving their automobiles, some kissing and embracing, others working. Some had all they needed to eat, while others, entire nations, were starving and dying of plagues and malnutrition. How could this be? After all, those with more than enough could just share with those who had none.

The more they saw, the more confused they became and the more questions they had.

They flew across emerald-green seas, the sunlight glinting like jewels on the waves, and still further on, they came to lighter, more serene turquoise lakes with small pleasure boats – how lovely! But a few miles on . . . what's that? There were seals dying on the beaches and dolphins, beautiful dolphins, committing suicide, their graceful bodies lying dead in silent testimony on the sand.

Ariadne and Jupiter wept in sadness. They looked at each other and decided to land on Earth once more, to see things close up. They wanted to ask the people and the animals what was going on.

The two walked through the streets of Earth, through miles and miles of cities: there was a feeling of violence and anger in many places, depression and cynicism in others. People were taking aspirin and lots of other things. When they asked the animals why, they said they didn't know exactly, but one thing for sure, they would never cover all the grass over with a thick layer of grey goo that became hard and ugly – concrete – then

12

look at it and declare it 'great'!

But Ariadne and Jupiter fell in love with other things on Earth. They were entranced by the small bright flowers called pansies, which bloomed in every rich, intense colour possible – yellow, purple, brown and black. Their soft, velvety jewel-faces shone up at Ariadne and Jupiter, glowing with life – it seemed they might speak at any moment. Butterflies liked the pansies too, and hovered round them – what butterflies were left, that is. Ariadne and Jupiter learned that in a country called Holland the first butterfly conservation park had been established.

Wandering happily along a path through the pansies, they came to a sign saying 'The Park'. They entered what seemed to be a large green area in the middle of the city. Jupiter, sniffing the cool, leafy air, bounded on ahead, twirling cartwheels in delight. Just as he was working up to full steam, he ran head on into a jogger wearing a red and white head-to-toe suit. The jogger was huffing and puffing with a lugubrious expression – as much of his expression as could be seen through his mole-type face mask.

After the near-collision with Jupiter, the jogger spied Ariadne. 'Hey! You'd better not let your dog exercise like that. This is a yellow-alert day! Take him home, or get a mask for him!' And he ran off, while Ariadne called after him, 'Yellow-alert day? What's a yellow-alert day??' Really irritated, the jogger stopped and turned back, 'Air pollution, of course! You can't breathe the air without injuring yourself. Unless you take scientific precautions like I do. . . .' And satisfied with his statement, the jogger took off again.

Ariadne looked at Jupiter. Could this be true? Maybe it was only true at *this* place in *this* park – so they rushed on in the other direction, to get away from it, the yellow perilous It. They left the park, and came to a large shopping street.

Like sightseers anywhere, they strolled down the street looking at the people and the enticing displays in store windows. Crowds of elaborately dressed men and women clattered and clicked past them, coming and going, chatting and laughing, in and out of the stores. They seemed to be having a heavenly time, so heavenly that Jupiter and Ariadne soon got into the spirit of things, and began breezing in and out of shops, too. But they noticed that there were others, people along the sides of the streets dressed in old, shabby clothes, who walked slowly, separate from the throng, glancing almost furtively at them, not laughing at all. One was sleeping over an air vent in the street, face hidden. As people stepped around the huddled figure to pass, they seemed relieved. Jupiter and Ariadne learned that this was because the person's face was hidden, and the passers-by knew they would not be asked for any 'spare change'.

Jupiter and Ariadne couldn't get over the contrast – so much good and so much bad! It was confusing. . . .

One final curiosity they observed was that Earth is divided by gender. Those who could reproduce were required to work twice as hard, both outside and inside their homes, as those who could not. However, they were not given greater status and respect because of this, just the reverse! They were seen as inferior. They were not allowed to run governments, large corporations, or to be in charge of the groups that collect and disseminate information ('the news'). Ariadne decided to ask women how they felt about this.

Despite these unnerving observations, however, Jupiter and Ariadne were enjoying themselves enormously, catching the afternoon sunlight as they strolled along, happy to be together on their adventure. . . .

In a store window they now passed, they saw a screen with moving pictures of the people in the street . . . in fact, themselves!

'What's that?' Ariadne asked someone passing by.

'TV, of course,' he replied, not pausing.

'TV . . .?! . . . Jupiter, look! There you are! And me!'

They both practised waving at themselves on the screen, watching themselves wave back. Then they noticed a sign: 'Show Today! Live Audience Needed. Enter Next Door!'

In fact, there was a long line of people waiting outside the next adjoining building. As they approached the queue, they heard snatches of excited conversation about the TV show.

'Wait until they see me back home! This is the Number One show on television! I'm so excited!'

'Why are you excited?' Ariadne asked; she and Jupiter looked blank.

'What?! Why, television is the most important thing on Earth!

Everybody knows that! Everything that really matters is on TV: the people who really count, the people who know what is going on behind the scenes, secrets of the rich and famous. The Truth of the News! On TV, you find out what's going on; the news tells you! Oh, what a great democracy we have!'

Jupiter and Ariadne weren't sure they wanted to get all their truth from one place, but the waving game had been a lot of fun. This TV thing seemed pretty intriguing, so they joined the queue. While they waited patiently under the hot sun with the others, a conversation started up. 'Where you from?' people asked each other. Some were from Texas, some from Nebraska, two from New Jersey, three from Kentucky. When they asked Jupiter and Ariadne, who had been notably silent, where they were from, Ariadne managed to duck the question. 'Oh, we've been visiting here since yesterday. Quite a place you've got. Unusual. Say, are you sure TV is so important? We're beginning to think this is too long to wait in any queue.'

'But our participation in TV is important! TV is one of the pillars of democracy.'

'What is democracy?' Ariadne asked.

Somewhat surprised at this question, a woman exclaimed, 'Why, that's what makes this country great.' Poor girl, she must be one of those new refugees from The East.

Ariadne still looked uncomprehending, so the woman elaborated. 'It's wonderful here. We have a democracy and you can say anything you want. People here think for themselves.'

'Who else would think for them?' Ariadne wondered, feeling confused.

'Yes, and democracy is great because it means equality. . . .'

'Equality?'

'Sure, men and women, blacks and whites, everybody has the same rights,' said the woman with great pride.

'Where we come from there isn't any word for this, since it's automatic. But I've noticed some strange things here on Earth. Like –' and Ariadne looked particularly amazed, 'Do you know that in some countries, even here, people are addressed with prefixes before their names which identify them by genital anatomy?! "Mr Smith" means genitally male person, "Ms Smith" means genitally female person, and "Mrs Smith" means genitally

15

female person who is officially understood to be having sex with Mr Smith; "Miss Smith" means genitally female person not yet having sex (?), or in a respectable family.'

Ariadne and Jupiter laughed until tears came to their eyes at such barbaric references to genital identity. Jupiter wondered how "Mr Jupiter" would sound.

The women looked startled, and didn't know whether to turn away from people who would make such impolite references to genitals – or to stare at them in fascination.

'Asks a lot of questions, don't she?' one of the men muttered to another.

Ariadne, happily oblivious, continued thinking out loud, 'And it's strange too, the way people can be so aggressive with the other animals. It's like they don't think they have *any* rights.' (Jupiter had not seen any other animals talking since he had been there, so he decided to keep his snozzle shut, and let Ariadne do all the talking.)

The woman looked more confused, so Ariadne added politely, 'Well, of course, people are animals too.'

The woman, now highly suspicious (what was she dealing with?) remarked rather defensively, 'But women *do* have the right to equal pay. It's their own fault if they don't get it. As for animals, my dear, I'm sure you take very good care of your little dog, but would you trust him to elect your president? No, my child, believe me, this is the Best of All Possible Democracies.'

How very curious! Ariadne thought. But now the queue was beginning to move.

'Good afternoon, ladies and gentlemen! And here's your host, the man whose name is always a greeting. Ha-a-al Low!'

The small band of musicians played a wild fanfare and the audience cheered and clapped as a man with dark wavy hair ran on-stage, smiling and bowing in all directions.

'Hello, hello, hello. It's just great to see you all here on this beautiful day. Yessiree, it's a glorious day and I'm going to start today's fun-filled show by talking to some people in the audience. Now, I wonder if we have any visitors to our fair city in the audience today? Just raise your hand! Yessiree, that pretty little lady over there!' He pointed to Ariadne.

16

A man with a microphone ran to her side, as Hal Low chattered on. 'And tell me, my dear, what do you think of this fine city of ours? Have you been here long? Isn't it just grand?'

Ariadne thought it was very nice that they wanted to know her opinion, here in this place where you could say anything you wanted – so she began to speak up. 'I've only just arrived, and it is grand! You really have a beautiful place here – shining blue lakes, cheerful birds, huge spreading trees and all kinds of colours – it's magic! But what I want to ask you is, why are so many people unhappy? Are some of them hungry? Why are the animals on chains and leashes, and behind fences? Is there a yellow-alert everywhere, or just in the park? Don't you think it's awfully authoritarian here? Things are not enough fun!'

And she and Jupiter began to chant, 'We want more fun! More fun! More fun!'

Suddenly there was a huge uproar, a commercial for air freshener was slammed on, and she and Jupiter were rushed out of the studio. The once-smiling Hal Low snarled and his producers hissed at Ariadne and Jupiter: 'What's the matter with you? Whaddya think you're doing? Are you crazy or something? From another planet? Need psychiatric treatment?'

'But I thought in this democracy everybody had a right to their opinion, everybody could say what they wanted to. . . .' Ariadne said over her shoulder.

'Yeah, but you're too much. Troublemakers like you who rock the boat usually end up overboard!'

And a woman all in black leaned very close to Ariadne and uttered the chilling words: 'You'd better watch out, My Pretty! Or you'll find yourself in Big Trouble – you, and your little dog too!'

Outside, Ariadne and Jupiter stared at each other in shocked surprise, then burst out giggling.

'Did you see that??!'

'Heaven was never like this!'

'Oh,' Ariadne said, 'this is too much! Maybe we should just go home!'

'Do you want to?'

'Well, let's go sit down on the grass right now. I'm tired!'

So they went back to the park. But soon it began to get dark, and Jupiter felt anxious. 'Shouldn't we go, Ariadne? It's getting dark.'

But Ariadne was writing something in a little red notebook. 'Just wait a minute, Jupiter. I want to get this down.'

'OK, I'll wait. . . .'

Too late. Now it was very dark and, amazingly enough, they were sleepy again! What to do? Get an apartment? A room to sleep? But for two creatures like Ariadne and Jupiter . . . with no references?? . . . Well, fortune shone on them, and before they knew it, they were firmly in bed in their own cozy little apartment.

The days were slow and languid now. Jupiter and Ariadne especially loved the afternoons, when they played in the park with a red Frisbee they had bought at the supermarket. It matched Jupiter's red collar (on Earth all dogs have to wear collars). They went for hot dogs (artificial ingredients, of course!) and ice cream at a stand near the zoo. Jupiter considered 'hot dogs' a real tribute. They enjoyed taking long walks, watching the leafy green trees swaying in the breezes, hearing the birds sing, and talking to each other.

In the evenings, they sat at home on the couch and listened to music. Their favourites were choral pieces like *Der Rosenkavalier* and *Tristan und Isolde* (with Kirsten Flagstad). Ariadne would often tease Jupiter affectionately by running a playful finger down his head, then back up – all the way from his wet black ball-nose tip on up, up, up, to between his eyes, back over his forehead – to wind up patting his head while he smiled up with his big brown eyes, his head bobbing. Sometimes Ariadne would whisper, 'My Angel. You are so adorable.' And Jupiter would purr happily in accompaniment, nudging his head closer, his eyes full of bliss. They could dream together like this for hours, playing all kinds of games they made up, snuggling and cuddling.

On other evenings, Ariadne would take a long bath, very warm and steamy. Jupiter (who preferred not to immerse himself) sat on the floor on a small green rug to keep her company; beautiful perfumed oil from a place called Floris scented the room.

Even though they were far from home, here they felt at home. It was a deep, satisfying feeling.

Most evenings, Ariadne wrote in her red notebook. She was writing down everything they had seen: the people sleeping on the streets in cardboard boxes, the splendid houses, the art museum, the dirty pavement patched over hundreds of times with different blobby grey masses (the animals said only one-third of the planet was left untouched by human enterprise), the garbage floating in the rivers and seas, the pansies, the wonderful people and the awful people.

'What does it all mean?' she asked. 'Oh, Jupiter, why do you think some people want to control and dominate all the others?'

Jupiter, just as perplexed (he shared her love of questions), reflected on this. 'Most of the trouble on Earth seems to come from that aggressive way of looking at things. . . .'

'Do you think it's inevitable? "Natural"? If I write about how unnecessary it is, will it make a difference?'

'Hmmm . . . yes . . . and you could even talk on TV about what you wrote! That's how it's done on Earth, isn't it?'

Earth: Act I

★

Earth-TV Meets The Meaning of It All

After a few weeks of asking more and more questions, Ariadne took her small red book to a publisher.

'We like your red book, my dear – but the Marketing Chiefs always make the final decision about writers. They want to know how you'll be on TV. But don't worry,' he reassured her, 'you're young, you're white and you're female!'

Some months later, Ariadne found herself getting ready for her First Big Chance on TV.

Jupiter lay under the couch, his head stretched out in front of him between his paws, Egyptian Middle Dynasty dogstyle. Only his nose protruded into the room. He could just see (peering between the fringes on the bottom of the couch) Ariadne walking to and fro, as she got dressed for the television appearance.

Remembering her first, naïve experience on TV, Ariadne was determined to make her point today with more sophistication. She had watched enough TV to know how to do it. You had to wear a suit, so she had bought a navy blue one, and combed her hair to look very 'adult'. But she was nervous. Jupiter was nervous too, and the small black antennae above his expressive brown eyes twitched agitatedly, punctuating his eye movements.

Ariadne stopped in front of the mirror to make a few last minute adjustments to her long red-golden hair, then turned, as the door opened. It was Kate.

Ariadne and Jupiter had first met Kate when they were visiting the sea-lions at the zoo in the park. At first Ariadne thought Kate's short, dishevelled, dishwater-blond hair was a mistake, that she hadn't combed it that morning. Then, when she saw Kate's green eyes peeking out from under her uneven fringe, and noticed her orange fishnet stockings and turquoise shoes, she knew this was not a matter of chance! She decided it would definitely be fun to talk to this person, and soon they had become fast friends; Kate had decided to help Ariadne while she finished her book. Jupiter adored Kate too. She threw a mean Frisbee.

'I came by to wish you good luck!' Kate said, adding, 'Your hair is getting long. I like it.'

'Yeah,' Ariadne smiled, tossing her head shyly. 'What a miracle it looks right today. Hair is very important for women on television, I've heard. I've read that the better your hair, the higher the ratings.'

'Don't worry,' Kate assured her. 'Yours looks great!' Then Kate put a copy of *The Meaning of It All,* Ariadne's red book, right in the middle of the coffee table, so that the TV crew couldn't miss it. 'Let's have a cup of coffee while we wait, Ariadne.'

Jupiter came out from under the couch to sit with them, ready to socialize and schmooze. He had to restrain himself from barking out loud when he heard Kate first address Ariadne as 'Ms Rite'; it sounded so funny to him – but Kate explained the necessity of having a surname: 'Calling you just Ariadne would make you sound like a child,' she said. 'There are a few people who go by their first name only, like Cher, and there is Sappho, of course. But trust me, you'll get better PR with a last name.' So Jupiter had suggested 'Rite' because Kate kept saying, 'You're right!' to so many things Ariadne had written about Earth. Spelling wasn't his strong point, but Kate said 'Rite' had more flair than 'Right' anyway, so Ariadne Rite it was.

They started chatting about Kate's social life. Ariadne asked, 'How was last night? Did he show up?'

'Late – very late!' Kate threw one of her adorable wry smiles at Ariadne, then added, 'We made up, of course!' They both laughed.

Then the doorbell rang. . . .

'Hi, I'm Susan Power, the producer, pleased to meetchya. This is Pat Prying. He's going to be on camera with you. Just you and your little dog sit right there at the side of this desk and we're ready to roll.'

Ariadne was impressed. This network must really be progressive, having a black woman as the producer. They must realize how important women's issues are. They're really trying to do the Right Thing.

'Ms Rite, we understand you've crisscrossed the country with your dog, Jupiter, interviewing people. Now in your book, *The Meaning of It All*, you say that humans are too aggressive – that they are unfair to animals. You even say that the majority of women are unhappy. Why is that?'

'That is not exactly what women told me, they didn't say they are unhappy (what a cliché)! What they said was – '

'Oh, now you're saying they're not unhappy? Changing your story, are you?'

'You didn't let me finish. I was about to explain – '

'Were you still speaking? Sorry, I didn't hear. Well, say what you mean.'

' . . . that women are frustrated with trying to build better relationships with the men in their lives,' Ariadne continued patiently. 'They want a man who will listen and talk, have a real conversation. Eighty-eight percent said that if he picks up his socks, too,' Ariadne smiled, radiantly, 'so much the better.'

'Psst! Ms Rite,' an off-stage voice whispered, 'not so many big words please. Let's keep it simple. Go on, Pat.'

'Well, Ms Rite, would you be surprised to hear that we've conducted our own poll and that's not the way women feel? Just look at this!' He held out his hand and a sheaf of papers appeared in a flash.

'My goodness,' Ariadne replied, startled, 'I am surprised. I haven't seen that before.'

'Well, here you are,' he chuckled, pleased with the effect, and handed her the papers. 'Now, what do you say?'

Reading quickly, Ariadne replied, 'But you didn't ask the same questions I did.'

'That's right! And we got different answers too! Isn't that amazing? And look at these results to our sex survey,' Pat enthused, another set of papers appearing in his hands. 'We found that hardly any of the women we spoke to are having extramarital affairs!'

'That's getting very far afield from the point of my book, but how did you find that?'

'Why, we called them up and asked them!'

'You can't be serious!' Ariadne laughed, wondering how on Earth this could be happening. 'Do you mean to tell me you called women up on the telephone and asked them if they were having extramarital sex? Good grief! What time of day did you call? Were they alone? Why did they agree to answer? Were they paid to participate? Were the women's husbands or children present when they were called? I'm surprised they didn't hang up on you!'

'Well, as a matter of fact, some of them did. Not at all well mannered if you ask me. Excuse me, could you look towards the camera again?'

'What?'

'The camera, Ms Rite. You're not looking at it and –'

'You're not still filming, are you?'

'Sure, we want your reaction to our poll.'

'My reaction?! You can't mean it. You haven't even given me a chance to read it, and you want me to react, right here, on camera? Why don't you stop and let me look it over?'

'Why do you need to read it? I've told you what it says.' Pat sounded irritated and impatient.

'But,' Ariadne said, 'this is like what women told me: men don't want to listen to what they have to say. I think I'd better talk to Ms Power.' Jupiter sighed, fearing the worst.

'Yes, Ms Rite. What can I do for you?'

'Please stop your camera and tell me what's going on. I agreed to do this interview so I could discuss environmental problems as well as women's assessment of what is going on and –'

'Well, we don't think our viewers are interested in the environment, and we have mentioned your book.'

Jupiter groaned.

23

'Yes, Mr Prying mentioned the title, but there's been no discussion of what it's really about. Instead I'm being told my conclusions are wrong, according to you. You don't stop to analyse what I or the women are saying!'

'Well, of course,' Sue Power replied soothingly. 'This is American Reality Commercial TV, you know. We're here to entertain people and keep the sponsors happy. We could hardly discuss your book in detail, could we? Now that that's clear, tell us something juicy about sex, Ms Rite? Ms Rite, come back!'

Ariadne and Jupiter were so glad when the TV people left that as they closed the door, they both sighed almost simultaneously with relief. Ariadne slumped onto the couch, staring into space, Jupiter shook himself off and sat close to her, trying to comfort her with his presence.

In a little while there was a knock on the door, and Kate walked back in.

'How did it go?' she asked, bright-eyed and expectant.

'It was an ambush!' Ariadne said with a little cry of pain. 'They were never really interested in what I had to say. They just wanted a confrontation to entertain their viewers, so they pulled out their own survey, right on camera!'

'What?!'

Ariadne looked gloomy, Jupiter looked surly and Kate looked amazed.

'And when I tried to tell them Jupiter and the animals deserved respect too, they just laughed and hooted. They sure weren't interested in *The Meaning of It All*.'

Kate became pensive. 'This big reaction shows that what you're saying must touch something important. They're hiding behind the statistics rather than discussing the points women raise about what's going wrong in relationships.'

'I wonder,' Ariadne mused, 'if it's hard for them to accept that women are changing their value-systems and their lives. . . . They probably would have accepted it if I had said there was something wrong with women, that women have to change – that it's women who are neurotic!'

'They don't like women challenging the system – in love or anywhere else!' Kate fumed. 'Oh, Ariadne, it makes me so angry!

24

We are their viewers and that's not the kind of programme we want. Well, never mind. It's all over now.'

'That's just it – it isn't over. They're still planning to use the interview.'

'But how can they?' Kate asked, stunned.

'It was taped. I'm so worried; they wouldn't tell me how they plan to edit what they taped me saying. When I tried to ask how they were going to edit my words, they accused me of wanting to suppress freedom of the press!'

Jupiter, who had been listening with growing despair, just lay down on the carpet, covered his head with his paws, and groaned.

The next morning Ariadne was at her desk in an old red plaid flannel shirt and black pants, her hair in total disarray, facing a mountain of papers that needed attention. She had turned on the TV to keep her company. *The Wizard of Oz* was showing, a perfect counterbalance to the work she was doing (not colourful at all!). When it was over, she turned down the sound so she wouldn't hear the commercials.

Glancing up from her work, she was dumbfounded to see herself on television. She looked up just in time to see 'Is Rite Wrong?' emblazoned above her photo. It looked suspiciously as if the 'g' was dropping down to form a noose around her neck. She turned up the volume as the announcer was saying, 'Tune in tomorrow at six for *Our View of the News* and find out.'

The phone began ringing. First Kate, then Robert, her publisher, called to tell her they had seen the promo. Ariadne invited them both to come over to watch it with her. And then there was another call from Sue Power.

'Listen, Ariadne, I'm over here at the editing room, looking at your interview. To tell you the truth, I'm a little worried. It's not going to sound like what you said any more.' In a whisper she continued, 'There's just nothing I can do about it, the editor-in-chief's adamant. I'm sorry, I didn't know it would go this far.'

A bewildered Ariadne put the phone down slowly. She knew she'd had some kind of warning, but what could it mean? She went over to the couch and curled up with her arms around Jupiter, burying her face in his warm furry neck.

'Good evening. It's time for *Our View of the News*. You may have heard about it, perhaps even argued about it, but you won't have read it. Yes, even though it won't be published until tomorrow, lots of people have already formed an opinion about it. We are talking about *The Meaning of It All*, by Ariadne Rite. ARC TV's Pat Prying has this report.'

'According to *The Meaning of It All*, the majority of women complain that the men in their lives don't communicate with them and don't do any work around the house,' Prying intoned.

The picture cut to a clip of Ariadne's interview. Ariadne was saying, ' . . . women are frustrated with trying to build better personal relationships with the men in their lives. They want a man who will listen and talk, have a real conversation.'

Pat reappeared on screen standing on a busy downtown street. 'In order to see if we could confirm these revolutionary claims, ARC TV telephoned two hundred men and women in a nationwide sample. We found that the majority of men didn't think women had anything to complain about: they talked to their wives at least once a day and even helped with the dishes sometimes.

'Now I've come down to the heart of the city to ask this fine rush-hour crowd what they think. Excuse me . . .' he said, putting out his arm to stop a couple hurrying by. 'Excuse me, sir, do you agree with the claim by Ariadne Rite that men don't communicate with the women in their lives?'

'No.'

'And do you agree with this gentleman or Ms Rite?' Pat turned the microphone towards the man's companion.

She opened her mouth but before she could get a word out, the man pulled the microphone back in his direction. 'She agrees with me of course. I'm her husband. Come on, dear.'

'Well, there's one man who certainly talks to his wife,' said Pat happily. 'Now let's ask these ladies their opinion,' he continued, walking over to two women who were holding an open book and peering up at the street sign. 'Tell me, ladies, what do you think of Ariadne Rite's claim that men don't communicate with women?'

'Σορυ ψε δοντ σπεακ Ξνγλσιη'

'Uh, sorry, I didn't quite catch that. Would you like me to repeat the question?'

'Σορυ ψε δοντ σπεακ Ξνγλσιη'

'Well,' Pat turned back to the camera unperturbed. 'Looks like it's the women who can't communicate, heh, heh. This is Pat Prying investigating. And now a message from our sponsors.'

Ariadne sat on the couch between Kate and Robert, too stunned to say a word.

'At least,' Robert sighed wearily, turning off the TV in disgust, 'they mentioned your name and the book's title several times.'

'But, Robert, it's a nine-hundred-page book and they talked as if it contained only one question! Not one word about what it really says. . . .'

'I know, I know,' he sympathized. 'But this kind of thing happens all the time. Don't let it get you down. Now, why don't you get some rest? You look knackered.'

'Good idea.' And Ariadne feigned lightheartedness for her friends, 'Good night, Kate darlin', good night, Robert! Thanks for your support. You're tops!'

When they were alone. Ariadne said mournfully to Jupiter, 'I certainly wasn't prepared for this. Nothing is what it seems.'

'Do you want to go?' Jupiter asked, giving her a kiss. Then, with that devil-may-care expression she adored, 'I'm ready to go flying if you are!'

She perked up and began to smile. 'Gadzooks! Let's get outta here!'

Ascension: Flying to Heaven

★

No sooner had they said this, than they suddenly felt themselves rising! Up, up, up, into the sky! Lifting away from the city, away from the Earth!

In minutes they were flying through a vast dark-blue velvet space, full of twinkling stars. It is so cool, Ariadne thought, so lovely, to feel the breeze blowing through your clothes, your hair. . . . She could feel her hair streaming out behind her in the wind. A deep sense of peace came over her.

By her side she could see Jupiter, his eyes looking straight ahead, dark brown pools of concentration. His small black whiskers and the antennae above his eyes stood alert and twitching, helping to guide him as he charted their course.

Ariadne began singing to herself, a song about their trip and the mysterious blue sky that seemed so infinite. It was a long trip, and Ariadne, drowsy, dozed off, her head resting on Jupiter's familiar neck, her arm still round his shoulders, holding him.

When she opened her eyes, it was daylight, and the morning sun was again spreading its creamy shafts of light through the golden air, all new and shimmering with life. Butterflies and birds circled and hummed round them as they came closer and closer to landing. Jupiter was smiling now, a big, bright smile, his pink tongue hanging jauntily out of the side of his mouth as he concentrated on his goal, the little bit further they had to go. Closer and closer. . . .

A perfect landing.

Up in Heaven

★

In Heaven, everybody was playing baseball. They all had on white robes and there was radiant sunshine and clean air everywhere.

Just as Ariadne and Jupiter were setting out to enjoy all this, they were spotted. 'And what, pray tell, do you think you've been doing?' demanded one Angel. 'you should have asked our permission before you went to Earth! Don't you know this is more than you should have taken on? Look what a mess you've made!'

'Those people on Earth,' chimed in another, 'you can't just talk to them. You have to go through channels – and I don't mean TV channels. You can't just shout out what you think, not even the Truth – especially not the Truth!'

'Listen, you just happened to pick on the hottest topic on Earth,' said a third Angel. 'Family politics! That business about which sex does what has been going on down there for a long time. They have been fighting over the democratization of the family for a whole century, which is quite a long time in their terms. What makes you think you can just walk in and change all that?'

'And the Planetary Affairs Department here could have warned you about the environment. It's Earth's problem, not yours!'

Jupiter and Ariadne were anxious to get away from such unheavenly scolding, to forget everything to do with Earth – just relax! As soon as they could, they made an escape and went to watch the baseball game, like everybody else.

A Scottish terrier was just arriving at the game, jumping out of a 1939 Ford convertible. He took a seat near Jupiter, and gradually they began talking – about the pitcher, the third baseman and so on.

This terrific terrier turned out to be Fala, the friend and long-time companion of Franklin D. Roosevelt, a former president of the US. Naturally, Fala knew all about politics, so when Jupiter told him that he had just come from Earth, Fala wanted to hear all about it. The more he heard, the more excited he got, and soon he offered to take Jupiter to meet the other dogs of Heaven who had lived on Earth. Off they went together.

Jupiter Meets the Famous Dogs of Heaven

At the dogs' hangout, all the dogs were chatting and having a good time. Fala introduced Jupiter all around, and explained that he and Ariadne had got all tangled up in things on television on Earth. Then lots of dogs, who all had tons of experience with reporters, started talking and swapping their stories.

'You know,' said a charming brown-and-white spotted dog who looked like she could be Jupiter's cousin, 'I wouldn't take all this too seriously.' She smiled at Jupiter, then introduced herself, 'By the way, I'm Rughetta! When I lived on Earth with Tito Gobbi and those reporters would interview him about opera, most of them asked the most absurd questions. For example, they asked him if his wife minded him singing in the shower! Most of them didn't know a thing about music – or even the name of the opera he was actually singing at the moment!'

Pluto, the famous comic-star dog (who had always dreamed of working with Margaret Mead, and studied anthropology when he could at the studio), chimed in, 'Oh! And their "research"! Why, their "research",' he rolled his eyes dismissively, 'often consists of nothing more than reading other reporters' articles. The problem with this is, if enough articles agree on something – and they do, of course, since they repeat each other – all the reporters believe it's a fact. Then, even if the one they're writing about tells them it's *not* a fact, they tell him *he's* mistaken!'

'That's just what they do,' Jupiter agreed. As the other dogs nodded knowingly, recalling their own experiences, Jupiter felt relieved to know that he wasn't alone. There were so many other dogs with their stories: Vulcan, George Washington's dog (who was famous for stealing a big ham from George and eating a bit of it each day until he was found out); the loyal dog of Ulysses, who was the first to recognize Ulysses when he came home after his long odyssey; and there was Laika, the first Russian cosmonaut dog who went into space. ('Wow! Was that a trip!' she told Jupiter.)

'You know the story about Fala, don't you?' Vulcan whispered, when he and Jupiter had a moment alone. 'No? Well, the Secret Service didn't like him because every time President Roosevelt went somewhere, it was their job to hide him. But Fala would go running around all over the place and then everybody would know that the President was there. The Secret Service would get furious, but FDR refused to leave Fala at home.' This endeared Fala to Jupiter even more.

'Once,' continued Vulcan, 'Roosevelt forgot Fala on an island in the Pacific. He sent a cruiser back to get him. The press made a big scandal out of this, saying that the taxpayers' money was being wasted. So Roosevelt made the "Fala Speech". "The Republicans have attacked my wife, my children and now my dog. But when my dog heard that he had cost too much money, this raised his Scottish blood, and he became very indignant indeed. He said he would be quite surprised to meet a Republican who ever spent less money than a Democrat!"'

They both had a good laugh at that, and Jupiter hoped to meet FDR.

Checkers had approached them rather shyly. There was a tendency among the dogs to snub the companion of Richard Nixon. But he'd been on TV himself and, even though he was usually barked down, he couldn't resist joining in. 'Have you ever heard a reporter ask a complicated question?'

'No,' Jupiter admitted, 'almost never! They kept asking Ariadne where she got her information. Well, I can tell you we travelled more, and talked and listened to more people than most of the people who live there all their lives. But after the first two sentences of Ariadne's answer, the reporters' attention would wander. They couldn't care less. And then,' Jupiter's eyes rolled upwards, 'they would ask her, "How do men feel about you? Are men afraid of you?"'

Some of the dogs roared with laughter at this, and shook their heads. But Checkers said defensively, 'Well, in the paper it says "Ariadne Doesn't Like Men".'

'Checkers,' Fala sighed, 'if you still believe what you read in the papers, then you didn't learn a thing in all this time! You of all dogs should know how frantic reporters are to get a story, particularly a "scoop"!' He looked disdainfully at Checkers. 'Why, they'll even invent stories to get something "first", like that non-sense about me, that I did you-know-what on Stalin's leg. Geez, give me a break!'

Checkers, his tail between his legs, apologized for being so thoughtless. Hoping to make a better impression, he decided to tell a joke: 'Have you ever noticed that most reporters don't take shorthand or use a tape recorder either? And since they can't write longhand as fast as anyone speaks, they just jot down the few words they happen to catch. At press conferences most reporters spend their time elbowing the next one, saying "Psst! What'd she say? What'd he say?" What they finally write reminds me of that game where everyone sits in a circle and one person whispers some-thing in the ear of the next, who repeats it to the next person, and so on, until by the time it reaches the last person, it has nothing whatsoever to do with the original story!'

The dogs laughed loudly in agreement and Checkers beamed at his success – he was a hit!

One of the Pavlov dogs, who had maintained an interest in science, remarked, 'It's interesting that reporters didn't find anything strange or unbelievable about Ariadne's statistic that seventy-two percent of men who'd been married more than two years had had extramarital sex, but they were outraged that a figure anywhere near that – seventy percent after five years, wasn't it? – could be recorded for women. They couldn't believe it, so they called Ariadne a fraud, denounced this figure hysteri-cally and did their own slapped-together surveys to try to prove they were right and she was wrong!'

'Yeah,' growled another Pavlov alumnus, 'what they don't want to believe, they try to discredit. Boy, times don't change much. Just because we dogs were bright enough to learn a routine, "Pavlovian" became a derogatory term, like stupid.'

'To make it worse,' Jupiter added, 'the press runs like a rat pack. They all copy the Beltway boys (and girls) now, the media "superstars". They're so eager to look "in the know" that they're afraid to have their own opinion. And, a lot of the papers are owned by the same big companies, so if one paper wants to push a certain point of view, and especially if that paper gets it first, then almost everybody takes up the theme, puts the same spin on it. Why? Because they all hope to get jobs someday on the Big Beltway too!'

Fala nodded, a worried look on his face. 'Some of the press were like this when we were in politics down there, but this consolidation of newspapers and television into just a few hands, that's new. It's got to be dangerous for democracy. A few media owners covering a person – or an issue – favourably or unfavourably, beaming their view at people day and night, control a lot of public opinion. It's not only Ariadne's problem. It has an effect on politics at all levels. Why, well-qualified people may become afraid to run for office (or support a policy) in case the media attack them and ruin their reputations.'

'They'll decide it's smarter to go into business,' another agreed.

The other dogs murmured their agreement, looking worried. But the meeting had to break up. Jupiter said good night to Fala, then to Rughetta, and went to find Ariadne.

He found her out swimming in a small lake. She was playing a game of hide-and-seek with a giant green water-turtle. Jupiter loved hide-and-seek, so he jumped in and joined the game. After the turtle won every round, the two of them climbed out and rolled around on the grass to dry off. They they sat there panting, their hair still wet and dripping.

Jupiter began to tell Ariadne excitedly about the meeting. 'Oh, it was great! Fala introduced me to a whole bunch of dogs who belong to Earth-Watch Political Club. It's quite a big deal. I met Laika, Vulcan, the Pavlov dogs, Checkers, and Rughetta Gobbi. We talked about you and the crazy events on Earth, and they told me their stories.' And Jupiter recounted every word for Ariadne.

Listening to him, Ariadne became curious about what had happened on Earth since they had left, and decided to look over the edge of Heaven through a large telescope (coin-operated). Focusing on her adopted city, she adjusted the lens until she could see it in the finest detail. Unfortunately what she saw was newspaper headlines declaring 'Study Says Men Are Meanies!', 'Men Bashed by Woman' and 'Anti-male Book by Mean Woman!'

Horrified, she cried to Jupiter, 'Oh, why did I look? This is just ridiculous! I don't even want to know about it anymore. Earth is so ... so ... *weird*! I'm going for a walk, Jupiter. I'll see you later.'

And she wandered off down a little lane, her shoulders drooping. She felt downhearted. She wanted to stop thinking about all the things that had happened on Earth, and almost wished she had never gone there.

Ariadne Meets Cleopatra

A little further on, still absorbed in her thoughts, she heard someone coming. Looking up, she saw none other than ...

... Cleopatra! The Queen of the Nile!

'Wow!' Ariadne thought, in awe.

Without bothering to introduce herself (it was hardly necessary, after all), Cleopatra remarked off-handedly, 'Baseball was invented after my time. I don't like it. It's boring. Who are you?'

'Ariadne.' She was conscious that her hair was still wet and drippy from her swim, but marvelled at how wonderful Cleopatra was to look at.

Cleopatra surveyed Ariadne from head to foot, thinking, Doesn't she own a hairdrier? Really, she looks like a drowned rat. Still, she could be fun.

'Come on,' Cleopatra said, 'let's go try on make-up.'

They sat down on a bench and took their make-up out of their purses. Ariadne's bag was pink plastic with gold specks on it and a rhinestone clasp. Cleopatra loved it. They traded eye-pencils and lipstick colours, spreading them all out and having a grand time trying them all on. Cleopatra said she thought Ariadne should shape her eyes *à la Egyptienne*, and showed her how to use kohl to tilt them up at the outside edges. Holding Ariadne's chin with her left hand, she began to apply the make-up on Ariadne with her right hand. Ariadne could smell an unfamiliar heavy musk oil when

Cleopatra came so near to her and, as Cleopatra leaned forward to reach her other eye. Ariadne could feel Cleo's warm breasts underneath the leopard-skin mermaid dress she was wearing. What fun to have a friend like this!

She gave Cleopatra her bright yellow cat-eye Earth sunglasses with the mirror lenses, which she had bought in Greenwich Village, as a token of friendship. They looked great on Cleopatra, against her ravishing dark-brown skin and black hair, under her fringe. Cleo wanted to know if Ariadne had any yellow fingernail polish to match, but Ariadne had left it back on Earth.

They were having a wonderful time, getting on really well. Ariadne was just about to ask Cleopatra a host of questions (so what's new?) – starting with, 'What was really in the library at Alexandria when it burned down?', 'What did the books say?' 'Did they tell about pre-patriarchal times?' 'Are they in the Vatican Library now?' She wondered whether Cleopatra thought of herself as a sex symbol? or whether she was really a military and political genius whom history had trivialized – or both? But they were interrupted by Gertrude Stein.

'Don't you two realize that it's women like you who give others a bad name? Make-up! Sunglasses! What do you want to be? Toys for boys?' Gertrude looked haughty and smug.

'Oh, goddess! Do leave us alone and go boss someone else,' Cleo retorted, stifling a yawn. Turning to Ariadne, she said, 'I must go now anyway. Come to my place later and we'll try on clothes. They wouldn't suit you, Gertrude,' she added mischievously, 'you are much too minimalist!'

Cleo and Gertrude walked off in separate directions, leaving Ariadne looking slightly bewildered, and thinking that Gertrude Stein seemed snotty – in the best girls' school tradition.

Visiting Cleopatra at Home

Ariadne could hardly wait until it was time to go to Cleopatra's house that evening. She found herself walking so fast that she arrived early. Comparing the street numbers of the houses to the address scribbled on the little crumpled piece of paper in her hand, she stopped in front of Cleopatra's.

She had thought she was looking for an Ancient Egyptian house, sort of dark and musty. Instead, she saw a white luminnescent spaceship with a plastic neon door. As she pressed the bell, the door glowed and changed from fuchsia to cyan, then mysteriously and soundlessly slid open. Ariadne walked in. There were pearlized plastic chaise-longues in lime-green, shocking pink and chartreuse, also a yellow latex TV taken from a Dali painting, soft and melting like a half-inflated inner tube, and small reading lights everywhere that said 'Cleopatra, Queen of the Nile' in gold. The wallpaper was Chinese-red covered with large giraffes. This must be the living-room.

Cleopatra appeared in a mermaid-like outfit made out of chartreuse latex, and serious-looking mock-tortoiseshell eyeglasses by Arletty. Did she need them? Were they for effect? They gave her that sort of Intellectualesque *Vogue* Look. Cleo steered Ariadne to a bright yellow chaise-longue, gave her a small blue glass with a strange gold design that looked very old, and said, 'Drink this.'

'What is it?'

'Well, it's like the *arak* that comes from Beirut. You drink it cold, in one quick gulp.' They toasted 'Women Friends Forever', an old Egyptian toast. Ariadne gulped it down, wondering if she might suddenly grow very tall or shrink to a fraction of her size.

Next, Cleopatra said, 'Come with me into the bedroom.' It was a bedroom like none Ariadne had ever seen – in fact, an endless series of rooms, draped with sensuous, shimmering golden brocades and Middle Eastern fabrics in intense pastels, turquoise and pink-gold.

Multicoloured fresh flowers were everywhere in abundance; clothes, jewellery and stockings were draped on various chairs around the room. Everything looked so exciting and inviting that Ariadne wanted to dive in, rub herself against the cushions, roll around in the soft fabrics, lie on the bed, drink in the colours and stare at the wonderful pink ceiling.

Cleopatra continued the tour. Between the series of secret rooms were soft velour curtains, so that everything seemed to be in its own little niche. In one niche, an antique bed with a deep moss-green and gold tapestry coverlet was set off with rosy pink silk pillows. Its dusty-rose satin headboard, framed by carved wooden edges seemed alive, or almost to be endowed with magic powers. Topping it off was an elegant snake emblem in gold – pulsating and aglow like the sun. It too seemed alive, breathing. Large mirrors with golden frames and fanciful paintings of birds, deer, dogs and other creatures Ariadne couldn't quite place covered the walls.

Travelling through this secret passageway of rooms, they arrived at Cleopatra's clothes closet – an enormous room with a magnificent display of hundreds of her royal outfits. In the centre was a large circular chrome clothes-rack that rotated at the press of a button – like at the dry cleaner's. Small atomizers dispensed perfume into the air at regular intervals to make sure the clothes were Heavenly Scented, ready for use at all times. The clothes were organized by colour. There was no differentiation between daytime and nighttime clothes. 'That was an unnecessary bourgeois invention,' Cleopatra pointed out briskly.

Ariadne was trying to absorb all this, her mind filled with confusing ideas. Do I care if there are Day and Night clothes? Do I care if there's Day and Night? Which is more important? For her part, Ariadne couldn't decide whether she liked day or night better: whichever it was, she was always sorry when it ended.

In a chest of drawers, Ariadne noticed that Cleopatra kept beautiful underwear from various Earth centuries – Egyptian underwear, Victorian underwear, even medieval underwear – pretty hot! But what really caught Ariadne's eye was a flesh-pink camisole which laced up the front. When Cleopatra saw that Ariadne couldn't take her eyes off it, she helped her try it on. The most feminine tiny satin blue ribbons marched round the top and bottom. Ariadne decided she really liked pulse-pink with her pale skin and red-gold hair. Wow! she thought, as she looked at herself. This is all Really Major. Really exciting! But . . . now what? she wondered.

Cleopatra led her to a little mirrored dressing-table with a dainty lavender-silk upholstered chair. Ariadne loved the way she felt, sitting in it, and was ready to trust Cleopatra with anything. Cleopatra gazed at her in the mirror, then tried her hair (which had finally dried – with that 'windblown' look) in different styles. Using a curling iron, she made Ariadne's hair stand out in waves all around. They fell down her shoulders luxuriantly, much wilder than before. 'Now, Ari! You look pretty sexy – a little different from a while ago when I met you!'

'But, Cleopatra, where am I ever going to go like this?' Ariadne asked.

'You'll think of something, I'm sure,' Cleopatra said, giving Ariadne a withering look that implied, 'How dumb can you be? Do I have to teach you *everything*?'

Even though there was nothing Ariadne liked better than playing around with clothes and make-up, her attention eventually began to wander. Cleopatra, seeing that she was distracted, asked her pointedly, 'Come on, what's on your mind? Is it a man?'

Ariadne made a funny face, but then settled into a large, over-stuffed cream-silk chair, and told Cleo the whole story of her Trip to Earth. 'Oh, Cleo, I can't figure Earth out!' she cried. 'It's such a beautiful planet – the flowers, birds, trees, the thousands of kinds of animals, the miraculous colours. But the humans are killing each other and lots of the other species now, along with acres and acres of forests where the animals live. Why??? And they treat each other shamefully too, sometimes. . . . I was writing down stories women told me, I wanted to find out why these things were happening. But when I finished . . . well! I thought I could just write down the things people told me, then give my opinions of them – but when I tried, I got wildly attacked!

'It's funny, but in lots of ways it was like what some women told me happened to them privately – men didn't listen to them, wouldn't take them seriously. The same thing happened to me! Some men in the media (well, a woman too) insisted I was wrong, that my research was rotten, that most people were happy the way things were, and didn't want to change things! Some tried to say there was no emotional violence against women in relationships – and if there was, it certainly wasn't linked to other kinds of discrimination against women – or to the physical battering reported in all the newspaper headlines every day! And they all said that human aggression against the environment was "natural", and in general, the world was just about as perfect as it could ever be. I was a troublemaker who should shut up! A real drag!'

'Hmmm . . . a messenger with an unpleasant message. But such

38

a lovely messenger . . . Well, I think I know how to deal with this kind of a problem,' Cleopatra winked, looking wicked.

'But,' Ariadne continued, 'I don't know what to think now. Originally I believed that, hearing there was injustice, naturally people would want to fix it. Was I wrong? When I pointed out that lots of women were leaving men, that they wouldn't take it anymore, some men got angry. Were they frightened? Maybe they didn't want to believe women could leave. But the women only wanted men to change; they didn't want to hurt them. . . .

'One of my friends said those guys were over-reacting because this is a bad time for Western white men. Everybody has been giving them a hard time, calling them names, and saying they are to blame for everything, and letting them know they aren't Number One anymore! Minorities around the world are attacking them – and now women too! Maybe they just can't take any more. But how can they expect love from women if they don't listen? And they need women.'

'You better believe it!' Cleopatra said.

'Well, did I frighten men by saying women should take more power? And lots of people said I asked too many questions . . . But . . . equality would only make sense, wouldn't it?'

'Ariadne!' Cleopatra exclaimed, looking bemused. 'You're so naïve! What an idealist! A great big innocent – but a thinker. Where did you come from, anyway??' Getting up, she threw a white satin dressing-gown over her shoulder, and took Ariadne by the hand. 'Come with me,' she said, leading her into another room, 'I'm late. I've got to take my bath. Anyway, we can talk better about the Nature of Reality on Earth from a nice humid room.'

Ariadne happily followed Cleopatra into a large, frescoed bathroom filled with fresh pink peonies and pale yellow orchids. A green marble pool sculpted like a shell occupied the centre of the room. Marble steps led down into the water, which was covered with a pale green foam from which a mysterious, fragrant mist was rising. A steamy, luxuriant languor enveloped Ariadne, as she picked out a white pearlized latex hammock next to the pool to lean back in.

Slipping into the water, Cleopatra continued, 'Well, it's clear to me already that the media are not engaging you in a direct battle, but an indirect one. They know they can't win by arguing the real point, arguing against what you and the women say – that women still don't have equality in private with men, that stereotypes are used to denigrate women, and that women feel shocked and hurt when men do this, especially men they love. No, instead the media say, "Her hairstyle's terrible" or "She can't write" or "She's no scientist!", no matter how many academic luminaries may praise you to the contrary.'

Ariadne closed her eyes and leaned further back, swinging slightly in the hammock, her golden-red hair spilling over the edge. It was relaxing to feel the fragrant mist wafting around the room, and the water lapped gently against the pool's edge. Ariadne was listening to Cleopatra (sort of hazily), but she wanted to change the subject – even though she was the one who had brought it up. It was hard to feel overly Earth-concerned here.

'Why do you let all this bother you?' Cleo was asking. 'The newspapers want to sell papers. They don't represent "the people". . . .'

Ariadne sat up, unable to let this pass unanswered. 'But I do care. It's important what the media say because that's how most people on Earth get their information now. Even with a bestseller, only ten percent of the population will read a book. So the rest rely on the news media for their information. The only way to disseminate ideas, to inform people about them, is to utilize the media. If TV and the press go off on the wrong track. . . . Well, the basis of democracy is free speech and debate in the press.'

'Hmmm, yes, that really is a problem,' Cleopatra agreed. 'But if you don't mind an opinion, I think you're becoming terribly Earth-bound.' And she sudsed her leg lazily. Yet a minute later she put her pink sponge down on the side of the tub, and looked earnestly at Ariadne. 'Really, Ariadne, you must realize you are making some very serious statements. Probably some of the press are quite aware of their truth – they just won't talk about it, lest people start thinking too much, and take action. What if women did unify and start demanding half the places in Congress or Parliament? Just imagine!'

Cleo leaned back and smiled again, submerging her gorgeous brown body in the foam. 'Oh Ariadne, stop being so serious! A little sex appeal will fix all your problems. You can have fun on

Earth – and I'm going to show you how!' Cleopatra's face lit up at this prospect.

Ariadne looked sceptical, sitting there in her pink camisole. But she didn't want to offend her new friend by questioning whether this was really a good idea. It would take a long time to explain to Cleopatra about Recent Developments, that sex appeal might not be the best way to get her point across. Where to start? Ariadne began by explaining to Cleopatra that maybe it was a question of her honour being at stake.

Cleopatra looked at her disdainfully, then took a deep breath and resumed carefully. 'Now look, Ariadne, I'm going to explain something to you. Once I was criticized too. Horatio wrote a whole ode about my defeat, gloating, "Now is the time to enjoy life because Cleopatra has been destroyed!" You think you've had it bad! Well, being criticized by the Romans was just as frustrating for me. They didn't understand me at all, and they really had it in for me.'

Cleopatra closed her eyes, a positively dreamy look crossing her face. 'I was so happy being with Antony. But the Romans thought I wanted to be the Queen of Rome. Well, I did and didn't, but that's another matter. They thought that was my motivation for everything. But that wasn't really how I felt. I was just happy being with Antony, and to be with him, I had to help him, because he wanted to take Rome.'

She propped herself up. 'I was defeated because I was so upset when I thought Antony was dead after the battle. He was leading our army and we got separated. I decided all was lost and I took my own life. Believe me, I could have turned that defeat into a triumph. If I hadn't been in love, I could have handled those men in Rome! I wasn't afraid, I was only devastated because I thought my beautiful Antony had died. Then he killed himself because he thought I was dead. Why doesn't anybody believe this is the real story? Don't they know that real love exists? Instead, they want to make me out to have had devious reasons for fighting with Rome. Listen, I can be devious with the best of them, but in the case of Antony, it was pure and passionate love. It was that simple. . . . So your book sounds very interesting to me, since women talk about what it's like to be that much in love. Can I have a copy? I want to know if any of them ever felt as I

41

did with Antony . . . and what happened — did things work out for them?'

Ariadne began to tell her what the women had said, but Cleopatra continued. 'Ariadne, don't you see? What they're saying about you now, it's like what they said about me then. Nobody believed I might be an Idealist or a Revolutionary, they just said I was out to make Big Bucks! "She wants to take Rome," they said. That wasn't it, not at all! The Romans said I was intelligent, shrewd and ambitious. Well, they were right about that. I was and I am. But all this other stuff, pooh! They're just the normal, everyday put-downs of women!'

'Cleo, did they dislike you more because you were Queen of Egypt, and powerful, or because you were a woman — and a dark-skinned one, at that . . . ?'

'Well, they said it was because of Egypt, but I think it was really because I was a woman and saw things differently than they did. But listen, kiddo, you need some help in handling those men down there. Believe me, I can help you, I've been dealing with men for aeons.'

But Cleo, you lost, Ariadne thought to herself (she was too polite to say this out loud). But Cleo, reading her thoughts, burst out, 'I didn't lose! I *told* you: I killed myself out of despair. My love, my Antony, was dead. I didn't feel like trying anymore. Of course, I was a military genius and a great strategist. Otherwise, how did I survive twenty years in power in Egypt?

'Remember, you know only what the Romans wrote about me, and that was after they defeated me! Most of our books — everything we Egyptians had written — were destroyed in the Great Fire at Alexandria. Our Great Library contained all the wisdom of history before patriarchy, remember that. There was a grand and glorious tradition of women ruling in many parts of the Earth. And here in Heaven, there is a pre-history section . . . if you are ever lucky enough to be invited to go there. . . .'

'Oh, Cleopatra! I'm so glad I've met you! I like you very much! Everything about you — your ideas, your house, your clothes, your make-up. . . . By the way, though, on Earth lots of women today think wearing make-up is a sign of oppression, that it means the woman is just desperate to get a man, she's a wimp, a coward!

They say going without make-up and sexy clothes is a sign of solidarity with other women.'

'Oh, Ariadne, get serious!' laughed Cleopatra. 'To be a powerful woman, a "feminist", as they call them now, you don't need to wear drab clothes! You sound like Gertrude Stein. I know a lot of the nineteenth-century feminists, and they like clothes, some of them quite a lot!' And she reached for a towel, getting ready to emerge from the foam. . . .

Cleopatra was convincing. Nevertheless, Ariadne thought, what's on Earth is what's on Earth, and the climate of opinion had changed. Besides, Beauty Culture and the Beauty Industry are no joke, and Ariadne decided Cleopatra should know about them. 'Come here,' she said, taking Cleopatra's arm and sitting down with her on the edge of the hammock. 'Cleo, a lot has happened since you were on Earth. . . .'

'Ariadne, darling! Lighten up! You worry too much! You and your social issues. Maybe you should visit the Whist Club. That's where all the Intellectuals hang out, mostly boring – well, some of them are rather bright – a few are my lovers, actually! They're always talking about this kind of stuff. I can't take you there myself now, because I've got a date. But maybe tomorrow.'

Cleopatra pulled on a black lace body, then a pair of leopard-skin spandex tights. She wrapped a gold snake bracelet round her arm. Wow, this woman had style! Ariadne wondered how she would look in an outfit like that. 'I'll see you later,' Cleopatra called out as they parted.

Ariadne and Jupiter Under the Stars

Ariadne was floating now, her feet hardly touching the ground, so enchanted was she by her visit with Cleopatra, and the friendship Cleopatra had shown her. She walked along energetically, singing to herself, on her way to find Jupiter. She spotted him in a little clearing under the stars.

As soon as she saw him, however, she stopped immediately, realizing she had come upon a private scene.

Jupiter was with another dog – Rughetta. The moonlight

shone down on them as they performed a kind of ecstatic dance together – jumping, leaping, entwining, embracing, putting their front paws on each other's shoulders, smelling, nuzzling, licking each other's faces, excitement showing in every movement of their bodies. Sometimes their lips touched sweetly, as they put soft quick kisses on each other's furry mouths.

Jupiter's expression was ecstatic. So in love was he, that his whole body showed how he was feeling. Ariadne didn't want to pry, but for a while she stood watching, captivated by the magical scene before her. Then she tiptoed away and sat down by a tree. The stars were crystal clear, and looking up, she found the Little Dipper, the Big Dipper, and Uranus, the bear. Ariadne's grandfather had taught her all about constellations, long ago.

Suddenly she felt a nuzzle and Jupiter joined her, sitting beside her. Now they both looked up at the stars, Ariadne with her arm round Jupiter. Turning, she kissed his ear. Warm and soft, under his ear was the finest fur ever. He smells wonderful, she thought. Then they talked about being in Missouri together, and all the stars they could see from there.

Harry Truman Says Hello

Suddenly they heard a faint sound of footsteps; someone was approaching. Who could it be, but Harry Truman!

'Must be something I said about Missouri,' Ariadne whispered to Jupiter, wondering if Harry would notice them.

He stopped right in front of them. 'Howdy! I was looking for you two. I'm always interested in events on Earth, particularly the escapades of the press. I saw you on TV and I wanted to give you some advice. After all, you don't know politics the way I do! Listen, Ariadne, in one respect what's happening to you is what happened to my daughter, Margaret. The press loves to make fun of women, like they made fun of Margaret's singing and playing the piano. Like they make fun of Hillary Clinton. That's just the way they are.'

He sat down on the grass too, next to Jupiter, smiling at Ariadne. 'You see, on Earth things can happen for really silly reasons. (It doesn't make a lot of difference where on Earth you are, this is always true.) The *Power Press* fellows and Biggest Brother's Staggeringly Big Money Holding Corporation's members are just like small town boys – they love to gossip! I heard you refused to talk to their yellow sheet, the *Daily Rumour*, when they wanted to do a story about Jupiter's and your personal life – good for you! But, boy, did that put you in the doghouse (sorry, Jupiter, no offence meant) with the editor. . . .

'He put out lots of rumours about you, to get you for that! That you were a real difficult babe, that you were on the verge of a nervous breakdown (and that's why you couldn't talk to them), and so on – oh, don't ever underestimate the repercussions of saying no to the press! When press barons say "freedom of the press", in my experience they mean freedom for them to write any damn thing they please!' He slapped his knee and burst out laughing.

Ariadne and Jupiter stared at him in amazement. They might have said something, but Harry was a great talker and went right on.

'Say, honeybunch – there's something else I wanted to tell you. You're up against some right-wing fundamentalist types who insist that the "real" news (despite any annoying statistics to the contrary) must be that women are happy, that families (as *they* define them: dad-in-charge) are The Best. They think that if they copy the Japanese family, they will copy the Japanese economic miracle! Keep America profitable! Funny, *nyet*?!?' Harry, really tickled at his new joke, was smiling ever more broadly. Ariadne wished she could have the distance on things that he had!

He got up to go, then stopped. 'One more thing. That group of guys I mentioned who call themselves Biggest Brother's Staggeringly Big Money Holding Corporation – who own ARC TV – they own tons of things besides TV stations – soaps and airplanes, newspapers and paper mills, deodorants and spark plugs – all kinds of things. Yessiree Bob! They've got 'em all! So their policy is to keep the country's women happy (or at least passive), sell them more soapsuds or whatever, stop them from complaining – and especially from organizing! They think equal pay would kill their profit margin! Sugarpie, it's so easy to see from Up Here; much more difficult when you're Down There. It's like a giant Disneyland.' He looked at Ariadne and Jupiter sympathetically, as he started again to leave.

'Oh, don't go!' Ariadne cried out. 'There are so many things I want to ask!' (Uncharacteristically, she hadn't got even one question in yet.) 'I mean, who am I fighting? Should I fight Biggest Brother's Staggeringly Big Money Holding Corporation or the Two Brothers? Could I convince them to be fair? Which brother should I talk to? Sometimes I feel like I've fallen down a terrible long tunnel and it's so confusing.'

Harry thought for a moment. 'The problem is, when you say that women are in the midst of a huge ideological transformation – well, you scare some Big Brothers! To them, equality just means *they* won't be on top! So they're scared out of their pants!' This time Ariadne and Jupiter joined in Harry's laughter, and waved at him fondly as he disappeared down the road.

Paradise on Earth:
Ariadne Falls in Love

★

Cleopatra, wandering home dreamily from her date, came up with an idea.

'Ariadne! I heard that Ben Badd, editor of that dreadful *Power Press*, and his wife Priscilla, are throwing a fancy costume ball at the Glitterati Centre on Earth tonight. Why don't the three of us, you and Jupiter and I, go there and crash the party, disguised?! All the Big Deal (and Hoping-to-be-Big Deal) media stars will be there. You can find out up close just what is really going on. We can just make it – come on!'

Ariadne and Jupiter agreed at once, thinking this could be a lot of fun, and rushed off with Cleo to search through her closets for something to wear.

Ariadne decided to go as a crossword puzzle, with words and question marks pasted like charms all over her short black velvet tutu and top. A tiny black lacquered tray filled with metaphysical questions on small slips of paper sat at her waist, slung from a black ribbon tied round her neck. She looked a little like a 'cigarette girl' in a 1940s nightclub. Jupiter decided to go as Harvey, the giant rabbit, in case his favourite idol, James Stewart, was there. He used a substantial amount of moustache wax on his ears to make them tall, muttering to himself as he had to add more and more to keep them up. Cleopatra, of course, could go as herself – nobody would ever believe it was really her.

The three of them made a grand entrance down the great red-carpeted staircase of the Glitterati Centre, which led onto the ballroom floor. (Shouldn't they have called it, 'Clitterati Centre'? Ariadne wondered.)

Jupiter went first, his chest puffed out proudly, his underfur fluffy and white as he walked impressively on two feet. Next Ariadne began her descent, throwing questions from her tray over the banister like confetti. People picked them up and began discussing them, opening them and reading them like the puzzles in Chinese fortune cookies. Then Cleopatra made a regal entrance in a strapless emerald-green satin gown, her pet asp coiled lazily over one shoulder, its head resting quizzically on her breast and its tail wriggling down her back.

Cleopatra was immediately surrounded by Fascinated Admirers, so Jupiter and Ariadne headed towards the refreshment table.

As they moved across the floor, Ariadne felt a tight grip on her arm. Surprised, as there appeared to be no one standing next to her, she glanced down and saw a commanding if exceedingly short figure of a man, his head at her waist. From there, she could see the top of his shaved head with its immaculate pink skin, glowing with health. It was so squeaky clean and shiny, so perfectly round, it was all Ariadne could do to restrain herself from patting it. He was wearing an impeccably tailored navy suit and enormous black eyeglasses. Altogether he resembled a happy otter or some other amphibious animal. He appeared to have a great sense of humour.

Still gripping Ariadne's arm a little too hard, the Otter rattled off in an authoritative, dictatorial, shotgun voice, 'Look, honey, don't worry! I've been watching all this TV stuff. I recognize you, even if the others here don't. They don't matter. Let me be your Agent, and I'll handle everything. Let me take care of everything. Now, here's what I want you to do. . . .' Ariadne, speechless, looked at him in amazement. 'Meet me next Monday – that's my birthday, by the way – for lunch at the Le Cirque Hotel. I'll see you there at one o'clock – *be punctual*! Tell them you're meeting me. Swifty!' and suddenly he was gone, disappearing into the crowd in a trail of dust.

Ariadne and Jupiter stared after him and then exchanged looks of such bewilderment they couldn't help laughing at themselves. Who on Earth was that? And what did it all mean? Before they could come to any conclusions the band started playing 'Cheek to Cheek', and they moved onto the dance-floor together in an improvised fox-trot.

Twirling to a step with the final note of the music, Ariadne and Jupiter bumped into a tall, elegant man, almost knocking his champagne glass out of his hand, spilling it all over him. He was wearing tails, with a medal on his lapel but no shirt, just a beautiful chest showing through – in fact, *the* most spectacular chest Ariadne had ever seen (even though now, drops of champagne were sparkling on it). He was tall, muscular and had a rather wild, daredevil look about him. His eyes flashed at her.

'Who are you?' Ariadne asked.

'Can't you tell? I am a Pianist's Understudy.'

'Is that a joke?' Obviously, it was.

'Look.' He took her lightly by the arm and motioned across the room, brushing the champagne off his chest. 'Do you see that ancient musician, Horshovsky, at the keyboard? Well, if he can't make this performance, I take his place. Yes! You see before you the new Liberace! But I'm better, I'm German. We German musicians are always better!' He burst out laughing at his own joke and the serious look on Ariadne's face.

'By the way, my name is Friedrich.'

'I'm Ariadne.'

'Permit me to introduce you to my friends,' he said, indicating three rather jolly-looking fellows standing in a row, their arms thrown over one another's shoulders, having a fine time drinking schnapps and champagne. Everyone exchanged merry hellos and Jupiter joined the line-up. Then they all swayed back and forth to the music. Jupiter was obviously enjoying himself with his new-found friends.

During the orchestra break, a strange record from the 1950s started playing: 'Volare', sung by Dean Martin. Friedrich began to pantomime a very exaggerated version of the number, pretending he was singing, slicking back his hair and trying to look oh so glamorous. . . . Ariadne did find him Seriously Glamorous. And very witty. She doubled up with laughter at his act, and at the same time began to feel a little shy. She was beginning to understand what Cleopatra had been going on about.

The Plastique Bertrand

'Let's get out of here,' Friedrich said. Ariadne saw that Jupiter was in great form, swinging and swaying with the three merry fellows, so she agreed, and followed Friedrich out to a small café.

The Plastique Bertrand, an all-nighter, was mobbed. Ariadne and Friedrich sat down on a velvet zebra-skin banquette where they could see everything – but they only looked at each other. They began talking – about music and composers and writers and the history of art and archaeology, politics and philosophy. Time ceased to exist.

Ariadne thought Friedrich was splendid. She loved his intensity; he seemed to care about those things as if nothing else mattered. And he seemed to care about Ariadne. His eyes were totally fixed on her as they sat close together at the little table. He was watching her with an expression of elation, listening intently to everything she said. Ariadne thought to herself, Can I be seeing what I think I see? His eyes – are they making love to me . . . ?

Ariadne was excited and confused, her head filled with conflicting voices: *Of course, this can't be a romance.* Gosh, he's wonderful. *Just a friendship. Just a really good, close friendship.* My heart is pounding! *There's no reason you can't be just friends with someone of the opposite sex.* Something is wrong with my eyes – I can't see anything or anyone except him. *Certainly I'd never make any physical advance, at least not the first one! I feel much too shy.* It's extraordinarily warm in this café! No, she promised herself for the tenth time, *it will be just a friendship, nothing more.*

At the table directly in front of them a couple started kissing. Since touching was a subject Ariadne was avoiding, she tried to look away, but the passionate couple were so close to them, they were almost forced to watch. Ariadne and Friedrich began to avoid looking at each other now, and fell silent. The silence grew louder and louder, longer and longer. . . .

Friedrich was saying something, but Ariadne couldn't hear it – she was staring at his sensuous mouth as he talked. He had the most beautiful lips she'd ever seen. He was so elegant, so urbane, yet shy. He was polite and considerate too, and his body! So perfectly proportioned and muscular, like an athletic ballet dancer. When he turned to the side, lost in thought, she was astounded by his profile. His eyes then took on a profound, mysterious look – a metaphysical quality.

Get a grip on yourself, Ariadne snapped to herself. You hardly know him. You're being silly. Anyway, what would it be like? Could we ever have anything but 'an affair'? Especially on Earth. Talk about a long-distance relationship! She promised herself for the fourteenth time that night she would keep it just a friendship. Anyway, she didn't have the guts to show him how she felt. What if he rejected her? Oh, Ariadne, pull yourself together. Feminists aren't supposed to be afraid of rejection. But she was.

Friedrich edged closer and closer to her. Taking her hand in both of his, he looked into her eyes. What was he thinking? He looked at her passionately, telling her that she was beautiful, how much he liked being with her. But could she really believe him? Could she trust him? She'd heard thousands of women tell stories about men who had romanced them and then up and left rudely the next day. Why should her experience be different? But she couldn't stop the feelings she was having, even if she had wanted to. So why try? And how on Earth could she ever fall in love if she kept thinking this much?

First Night of Love

At 4 a.m. the Plastique Bertrand began to close and they had to leave. Ariadne told Friedrich she could take a cab to her apartment (he'd really wonder if she said she could fly!) but he insisted on riding with her. Only when they reached her building did Ariadne discover that Friedrich lived out of town. It would take him more than an hour to get home. 'It's so late,' she said, 'you can't start back now. Why not sleep on the couch?' Friedrich accepted, and they went in to her apartment.

Inside, they found Jupiter, who had returned from the party very gay and full of champagne, busy taking a nap. Ariadne made up the soft-cushioned couch for Friedrich. Then she sat on a chair nearby, knowing she should say good night and go to her own bedroom, but unable to leave him. He clearly felt the same way, and to prolong the evening for just a few more minutes, he offered to tell her a bedtime story. With this excuse, they could pretend that nothing unusual was happening. Friedrich made up a wonderful, silly story about bears in the woods who liked to eat berries, and the trouble they got into.

When he'd finished, they both fell silent, looking at each other.

Friedrich got up, silently walked over to Ariadne's chair, and picked her up in his arms. He carried her into her bedroom. Jupiter followed them, watching carefully, concerned about Ariadne. Friedrich gently placed her on the bed, atop the soft, yellow satin quilt, inside the pale blue tapestry curtains.

Her heart was racing. This couldn't be happening. She couldn't be falling in love this way. They couldn't make love this soon. 'Darling, my darling,' Friedrich murmured. What was happening? Ariadne hoped and yearned with all her heart that Friedrich would make love to her, but at the same time she wished he would leave her alone.

Friedrich lay down next to her. No one spoke. Ariadne felt Friedrich's breath close and warm on her cheek. She turned towards him. He was the most beautiful man she had ever seen. His eyes were so intense, so full of love; they said a thousand things. . . . He seemed to yearn for her.

It seemed like an eternity, the two of them suspended together in another world, before Ariadne felt Friedrich's mouth warm and soft against her own.

It was a wonderful kiss, an immortal kiss – a kiss to announce that kissing and everything that it meant were his intention. There, in the semi-dark room, the world so silent, time ceased to exist, and they were lifted up to an infinitely beautiful universe, a world where people could really be one, and all love was possible. In that instant, everything changed for Ariadne.

In the days that followed, bright autumn days, when the air

was crisp on their faces, Friedrich and Ariadne spent most of their time together. And when they were apart, they talked on the phone, often for hours. Sometimes, they would hang up only because they had just agreed to meet each other minutes later!

Jupiter started to feel a little jealous, even though a lot of the time, the three of them went out together, which he adored – he was now a 'city dog'. In fact, when he knew they were going out for a walk, Jupiter would grab his red collar and leash and leap up, turning somersaults in the air.

One day Ariadne confided to him. 'Oh, Jupiter, do you know how I feel? I'm so happy! Why, oh why, is it so wonderful? What does it mean? Can it last? Or is this just a game he is playing? Oh, he is so wonderful! It couldn't be just a wild fling, could it? Is he serious about me? Oh, Jupiter, tell me, tell me, what do you think?!'

Soon there were nights of sex together, both Friedrich and Ariadne telling each other rapturously that they loved each other, that life had never been complete before, that they never wanted to be apart. Friedrich told Ariadne he wished he had known her since she was a child. He wished they had grown up together and regretted all the days they had not spent together.

Jupiter was becoming more than a little jealous – in fact, terribly jealous – but, thinking it would be beneath him to show such a pedestrian emotion, he forced himself to smile and look interested, and listen.

Inside, however, he felt deserted, angry – almost desolate. Would Ariadne still be *his* best friend? Would they continue to be as close as before?

Earth: Act II

One of those mornings, Ariadne sat on the floor of the living-room in her pink and blue flowered pyjamas, petting Jupiter, a broad smile on her face. 'Oh, I'm so happy! Life is so wonderful! The sky so blue! Why can't everyone be as happy as I am?'

A knock at the door announced Kate. 'Wait until you get a load of today's papers . . . I'm afraid. . . .'

'Oh Kate, I don't care! I'm so happy, so in love – the roof could fall in today and I wouldn't care! All that matters is Friedrich. How I love him! He's so handsome, so intelligent, so wonderful! So exciting . . . he left just a little while ago. . . .'

She stopped, suddenly noticing deep black circles under Kate's lovely green eyes.

'Kate! Terrific one! What's wrong? Did you work too late last night?'

'No . . . I had a big fight with Roger. He was furious because I stayed here so late, we argued all night. I hardly got any sleep. And this morning he walked out in a huff, calling me a "cold bitch" and saying he was going to go see his ex-girlfriend.' Kate stifled a sob.

'Would he really go see his ex-girlfriend? He wouldn't!'

'I don't know and I don't care. Damn it, the trouble is I do care.'

'Listen, why don't you invite him over here for a while, so he can see what goes on? Would that help?'

'Oh, I don't know. I'm so mad. And I don't even know where he is right now.' Kate began to cry again.

'How awful . . . oh, don't cry. Look, he's sure to call you today. How about some breakfast? Would you like some eggs?'

To comfort Kate, Ariadne put on a cheerful recording, *Boutique Fantastique*, and began cooking. She made coffee, scrambled eggs and biscuits for the three of them.

The Ministry of Truth

The telephone rang. Kate picked it up. 'Yes, I see, I'll call you back.' Turning to Ariadne, she explained, 'That was Ms Light from *Power Press*. She's called several times for an interview.'

'Has she read the book?'

'I doubt it, she didn't say anything about the book at all. . . .'

Ariadne mused aloud, 'But maybe she is serious. I've heard that newspapers give a more in-depth report than TV. TV does short, simplistic stories (and that's all one can realistically expect), but in newspapers, serious ideas are discussed in depth. Could this be a good chance?'

'Don't forget, Ariadne!' Kate cautioned her friend in an urgent tone of voice, 'This is the same paper that has already invested money in that poll that "proved you wrong". You know, *Power Press* and ARC TV are both owned by Biggest Brother. . . . It could be in their interest to undermine you in the public's mind. They've got an investment in one point of view. They won't want to contradict themselves. . . .'

'Yes, but this paper has an excellent reputation. Its journalists are said to have real integrity. We shouldn't be negative. . . . Would Ms Light stoop so low as to come on false pretences, with a closed mind? And – after all – she *is* a woman!'

'Yeah, but so was the one from Whole Truth TV. . . .'

'But that was TV, this is a serious paper. It wouldn't have trivial people working for it. At least, I hope not.'

She looked at Kate uncertainly. 'Tell her, yes – tomorrow, at twelve.'

Ariadne and Jupiter were in a positive mood as they waited for Ms Light to arrive.

But when Ariadne opened the door, not a woman, but a man stood there. The man was in his late twenties, thin, wearing a plaid flannel shirt and blue jeans. Not even bothering to sit down in the chair Ariadne offered him, he scowled back at her smile of welcome, and jerked a tape recorder out of his pocket, thrusting it roughly towards her mouth. 'And *so*, Ms Rite, what do you have to say about what the papers are saying about you? How do you explain yourself?'

Jupiter stood next to Ariadne, looking as tall as he could.

'Oh, no,' Ariadne sighed, crestfallen. 'Maybe Kate was right.' She looked him in the eye, 'I didn't catch your name. Where is Ms Light? Is she coming later?'

'She didn't have time.' Snarling, he pushed his tape recorder even more aggressively at her face, and began repeating, 'Are you refusing to talk to me? Are you trying to manipulate the press? Censor what we say and do?'

'No, of course not. . . . I just wondered . . . Have you read the book?'

'Why are you so aggressive? I can do an interview without reading a book. You don't think I have time to read that whole thing, do you?'

Jupiter began to growl, showing his teeth. Ariadne put her hand on his head in reassurance.

'Well . . . uh,' she thought quickly, 'Can't we get things onto a better footing?' She looked placatingly at him, 'Mr . . . What is your name? Why don't we sit down here on this couch by the fireplace – would you like some coffee? – and I can explain to you the main ideas, some of what I found. . . .'

Elvis Trouble sat down, but still clenched his tape recorder, holding it threateningly near Ariadne's face. Ariadne tried to overlook these gestures, telling herself, After all, it's better than reporters who don't bother. Probably, he just wants to get the quotes right.

She began, 'Well, as I see it, relationships are a microcosm of the larger social system. There is an important connection between how women see their intimate relationships with men, the emotional dynamics, and problems of poverty and racism, as well as society's attitude to the environment. . . .'

'Sorry,' Elvis interrupted, 'I don't cover environmental issues, so could you stick to the point?'

'But that is the point.'

56

'Yeah? Well, our readers are only interested in why you say all these women hate men.'

Jupiter rolled his eyes. Not that old saw!

'But I don't say that, and neither do the women quoted in the book,' Ariadne explained, thinking she'd better speak more simply. 'The book is about love, and how it can be better. Not how to put men down. . . .'

'Oh, come on,' Elvis waved her reply away dismissively. 'Women have equal rights and equal pay and all that. You're really on about a bunch of frustrated old hags who blame all their problems on men!'

'How can you say that! Women may have equal rights in theory, but not in life. This book, with thousands of women speaking, could be the beginning of a great dialogue, don't you see? It could do so much good. Women are wondering whether, in order to gain equality, they have to become as aggressive as many men. At present even doing housework is non-negotiable for many women.'

'Negotiable! Why should a man have to negotiate in his own home? You're trying to make everything into a battle.'

It was almost more than Jupiter could bear. His nose and ears twitched, not in their usual charming way, but in nervous spasms. He wanted to bite Trouble.

'Mr Elvis,' Ariadne wondered how anyone with so little under-standing of the language could be a reporter, '"negotiate" simply means to agree on an issue by discussion. Women don't want battles, they want communication. Many women lie in bed at night, after their husband has gone to sleep or their lover has gone home, wondering, Why do I feel there's something missing? If only he would talk to me more, open up.'

'Yeah, yeah, yeah,' Elvis impatiently changed the subject. 'How many people helped you do your research? How equipped *are* you to do such research?' He arched his eyebrows accusingly.

Ariadne counted to ten, determined not to lose her cool. It had become clear beyond a shadow of a doubt that Trouble was looking for trouble – not the facts, ma'am, just the facts. Was this his idea or *Power Press*'s? she wondered. And what was the point?

'Really, Mr Trouble, do you care how many research assistants I had? Whether 5,500 or 4,500 women participated? That wouldn't make women's lives and thoughts any different – especially as this was a highly representative sample of the population. All the best researchers said so (even on the book jacket). You, dear sir, are not really interested in my research methods, and certainly don't understand them. Frankly, you're not even interested in women's well-being or the planet's survival. You just want to trivialize everything, and start a fight. You're looking for a way to discredit my work because I've dared to say women are rethinking our lives and men are no longer the centre of their universe.'

'You don't know what you're talking about!' Elvis Trouble blurted out, in a rage. 'Admit it, you're a fraud! Your research is a fraud! Your whole act is a fraud! You hate men! Admit it!'

'But there is a fifty percent divorce rate in this country, according to government statistics. I didn't make them up. . . .' Ariadne took a deep breath, and decided to try to reach him one more time, human to human, show him their common purpose. 'Listen, Mr Elvis, do we have to fight? Can't you help me? You represent the press. I'm talking to the press because this is the way to get ideas across in a democratic society. Public debate has to take place in newspapers and on TV. Certainly you must believe in free speech and in democracy! Why don't you show it?!'

The door opened, and Friedrich came in with Kate, who was asking, 'The papers are filled with stories about physical violence against women every day. Why can't they cope with some of Ariadne's reports of emotional violence?'

Friedrich hugged Ariadne. 'Hello, sweetheart!' Kate went towards the kitchen. Before Ariadne or Friedrich knew what had happened, Elvis had darted over and cornered Kate at the kitchen door, blocking her way, holding his ever-present black tape recorder an inch from her mouth. 'Who are you? Are you permanent or a temp? Did you do Rite's research for her? You can tell me. Isn't she awful to work for?'

Friedrich and Ariadne both walked over to Elvis. 'What do you think you're doing?'

Elvis winked broadly at Friedrich, then leered at Ariadne. 'Miss, oh, I mean Ms Rite, tell the truth: didn't you really write this

58

because you thought a book about sex would sell well and make you a lot of money?'

Friedrich was livid. 'You're totally off-base. Did you come here to have a discussion, or to make trouble? Your paper started it when you did that poll with ARC TV, and now you want to finish the job.'

Elvis kept trying the man-to-man approach. 'But, old man, women are always moaning on about things. They're never satisfied.'

Ariadne's face flushed, and tears of frustration sprang to her eyes. She wanted to throw something at that man. She felt so invaded – almost raped. She threw her book at him.

For Friedrich, Elvis's sleazy statement was the last straw. Towering above Trouble, his anger making him appear even taller than his six feet, he shouted, 'Your behaviour is outrageous. Who do you think you are, coming here and acting this way?'

Elvis looked nervous, but gleeful at the same time: here at last was a turn of events he could use to his advantage! This was juicy! A real story!

Jupiter, however, decided to take matters into his own hands, or paws. With one swift movement, he latched onto Trouble's flabby biceps with his sweet little teeth, shaking his head to and fro, and the biceps along with it. He growled fiercely.

Elvis saw it was time to go. Journalism school had taught him how to deal with irate humans, but not with irate dogs! He was out in two seconds flat.

Jupiter rolled over and gleefully waved his feet in the air. Friedrich had never felt closer to Jupiter. What a great dog! What a good friend!

The four of them sat there, at first laughing, then trying to analyse what had happened. They all agreed that no reputable paper would condone the actions of a reporter like Trouble.

At Friedrich's urging, Ariadne called the editor-in-chief of Elvis's paper, Ben Badd. 'The reason I'm calling you is that, as you may know, a reporter from your paper came here today to write a story about me. He is, of course, free to write whatever he wants, but he behaved so aggressively and unprofessionally, I couldn't believe he represented your paper. He didn't seem objective, he hadn't read the book, and wouldn't listen when I tried to discuss it. Was this some kind of a mistake?'

'Ah, Miss Rite . . .' Badd responded, bemused. 'We tried to get you, but now we'll stop.'

'What??' Ariadne couldn't believe her ears.

'We tried to get you, but now we'll stop,' Badd repeated, in a Looney-Tunes voice.

As calmly as she could, Ariadne thanked him and hung up, in shock. What had he meant? That they wouldn't run the piece? What article could there be, after all – they hadn't really even discussed anything. But how amazing that the editor would have used the phrase, 'tried to get you' – not to mention admitting to such a thing. What on Earth was she involved in?

'This could be hysterically funny,' Friedrich offered, 'except I don't feel like laughing.'

Swifty's Clairvoyant

Swifty had Connections. Everywhere. He belonged to all the Right Clubs and knew all the Real Players on every continent. Almost before Elvis's taxi could pull away from the curb, Swifty was on the phone. 'Ariadne, I've heard all about it. Listen, who the hell do you think you are? Jeanne d'Arc died a long time ago. Let me do the talking for you.'

It was the happy Otter, the one Ariadne had met at the Glitterati party – the very night she had first met Friedrich. . . .

'Hello! But if I don't talk to them, how do I get through to people in a democracy?' Ariadne wanted to know. 'Don't I have to talk to the press?'

'In this country you have to talk to the Right People, let them talk to the press for you.'

'The Right People? Do I have to know them to get a fair chance with the press? That doesn't sound very democratic to me,' Ariadne was dismayed and looked at Jupiter.

'Stop looking at that dog of yours. He can't help you!' Ariadne doubted that. 'Say listen, honey. . . . Here's what I'll do for you! Meet me later with your ice skates and I'll treat you to a Real

Good Time. And, yeah, yeah, you can bring the dog. I suppose he skates too!'

Swifty Takes Ariadne and Jupiter Ice-Skating at Rocky's Wonderland Centre

Ariadne had just finished tying on Jupiter's skates (they'd only been charged for a regular rental even though there were four legs involved) when Swifty streaked across the ice in his new designer bobble-cap, with matching scarf and mittens with pom-poms.

'Oh, how wonderful you look,' Ariadne wondered if she and Jupiter weren't a trifle underdressed.

'Yeah,' he said matter-of-factly, 'I saw Prince le Baron Rothmann wearing an outfit just like this the other day. I had to go all the way to Paris just to get an identical one.'

At that point Jupiter, unable to resist the Walt Disney cartoon music playing over the loudspeaker, took to the ice in a big way. Racing out to the centre, he performed the most spectacular somersaults, making a triple-axel with a toe-loop look like child's play. Zooming back to Ariadne and an astonished Swifty, Jupiter took both by the paw and led them out to skate round the rink in the skaters' traditional crossed-arm form.

Swifty, on the outside end, looked alternately thrilled and terrified as he accelerated and decelerated round the curves. But gradually he stabilized, and round and round they all went, their three very different voices chiming in with the music, all cares and worries banished – for now.

That night Ariadne, Friedrich and Jupiter were cuddled in bed together, half asleep. Ariadne, her head against Friedrich's warm shoulder, muttered drowsily, 'What a day. . . . Oh, I almost forgot, but it's very important. . . .' She opened her eyes. 'Twelve brilliant women, women I admire, all famous writers – are planning to defend me. One of them spoke to Kate today. They are drafting a statement saying my work is important, and that the personal attacks should stop. . . .'

She started to say more, but Friedrich was already asleep.

Ariadne played with Jupiter's paws until she and he, too, fell asleep. Ariadne's sleep was fitful, however, and she woke up later, thoughts racing through her mind. 'Why, why, is all this happening? Is there something wrong with the way I am going about things? Should I be speaking so honestly about what I see here on Earth? Who am *I* to do this, anyway? Maybe there's some mistake about the reaction. . . . Could they be intentionally misunderstanding? *Why?* Oh, this must be a nightmare, it can't be real. . . .'

Sensing her vague, fitful sleep, Jupiter woke up and stretched his sweet little body. Ariadne felt better immediately. 'Jupiter,' she whispered, tickling his soft ear, the white furry part and the pink part, 'I'm so confused. I can't stand not knowing what's going on. I need some *Answers*.'

In silence, understanding her perfectly, Jupiter dreamed them up to Heaven.

Harry Truman Explains Biggest Brother

Remembering Harry Truman's offer of help, Ariadne and Jupiter went to see him the minute they arrived.

'Hello, Jupiter. Sit down. What can I do for you, Ariadne?' Harry's desk was crowded with signed photos of great politicians.

'Well,' Ariadne began, 'I was expecting to be attacked, as anyone is who takes a stand – but on the issues, not on my personality. It's like sitting through an endless series of denunciations.'

'I know. I've been watching. It looks a bit like the old Stalinist show trials!' he laughed.

'Funny you should say that – it's exactly what the Defence Committee said on the phone: the media put women in the news on trial. Use blatant sexist stereotypes to belittle every major step forward that women take. But what I want to know is, what can I do now? You're a politician, do you know?'

Harry leaned back in his chair. 'Well, in most towns – just like my home town of Independence – everyone sucks up to the people with money and power (most people – but not people like my hero, Will Rogers!). I remember how sure these big papers were that I would lose the election – ha! Were they ever wrong! But what they're doing to you is damn vicious. It's like an old tom cat, knowing it has all the power, just toying with a fledgling bird.'

'You know,' said Ariadne, 'I feel like a character in a Hitchcock film who is going along, minding their own business – like Cary Grant in *North by Northwest* or Robert Donat in *The Thirty-nine Steps* – and suddenly I'm caught up in something I don't quite understand. Sometimes I wonder if it's a case of mistaken identity – the reports I read don't seem to be about me at all, and they're not about my book either.'

She began to stutter shyly, as if thinking aloud. 'I don't want to get involved in fighting back – that's just low-level mud slinging. But when they keep attacking me, I have to fight back or go under. Oh, I'm so confused. I thought everyone had the right to free speech, but when I speak out, they try to shut me up.'

'When the Biggest Brother was a boy in the forties – I knew his parents – he used to watch all those movies about tough guy reporters.' Harry sighed, 'It's sad. He decided, when he grew up, that he would be tough just like those guys! Today when you listen to him, you can almost hear James Cagney snarling, "This is a nasty business! People are out to trick you, so watch out!" He still hasn't grown up, he's still trying to look like a tough guy, impress the other boys on the block. He used to watch *Citizen Kane*, too, but I think he entirely missed the real message, though heaven knows he saw it often enough.

'Did you know he was once head of the sports division of their TV network? That's how he started. Then he got the bright idea of bringing a fighting spirit to the news, to up the ratings. And he did it. Under him, the news began to look like a giant sporting event. Fast and combative. Keep those viewers glued to their chairs. Soon all the networks followed this format, worried that they'd lose viewers if they appeared "wimpy" by comparison.'

'If they're such tough guys,' Jupiter inquired, 'why don't they go after tough targets, like the corporations that throw chemical waste into the oceans, or the ones that kill our endangered species?'

'Listen, Dog, of the eleven hundred members of the Society of Investigative Reporters, last year only five were assigned to investigate corporations, and none was assigned to investigate other reporters or news media. Anyway, despite all this news-as-combat, the TV ratings are going down. Maybe people don't like this way of getting information anymore.'

Ariadne suddenly got it. 'They are just grown-up boys playing cops and robbers!'

'You betcha!' laughed Harry. 'Don't be depressed, Ariadne, you're not as powerless as you feel. You've made a successful attack on the injustices of the system. You've criticized the powers that be and people listened to you. Why should those in power smile at you? Of course, I agree they should argue with you on the issues, not attack you personally – but that's politics.'

He took his feet off his desk and leaned forward earnestly. 'Plus, you're finding yourself beleaguered on all sides because of the extraordinary consolidation of the media. The result of all those damned corporate takeovers is that there are not many independent newspapers or TV stations left in America anymore. The real Big Brother has arrived. Used to be, only as far back as 1981, there were forty-nine major corporations controlling the media in the US, but within five years there were only twenty-nine. Soon, it will be only five, perhaps. Many of them have interlocking directorates, they're all friends.

'George – do you know Orwell? Well, he's been talking a lot about this, about how he was right. The Ministry of Truth is here. And the consequences for democracy . . . well, maybe you should meet him.'

'I'm so sick of discussing the media!' Ariadne cried. 'I set out to talk about equality and justice, just a few simple ideas, to let people speak out in my book, and I've wound up talking about defending myself against media attacks!'

Harry sighed. 'A diversionary tactic. I've seen it before. The press has created this controversy about the statistics to keep you from getting your message across.'

'But, Harry,' Ariadne sighed too, her hand on Jupiter's head for comfort and support, 'how on earth *do* you get things on Earth to change?'

Jupiter chimed in, 'Yeah, how can you make things there more fun, too?'

'Well, well, so you both want to know how to change things on

Earth? That means understanding Human Earth-History,' Harry smiled.

Ariadne looked excited. 'Harry, do you know any people up here who are interested in discussing history? I'd really appreciate your introducing me. The theory of revolutions, how society changes – I've been waiting for months for someone to discuss this with!'

Jupiter looked at Harry expectantly.

'Sure,' said Harry. 'I know plenty of 'em! I'll take you to the Political Debaters Division of the Whist Club. I'll make sure you meet the Right People. Or, maybe I'll call ahead for you, I might not go myself – I don't know how many more political debates I can stand!' And he picked up the phone.

While they were waiting, Jupiter and Ariadne began to wonder if Friedrich would wake up and miss them. Somewhat reluctantly, they said 'ciao' to Harry and drifted down to Earth, linked by hand and paw. . . .

Trouble Again

A grim Kate arrived at the apartment. 'Well, good old Elvis has actually done it,' she said, pointing to a huge article in the *Power Press*. 'He goes on and on, attacking your statistics (they're not "scientific" – that old saw!*!), and *you*: he says you're an impossible, weird, aggressive woman! He more or less implies you concocted your statistics to match what he calls your prejudices, and he gives the impression it would be terrible if other women listened to you – or ever tried to be like you, in speaking up for women!!! There's nothing, not a word, about the main concepts in the book, or the scholars who praise your methods – it's almost like disinformation.'

'But what about what the editor-in-chief said to me? Was he being manipulative? Cynical?'

'Well, you don't get to be a member of the Big Brotherhood for nothing,' Kate observed drily.

The following day another Powerful Paper carried a spin-off

article, 'Rite's Book Under Rising Attack', with the subhead: 'Social Science Fiction'.

That afternoon, the president of the Super-Professional Psychological Association called. 'Ms Rite, we consider the situation in the papers so inaccurate that nineteen of us, all well-known scholars in our fields, have sent a statement to the editor of the *Power Press*. It says,

> To the Editor,
> With regard to your article on Ariadne Rite's *The Meaning of It All*, we would like to make our opinions known as follows. We believe the Rite Report to be an authoritative and scholarly work that will prove extremely valuable as we re-examine our culture. While we believe it is particularly important for women, we hope that it will be read by as many people as possible who care about the nature of our society in the years ahead.

'We've all signed it, of course. Just thought you'd like to know.'

At last, Ariadne thought. Just wait until this letter appears! That will really change things.

However, only two days later Ariadne received a letter from another editor at the paper:

> Dear Ms Rite,
> The scholars' testimonial is wholly meaningless to the average reader of our columns, so I doubt that our letters column will publish it.

Pale and trembling, Ariadne sat down, her heart pounding. Why were the scholars irrelevant? Why wouldn't anybody be interested? Why did the editor write to her and not to the scholars who wrote the letter?

She read this hellish message out loud to Kate and Jupiter. 'What!?' Kate exclaimed. 'They're refusing to publish a letter signed by such eminent scholars? I can't believe it!'

Ariadne began to pace back and forth. 'I don't feel too well,' she said, 'I'm going to lie down for a few minutes.'

Later that night, Ariadne and Jupiter were in the kitchen trying to have a normal dinner when the phone rang.

Voice of Ariadne's publisher calling from Europe: 'You won't believe this: A reporter named Elvis called us today all the way from the US pressuring us not to publish your book! He found me out in the country at a sales conference, and asked me whether we are "still going to publish" your book. I said, "Of course we're publishing it – why?" "Well, after all the things they are saying about it, that it might be a fraud, and so on . . . !" (He said this with a nasty innuendo.) I fired back, "That's ridiculous. There's enormous academic and literary support for the book. Not only are we publishing it, but we are proud to publish it!" We were amazed! What cheek!'

Next morning, Ariadne got another call. What now? Robert, her editor, told her, 'Hi kiddo! We've had a call from some guy called Elvis Trouble, asking if we are going to withdraw your book from the market. He has called no less than four people here, asking all of us if Holy Grail isn't going to withdraw your book since it is being called a statistical fraud! I told him that this is ludicrous and that, in fact, we are suggesting it to the Pulitzer Prize committee for nomination.'

Ariadne was too stunned to speak. Robert's voice, as it continued, seemed to come from a long way off. 'This reporter Elvis is stepping way beyond the bounds of journalism. He is trying to create a media event. What outrageous behaviour! You could sue him for trying to interfere with your contract. I'm going to call the book chains, to see if he's been trying to intimidate them too.'

A shocked Ariadne just managed to mumble. 'Thanks for calling, Bob,' before putting the phone down.

'Kate,' Ariadne said, very pale, 'can you believe this? Elvis's plan was to take on two of the best publishing houses in the world, try to control them, get them to sever their connection with my book! He wants to ruin my reputation. He wants to make it impossible for me ever to publish again!'

Friedrich arrived with lunch for the four of them, and they told him this latest news.

'Listen, darling,' Friedrich said, 'to me, that reporter Elvis (and a few others, too) is pursuing you in a way that has definite sexual overtones. Don't think I'm exaggerating – his behaviour is that of a rapist stalking his intended victim. The baiting, the taunting, the "you like it too, otherwise you wouldn't cooperate" – while ostensibly offering "a chance to tell it like it is" – adds up to sexual harassment. . . .

'He, the pursuer, has more power, the power of the media, and doesn't mind using it. He sees your meeting not as an "interview", but as a one-to-one male – female encounter in which he should dominate. And if you don't act submissive, if you act authoritative and knowledgeable, he feels threatened and retaliates. You become "the enemy". And the fact that you wrote sometimes about sex, this makes you (in his macho eyes) fair game, a fair target.'

'How chilling!' Kate looked horrified. 'A rape mind-set – an opportunity for legal rape in which the "journalist" is actually commended for being "tough", and not "letting a woman fool him", or "control the interview"!'

They were all silent, thinking. Jupiter, too.

Learning How the Legal System Protects Your Rights

'Maybe it sounds extreme,' Kate interrupted the silence, 'But can't you sue Trouble for what he's done? This is a democracy. We have free speech and people's rights are protected. They can't just tell lies about you and get away with it. There are legal remedies for this. For example, you could sue the papers for not telling both sides of the story, not giving a balanced picture.'

Ariadne sighed, 'Maybe it's time I checked this out.'

In the office of Stanley Shay, Heavy-Duty Attorney, Ariadne was treated to the wood-panelled atmosphere of Power. . . . Clearly, he was One of the Players.

'Who's giving you the most trouble?' Shay smiled, genially.

'*Power Press*, their TV network, and another of their publications, *Truth of the Week*.'

'You – and everybody else! The Biggest Brothers have the greatest libel insurance around, so, frankly, they're not worried about the threat of a suit. Worse, the biggest problem is that you're now what is known legally as a "public figure".'

Ariadne looked blank.

'Public figures can't realistically sue for libel. The laws that used to protect them don't exist anymore in this country. Let me explain something very important. The media are no longer required to do a "balanced story", showing both sides, in the case of public figures. The Supreme Court ruled in a 1974 case brought by a politician against the *Miami Herald* that in this country we rely on a multiplicity of newspapers, magazines and television for different opinions, therefore any one paper does not have to present more than one side of an issue, even knowingly. No, you have to prove they had a malicious intent. And that's quite hard (if not impossible) to prove! So, it's almost impossible for public figures, such as yourself, to sue for libel. The press knows this. The public does not.'

'You mean, in the case of public figures like me, the press can legitimately report only one side of a story? Knowingly not telling both sides of it?'

'Right you are, you smart little cookie!'

'So if their paper says my work is not scientific, and lots of scholars say it *is* scientific, they don't ever have to report this?'

'Right again! Give that girl a prize!' He offered her a mint. 'Honey, it would be easier to sue Elvis and his paper for interfering with your contract – those phone calls he made to ask your publishers to withdraw your work – than for his defamatory article. So – you wanna play?'

He stood up, beaming at his own professionalism. 'Well, time is money! Now that you know the facts, what do you want to do?'

'Own a TV station or run a newspaper – that's what it seems to take if you want to have freedom of speech!' Ariadne replied with irony. 'Anyway,' she added, 'I see that suing them wouldn't get the real story told. It would just be more of a media circus.'

'It would cost a fortune, too,' Shay pronounced, a beatific smile on his delighted countenance. 'You have a few years before the statute of limitations runs out. Call me!'

At home, Kate inquired about Shay, 'Whaddid Shay say?' Almost laughing, Ariadne replied, 'If I could pay Shay mucho bucks, maybe I could defend myself. That's the bottom line.'

Kate blurted out, 'That Trouble and all the noise he makes – and gets his buddies at other papers to make – he's created this false "controversy". He wouldn't know what "scientific" was if it jumped up and smacked him in the face. What a shame this manufactured "controversy" doesn't sell books the way people imagine.' Kate looked furious.

'Yes, finances are a problem. All the research I did cost horrible amounts of money. Well, it was worth it – but sometimes I wonder how long I can keep it up, it's so expensive.'

'Oh, Ariadne, as long as I can pay my rent, I'll always be here! Don't worry about me!'

'Kate, you charming one, you're so wonderful and thoughtful. I love you.' Ariadne hugged her friend, tears in her eyes.

Ariadne's Dream

That night Ariadne dreamt she was standing on the roof of a tall building, where she'd been chased by a pack of reporters. She peered over the edge, looking for a way of escape, as they came up the stairs to get her. Down below she saw many of her friends, the people she loved, and many other people she didn't know. They were holding two large round mats, like the ones the fire department uses to catch people who jump out of burning buildings. They moved the mats into different positions, trying to get them in the right place so she could jump safely. But there was no way her safety could be guaranteed. There was nothing to do but to take a chance and jump. They so wanted to help her and to give her support, but there was very little they could do. They became tinier and tinier, and shrank into the distance. . . .

Ariadne woke up after her dream. She asked Jupiter, lying next to her, to come with her for a walk in the park, to be calmed by the tranquillity of the night sounds. The air outside was cool, and the stars shining above them were clear.

It was Jupiter who broke the silence. 'Ariadne, I have to ask you this. How important is all this trivial behaviour on the part of reporters? I know you care about the dignity of women, of people and animals – that's courageous and heroic – but I can't stand to see you hurt so much. All this involvement with reporters, does it have to continue?'

'I don't like it either. I hate it. I wouldn't even talk to a person like Elvis normally, but what else can I do? How else can I reach so many people? I never knew when I started taking notes that it would be like this. Oh, how I long to be doing something else, to forget all this!'

As they sat on the moist ground, she put her arms round Jupiter, caressing his soft warm fur, burying her face in his neck. He pressed his body against her.

Together with Jupiter, Ariadne began to feel like herself again. For the first time in days, she forgot her worries.

She looked at Jupiter and really saw him. She loved his furry face and his sweet shining eyes, which looked up at her, adoringly. Large brown orbs, his eyes, larger than her own, the white part surrounded by perfect black edges. His eyelashes, short, neat and shiny alternated in perfect symmetry, two beige palomino ones, a pale blond one, two palominos. . . . His whiskers sprouted from little black dots, rather like the antennae on his forehead, growing out of darker, furry areas. Sometimes when one fell out, Ariadne would find it and put it under her pillow at night, or in her jewellery box. These were Jupiter's 'antlers'. When he smiled, as now, Ariadne could see his baby-teeth. A little crooked in the front, they only made his smile more charming.

'I love you, Jupiter! You remind me of a deer, a lovely, flying deer.' Running her hand through his fur, she could see, just next to his skin, the soft, white baby underfur. His eyes sparkled softly like little lights, as Ariadne stroked him and talked lovingly to him.

Jupiter's antennae started twitching. He adjusted them and sat bolt upright, listening intently. 'Ariadne! A special report from the Intergalactic Animal Radio Emergency Network is coming in! They're featuring a Report on Earth's condition – "The Ecological History of Earth". Listen!'

The voice was faint at first, then a little stronger . . . it seemed to be coming from very far away, from distant galaxies, a sombre, dark voice, but steady and clear, speaking to them through the mysterious static of time and space, broadcasting back to the Present from the Future. Jupiter listened to catch every word, and now Ariadne listened too.

'Since the start of the Industrial Revolution, new vapours, two hundred billion tons of carbon dioxide alone, have been added to the atmosphere. In less than a century, thousands of new chemicals have infiltrated every living tissue and, like radiation, these are creating ominous biological alterations.

'By the late 1950s industry had extracted raw materials in such astounding volumes that by the year 2000, most were near exhaustion. The economic benefits of industrialization spread unevenly, and caused political turbulence. As ever, entrepreneurs contended for dominion over the Earth's crust, this time wielding its bitter fruit – uranium.

'By the 1980s some wastes of industry, seventy-seven billion pounds a year, were so hazardous that it was not clear whether the planet could safely contain them. They poisoned drinking water, land, food, and, in some cases, entire communities.'

Ariadne and Jupiter were riveted to the spot: this was what their own research had shown.

The voice continued. 'In many so-called democracies, corporation leaders gave more financial support than ever before to political candidates friendly to their business interests, ensuring the defeat of candidates they considered hostile. As a result, in the 1980s and 90s many Western nations were run by politicians dedicated to wiping out half a century of social legislation and regulation of business. The outlook for Earth is grim. Will people see the dangers to their freedom and their world in time? Will Earth survive? Tune in for our next report. . . . ' The voice faded.

Ariadne and Jupiter sat staring at each other, realizing all too clearly the implications of what they'd just heard. 'It sounded like the car radio in Cocteau's film *Orphée*, in which a banal announcement of the news turned out to be a great poem, if you listened closely,' Ariadne said.

Jupiter's ears suddenly stood up even straighter, and he leaped to his feet. He was getting another message. He told Ariadne he had to go to an emergency meeting of the Council of Animals, but would be in bed with her before she awoke in the morning.

He was gone.

The Council of the Animals

★

Fala was calling the meeting to order when Jupiter arrived. As the animals gathered they talked about the report they had just heard – the mass extermination of many species, widespread cruel industrialization of animals, and too, the danger of the poisoned atmosphere for all animals.

What were the humans doing to the Earth? Could they be stopped? How much longer could they breathe?

Fala opened the meeting: 'As you have all heard, chemical fumes are circling around the Earth in the jet streams of the upper atmosphere, injuring all Life. No one is immune: what starts in one place spreads out everywhere. No animals can escape it by hiding, not even in the deep forests. We are here today to discuss what can be done, and to hear your testimony for the Record.'

A sea gull stepped forward to testify. 'Every night I see drift-net fleets, the mass-fishing companies, strip-mining the Earth's ocean. Hundreds of ships drape out over thirty thousand miles of monofilament netting in the North Pacific . . . enough netting to stretch from the Arctic icecap to Antarctica . . . and from California to China and back again. They're looking for tuna, but they catch every kind of fish – dolphins included. It's terrible to watch them die. . . .

'Like a spiderweb, the mammoth net binds the frantic dolphins eight or even ten times around, pinning their flippers, cutting deeply into their flesh. Unable to surface for air, the trapped dolphins drown after a hopeless fight to free themselves. The fishers try to sell the dolphins as "fish" (called mawi-mawi) to restaurants, and the unsuspecting human public eats them.

'Whole flocks of seabirds are also entrapped in the cruel mesh.

In their desperate struggle to escape, they bite and peck at their own wings and feet, dying at last in agony. Time-tested survival skills are of no use against this new, virtually invisible predator. Dolphins and seals lie lifeless by the score in the nets.'

A hush greeted this grim story. What could the animals do? How could they fight against these "modern" barbarities? Millions of birds, turtles, so many animals dying needlessly. 'Vast areas of the ocean could be reduced to watery wastelands,' Fala cried out.

Silvia Rea, a gorgeous wolf, came forward next. 'Did you know that long ago, before the Romans cut them down, the Mediterranean areas were all covered with lush green woods? The Romans used the trees for houses, ships and fuel, but today, the land is stripped. The scrub-brush vegetation you see in Greece, Italy, Spain and Turkey is not like the beautiful old trees that were there in the beginning, when I lived there. After they cut down the trees, of course the soil went too. Then only the scrub-brush could grow.

'If I had never nurtured those boys, Romulus and Remus, then things might have been different. Just look at what they did – founded a country that dominated women and animals, violating them and the Earth every day. Then they spread their culture all over Europe. Why did I help them? We females are always doing this – giving and nurturing – but are we right to keep on doing it?'

Many of the animals, male and female, nodded at the justness of her question.

'Just imagine,' Silvia Rea continued, 'what would have happened if there had been no Rome! In the south of Italy, women had a lot more status and they believed in the animals. Maybe that world would have flourished, and Italy would have had a different kind of civilization. I often imagine what might have been.'

Rughetta went over to comfort her. 'Oh, Silvia, don't torture yourself. You did what you thought was right at the time.'

Next, Laika delivered her report on the atmosphere. Because she was part cosmonaut, it was very scientific: 'Acid rain is destroying forests thousands of miles from the coal-fired power plants that are causing it. The ozone in the upper atmosphere, which protects all life on Earth from the sun's harmful ultraviolet rays, is being depleted by chemicals released from air conditioners, refrigerators, styrofoam, aerosol sprays and other products. This is causing global warming.

'Research shows that the Earth is now about 0.5 degrees centigrade warmer, on average, than a hundred years ago. The warmest period in history, 6000 BC, was one to two degrees centigrade higher than today, whereas the Little Ice Age, from about AD 1550 to 1700, was only a few tenths of a degree cooler.

'Strangely,' Laika concluded, 'the humans have this information. They discuss it. They make endless TV programmes about it. They talk, talk, talk. But they do nothing.'

Messages had been left on the Animals' Intergalactic Network Answering Machine (AINAM) throughout the meeting by those who couldn't attend. The animals now turned their attention to one just coming in: 'I am a porpoise and here in California, where I live, we porpoises are in revolt. We refuse to reproduce. Some of the humans are very dismayed. The smaller fishes that ride our backs have been asking each other what they should do. In fact, they're meeting now to discuss it. Some are in favour of taking action, others want to wait. The former call the latter "passive", while the latter call the former "aggressive". I don't know how long our strike will last or if we'll decide to go all the way to the end with it. I'll call again – but I hope I don't have to speak into an answering machine!'

Worried and angry murmurs echoed through the meeting. Many of those present believed that the animals should be the decision-makers on Earth.

One of those they wanted to empower was a lovely young doe named Phoebe, who told them, 'I live in a green and pleasant land. Now there are plans to privatize all the water companies. My companions and I are worried that we won't be able to have water since we can't pay for it.'

As the testimony piled up, Jupiter took the floor. 'Should the animals be the decision-makers, not the humans? We know the state the world is in, and we care. Humans care mostly about their cars, stereos, and their TVs. So much beauty around them, and they miss it! What's worse, they are causing that beauty to die. They think birds and plants will always be there for them, no matter what. Should we continue to support them?'

76

As the meeting broke up, separate groups continued talking about Jupiter's question. One group contended that some humans did understand, that not all humans were the problem. 'Leonardo da Vinci was a vegetarian,' Argo contested. 'He even said there would come a time when it would be considered as immoral to eat animals as it is to eat people.'

But Frederick the Great's lovely whippet, Arsinöe, thought this insufficient proof. 'Oh come on! Animals eat animals, too!' Alcemene, her sister, was of a different opinion. 'Neither Frederick nor Voltaire ever said a word about animal rights.' Arsinöe defended Frederick: 'But Alcemene, how can you say that? Frederick had great respect for us animals; didn't he build us our very own burial crypt and ask to be buried with us?'

Alcemene bared her soul to her sister, 'Well, I didn't like hunting. I felt compelled to do it out of loyalty to Frederick, and to earn my keep. But it made me feel compromised.'

Nearby, Jupiter had put politics aside and was immersed in a more lighthearted conversation with Rughetta. Oh, how he loved her sweet brown-and-white spots! Soon they began to sing together, songs that Rughetta had learned from Tito Gobbi, and she helped Jupiter practise his Italian. The other animals began singing along too, and soon the whole room was swaying to their favourite songs.

Sex in Paradise

Back on Earth, one human named Ariadne was also thinking about something besides politics.

She was trying to write some letters quietly in her apartment, but then had a better idea. She telephoned Friedrich. 'Hi! What are you doing?'

'I'm practising the Liszt *Transcendental Études*. Come over!'

Ariadne grabbed her purse and a small parcel, and took off.

At Friedrich's, she opened the door softly, trying not to disturb his playing, but he stopped, happy to see her.

Ariadne walked over to Friedrich, smiling provocatively. She ran her fingers through his hair, saying, 'Getting lots of practising done? Can I help?' But her eyes said she didn't mean to

77

help, at least not with his work. She sat down on his lap, facing him, her legs spread, and pressed her crotch against his.

'Guess what?'

He smiled.

'Today I got a pair of great, incredibly tight, gold lamé stretch pants. What do you think I should do with them?'

'Mmm. . . .' Friedrich said, warming up.

'Would you like to see how they look on?'

Friedrich pulled her closer, so they were crotch to crotch on the piano bench. Kissing her lightly, he was just able to ask, 'How tight did you say they are?'

'Skin-tight. They're stretch pants. Would you like to know what I was fantasizing you would do when I wore them?'

'Try them on!'

Ariadne started to get up.

'Wait! No!' He pulled her back to him. 'Stay here. *Tell* me first.'

'I was imagining . . . are you sure I should be interrupting your work like this?'

'Go on, go on!'

'I was fantasizing that we would get dressed and go out to dinner, and I would wear this gold lamé outfit. We walk through the door of the restaurant, me wearing the gold lamé pants and top, high heels, and long black gloves, satin ones.

'We are standing at the bar, maybe waiting for our table. I know you think I look sexy. I'm trying to provoke you, to drive you crazy, by giving you certain looks. You seem unaffected, but then I feel your hand go round my waist. Then I feel it going downward, lightly touching the seam in my pants, going up and down, then just two fingers, up and down, up and down. I try to continue talking normally, although I know that you know I can feel everything you are doing.

'Then your fingers don't come up, they hover over my ass, circling just at the point of the seam. But you keep talking to me and appearing casually interested in the restaurant scene. As you move your finger around and around in small circles, I can think of nothing but your finger. I am so turned on, I'm dying for your finger to move lower. It does − first going slightly lower, then barely touching my crotch. I'm out of control and I spread my legs, ever so slightly. My whole body is tensing and I feel an inadvertent spasm. I am holding myself back from twisting – I want to twist up and down on your finger, but I try to stop myself.

'Suddenly, the restaurant darkens as they turn on the football game on TV at the end of the bar. With your other hand, you reach my front and fondle my breast. I let you because I don't care where we are anymore, all I can think of is I want to go to bed with you. Then, when no one is looking, you pull the stretchy gold lamé down off one shoulder, exposing my very pointed nipple. You pinch that nipple while I stand, holding onto the bar with one hand, and you with the other, about to faint with pleasure. . . .'

No more story. They had left the piano bench and were rolling over each other on the floor.

Later, when they were resting, Ariadne looked at Friedrich lying peacefully beside her and remembered the first time she saw his beautiful profile, that night at the Plastique Bertrand. She whispered, 'I love the spaces in your eyes, your eyes that seem to be looking at some very distant, faraway scene, some profound eternal landscape.'

They lay together quietly for some time.

Friedrich thought, How I loved it when we made love before, and she murmured, 'Friedrich, my love, Friedrich', over and over, out of control, and made other sounds – tender, passionate, indescribable sounds. And she said, I never want anyone but you – ever, ever. I will love you always.

Thinking of all this, he began to get an erection again.

When Ariadne woke up at home the next morning, Jupiter was there, true to his promise, sleeping soundly beside her on the big warm bed. His eyes, though still closed, were moving, and Ariadne imagined that he was dreaming. His little paws were moving too, as if he were running, so she thought he must be dreaming of flying through the sky – his favourite pastime. Or was he dreaming of dancing?

She tried not to wake him as she got up, but he raised his head with a start, and looked at her. When he remembered where he was, he smiled sleepily and stretched his graceful palomino legs. Ariadne kissed him on the top of his head.

'Hello, Jupiter!'

Heavenly Ascension II: Flying to Heaven Through a Green Venetian Mist

After breakfast, while Ariadne took a bath, Jupiter sat on the little green rug beside the pale pink bath tub, his head between his paws, his large brown eyes looking at her inquiringly. He was hoping Ariadne would remember her original reasons for coming to Earth, the things she really cared about. It seemed like they were getting bogged down here: no progress – although he had to admit, he loved sitting in this bathroom with Ariadne and the splashing water! But. . .

Ariadne must have come to the same conclusion – because suddenly she sat up, looked at Jupiter with a big smile on her face, and said, 'Jupiter! Let's go home!'

Jupiter was so overjoyed he could hardly believe his ears! Before Ariadne had a minute to change her mind, almost before she finished her sentence, and certainly before she finished her bath, Jupiter scooped her up, along with her pink robe, and off they flew, up into the clouds!

Climbing higher and higher, getting further and further away from Earth, once again they saw beneath them the great cities of the globe, the deserts and the farms.

When they saw cattle dying from heat exhaustion and thirst in parched, drought-stricken fields, while in nearby buildings people relaxed in air-conditioned rooms, sipping iced drinks, bemoaning the fate of the cattle, Ariadne couldn't help asking why some of the hotels, which could hold thousands of people, and were half empty, didn't make room for the cows, at least for a little while until the heat passed. . . .

From still higher, they could see the car and factory emissions rising in giant waves, reaching and destroying the ozone layer, and they saw the Big Hole over the Arctic.

They flew on, into a mist that obscured Earth and all the stars around them – a thick emerald mist, coloured with a patina like a Venetian painting. Passing through this dense, sea-green fog, Ariadne cried out in despair, 'Oh, Jupiter, am I a fool to think things can be better? A naïve idiot? Can't life on Earth be as happy as it was for us in the beginning? How perfect it seemed! How happy we were!'

Jupiter tried to console her, although it was difficult for him to talk while he was navigating. 'It's a surreal world. . . . I'm wondering about it, too . . . all the animals on Earth . . . What will happen to them?' Jupiter looked sadder than Ariadne had ever seen him.

But when they reached the other side of the mist, their spirits lifted once again. They came to a place where the air was clear and shimmering, like the opening strains of Stravinsky's *Petrushka* ballet, full of life and expectancy.

Heaven: What Heaven
to Be Back in Heaven!

★

After landing, Ariadne and Jupiter felt a lot better, and they began hopping around, doing an impromptu dance in celebration.

They heard that there was a message waiting for them on The Big Bulletin Board. They raced over to find it. It was from Harry. 'Dear Ariadne and Jupiter: There is a meeting of the Whist Club Political Debaters' Society tonight. Hope you can make it. Love, Harry.'

'How nice of Harry to remember,' said Ariadne.

After a refreshing lemonade, they combed their hair and fur and set off.

The Heavenly Debate: The Whist Club Debaters Revise the Canons of Western Civilization

As they approached the Famous Club, Ariadne and Jupiter encountered a highly imposing wooden gate. A small plaque read: 'Whist Club'. They strained against the heavy gate until it swung open, and they found themselves wandering down a long carpeted hall with mirrored walls. Following a sign, they went through a door and proceeded up a flight of stairs, which led them to a large room bearing a strong resemblance to a huge Cecil B. DeMille Technicolor set for *The Greats of History*. The ceiling was so high, they gave up trying to see it. There were long oak conference tables and wood-panelled walls on all sides. Men (and a few women) dressed in clothing of different centuries sat in comfortable, overstuffed velvet chairs, sure of their Importance.

Ariadne glanced around, thinking that Cleopatra might be there, but didn't see her.

A debate about Earth – what was going on there, whether it could or should be changed, and how change comes about in Human Earth-History – was just beginning.

The Best of All Possible Worlds (or, Does Democracy Really Work?)

'Democracy is a noble idea, but it just doesn't work.' A young man in an elegant eighteenth-century morning coat with a silk cravat and dark, shoulder-length hair (was he a rock star?) was quite blunt.

'I *said* that in my book,' he continued, 'two hundred years ago already! And *now*, I've been proven Right!' And the groupies all around him chorused, 'He's Right, He's Right, He's Right!' hopping up and down. Their star joined in, 'Oh, what a delight to be Right! It's so Right to be Right! Even when depressing, it's always less distressing when you're right!' And he added, 'Especially, Right Wing.'

Rex Harrison? Jupiter, spying the speaker's-tag, reported to Ariadne that this was Alexis de Tocqueville, the famous author of *Democracy in America* – who claimed democracy could never work, based on his visit (with his friend) to America.

With an elegant flourish, he continued, 'One has only to look at Earth TV to see what a Terrible Mess everything is in – although I myself refuse to watch it, can't bear it. Except for old reruns of *Dynasty* once in a while.' His eyes became dreamy and glazed over at the memory, but he straightened up, remembering where he was. . . .

'As I was saying! The theory that the masses can rule themselves and change the world for the better, From the Bottom Up, is idealistic poppycock. Utopianism! What most people want is a good strong leader to rule them – run things. Pity they don't have any! The politicians now – what a Motley Crew! What chaos they have made – the unbalanced budget, productivity fading, Western world-domination evaporating – and what do they do? Debate! Democracy leads to mediocrity and the tyranny of the majority! No wonder only fifty percent of the population vote – even the *people* know the system can't work!

'Yes, my friends, democracy is sinking into the sunset of history like the Roman Empire.'

Marx and Lenin, dressed in matching tweedy twin-sets, jumped to their feet, appalled, and shouted in unison, 'How can you be so condescending?? Haven't you noticed, the whole Eastern Bloc has risen up, there was a full-blown Revolution From the Bottom Up in 1989. This *proved* that the masses are good! If things are a mess, it's the fault of the capitalist bosses on top – not the masses!'

Ariadne and Jupiter looked at each other. This sounded condescending too: 'the masses'?

Lenin's flood of words continued, 'Those trendy new Capitalist Multimedia Masterminds, they're manipulating the masses through the media. That's why things are a mess!'

'Nonsense!' Tocqueville haughtily surveyed Lenin in his tweedy twin-set, 'The Media Masters are brilliant, refined men. They're simply putting on television what people want. You can't blame them.'

Lenin waved his cap, 'What an apologist for the system, Alex! You donkey, don't you have any courage? How many times do I have to tell you, it's not the people who dictate what's on television, but the media bosses who just want to make money!?*!'

'You romantic fool,' Tocqueville smirked, stuffing his handkerchief in his breast pocket in the smug manner he had picked up from watching a Mr Buckley on television. 'People can be swayed by any demagogue who comes along – like now by the new television Celebrity Evangelists. (I see them sometimes when I'm trying to find *Dynasty*.)

'No, no, I'm afraid, my dear Mixed-Up Mr Marx, they'll *never* think for themselves! Why don't you give up?' And his groupies took up the theme, 'Mixed-up Marx! Give up, give up!'

Rolling his eyes heavenwards, Karl shouted over the din, 'Alex, you wimp! You're super simplistic! You want Big Daddy to descend and make your life big and dreamy. Dictatorship is no answer! Look at history – it's studded with power-mad rulers who didn't make things work. Democracy is still the best idea, a great idea, which (I hate to say it) grew out of Christianity. Communism was supposed to be the ultimate form of democracy – the ultimate form of Christianity!' Here Marx stopped to laugh at his remark. 'BUT – it was never really tried in Russia, no matter how often the Soviet Union proclaimed itself a "communist" state.'

'What???' Lenin's head jerked round in its socket, his dignity wounded. 'My dear Karl, how can you speak like that? Maybe it wasn't pure enough communism to suit you, but I did my bloody best!' He gazed into the distance petulantly. 'You can't win 'em all.'

Marx (oh no, another relationship to repair) touched his shoulder. 'But, my dear Vlodya, I *told* you when we bought these matching tweed outfits that they didn't symbolize anything, they didn't mean I totally agreed with you. Of course I support you – but you have to admit you went off in the wrong direction when you got impatient and decided to let an elite group lead the masses. That's how our dear Mother Russia wound up with Stalin's dictatorship. He was so angry at his mother's incessant whippings, he just had to get even when he grew up, I guess. But – I don't want my name remembered for that!'

A businessman, newly arrived, looked round him in bewilderment. 'What *are* they talking about? Democracy is the best system anyone has come up with yet. Everybody on Earth knows that. Just like they know that communism has failed; it's dead as a doornail.' He smiled warmly. 'Just think of it! Russia will be a Great Capitalist Democracy! One Great Big New Market Place, all for us!'

'Yes, better even business in charge than the masses,' Tocqueville loved insults. But perhaps he had found an ally.

'Is that what democracy means, then?' Ariadne whispered to Jupiter.

He looked perplexed. 'I don't know, Ariadne. I thought it meant freedom?' They stared at the scene, transfixed, trying to grasp its meaning.

Meanwhile, the businessman, along with his new friends, Alexis and his groupies, began chanting happily, 'Dead, dead, we know it's dead!' until they wound up singing their refrain to the tune of 'Ding, dong, The Witch is Dead!'.

Marx, waving his arms Jehovah-like in the air, screeched, '*Stop declaring me dead*!! Nobody's forgotten me yet! My ideas will rise again. Even if they weren't perfect, they were idealistic. Doesn't anyone care about idealism anymore? The market, the market, that's all I hear. Capialism has won! Capitalism is perfect! Oy! I still believe there can be a more just organization of things than the survival-of-the-fittest, "free-market" economy.'

Lenin groaned, his head in his hands. 'The East . . . all our mystique going down the drain! It freaks me out to think what they might do without me. Oh, they might adopt . . . yuck, all those billboards covering everything! Ads for pancake houses! Toilet cleansers! Roach-houses! Bah!'

Ariadne couldn't hold herself back any longer. Even though she was new to the Political Debaters, she burst out, 'This is so abstract! Do you have to go on and on like this? Can't you think of something productive? Something up to date? Is there anything we can do to improve the situation on Earth *right now*?'

They all turned to look at the source of this bizarre suggestion. 'Who would have the nerve to ask such a question?'

'Why it's just a girl . . . and her little dog.'

'Go on,' they said indulgently. 'Speak up, dear. Spit it out, don't be shy. . . .'

With Jupiter standing at her side, Ariadne began her story, telling them about her Trip to Earth and what she saw there. Then she asked them her questions about it. 'I want to believe that democracy works . . . real democracy, equality for people, not just everybody racing to make money, with some having a head start. . . . But I don't know, some of the things on Earth make me wonder. . . . Surely, people must be basically good. If there is inequality, like racism, won't most people want to remedy it? Will they care? If they see something wrong, won't they want to change it? And if they do want to, why are so many doing nothing?'

'In Cincinnati, we have a booming democracy. Business is great!' the businessman interjected with civic pride. 'We've started selling light sockets to the Russians. This is a Great World! Sure, there will always be some injustice, life is imperfect! Some people will get dropped through the cracks, but never mind! This is the Best of All Possible Systems!'

Thomas Jefferson couldn't bear to see someone as idealistic as Ariadne being derailed. 'Don't listen to all that twaddle,' he advised her sympathetically. 'Yes, Ariadne, democracy really means more than just free markets. It means that everybody should have the right to an equally decent life, the right to education, to think for themselves, to speak freely, choose their own government, have access to culture and real information. In fact, true democracy means representing the interests of as large a spectrum of people as possible. Asking every question, no matter how uncomfortable.'

Tocqueville Continues His Discourse With Marx, Lenin and Two Dogs

Fala had come in during Jefferson's remarks, and now piped up, 'I may have missed something, and maybe what I'm going to say is out of order, but has anybody here said anything about the quality of life for the animals on Earth? Half of the species are endangered or almost extinct, many are in captivity to industrialized agriculture ... they have no life anymore. And the humans are not doing so well either. FDR says US farmers are losing their crops and homes because half the topsoil in the grain belt has been eroded. In 1988, for the first time in its history, the US imported more food than it exported! The US, with its great Midwest, which used to be the breadbasket of the world!'

Jupiter seized the moment. 'Dictators or democrats, whatever you're talking about here, it's only humans in charge. And it's humans who are causing the problem, poisoning the ecological system, killing themselves and the planet. They're not so intelligent ... why should they run things??'

Fala joined him. 'The animals, plants and forests are in danger. Humans know this, but don't do anything about it. Meanwhile, acres of ancient woods are dying from acid rain, their dried needles ablaze in forest fires, burning alive the thousands of animals who live there.'

'I saw one fire televised from Yellowstone Park when I was on Earth,' Jupiter spoke with urgency in his voice. 'While the fire burned behind them, men came on the screen, day after day, smiling and saying that everything was all right.' Here Jupiter was almost beyond words, 'And nobody even mentioned the animals who were dying in the fire.'

As soon as Tocqueville recovered from the shock of finding himself in discourse with two dogs (and not wanting to be accused of more élitism than he was already), a gleam came into his eyes, and he announced triumphantly, 'You see! That *proves* I'm right!!! The masses cannot be left to do as they please. They have stripped nature of its wealth in only two centuries – even less!'

'Bashing the masses again?' Marx was so weary. 'Stop mass-bashing and shut up!'

'Tsk, tsk. Such idealism cannot be reasoned with.' Tocqueville felt he had won the argument, and added in Lenin's direction, 'Can't you see that Utopian Revolutions lead to blood-baths?'

'Well, I did eventually have to stop them from killing all the dentists,' Lenin admitted, feeling his jaw.

The blood-baths theme hit a sore spot with Diderot, who was jolted into speech. 'Well, when we *philosophes* started with our revolutionary ideas, we meant only the best. Enlightened rationality, our philosophy, became the basis for theories of democracy and equality. I'll never believe we were wrong to declare that people can think for themselves, that they should have rights, and not be ruled by kings who claim to have a "divine right" to govern them, simply because of birth.

'I don't know if our group of writers was responsible for the blood-baths of the French Revolution, I've agonized over this point – but I believe the French Revolution was a step forward, despite it all.' He looked at his fingernails. 'Poor Robespierre, he must have been a tortured man . . . watching the guillotine, the purges, wondering if the end was really worth the means. . . . But, no, despite all the excesses, I still believe the Enlightenment was the greatest force for civilization of the last three centuries. It should definitely be the basis of the next.'

Mme de Pompadour, lovely in her famous blue and pink eighteenth-century silk dress showing a porcelain white neck, smiled warmly. 'Yes, the Enlightenment set off all kinds of wonderful things. You never had revolutions before that, really. Before the Enlightenment it was believed that injustice had to be accepted, that it was God's way: either a person somehow deserved poverty, or was being tested for the Afterlife. That one had to endure suffering and injustice. After the Enlightenment, it was believed people had the right to try to make life more just, more fair here on Earth – create a Better Social System right here. And voilà! Revolutions began.'

Herr Herrhausen of recent Deutsche-Bank fame (the real ruler of Germany, some called him), and relatively new to Heaven, drew a stunning conclusion. 'Say! That pre-Enlightenment system wasn't so bad! You would have a lot less social unrest with that! If anyone were poor or had a lot of problems, they would have to take them up with "the man up there", ask him how they had sinned. Look into themselves – not upset everybody else!!! (Not to mention bombing my car.) That would surely be an improvement!'

'I object.' Paul Claudel clutched his rosary ostentatiously. 'You Enlightenment philosophers shouldn't be so arrogant, you didn't create the ideal of democracy all by yourselves. It was the Church that first proclaimed that each man had a unique, individual soul, a soul equal before God. . . .'

Marie-Antoinette couldn't take anymore, and suddenly swished towards the front of the room in her wide lilac and yellow taffeta skirts, pronouncing the proceedings dull, dull, dull! 'Revolution, revolution! That's all I ever hear! It's only a silly old word and yet people keep losing their heads about it. It just means "revolving", doesn't it? For centuries and centuries, they didn't even have it. Some stupid fool in the seventeenth-century applied the word to those messy peasant uprisings, and it stuck. Now they glorify it!' She sat down, fanning herself peevishly.

'In a way you're right,' Marx looked bemused (he liked her fancy platinum wig, despite himself). 'Plato observed that there are always five stages in political life, which keep turning and turning round. I hate to say it, but no revolution has lasted. It's always followed by a dictatorship, then back to revolution against the dictator, then gradual corruption, bureaucratization of the revolution and so on.'

'In America they just skipped the dictatorship,' someone remarked cynically. 'At least so far.'

'Anyway,' Marie-Antoinette concluded (draping her silky lilac

skirts even more stylishly in the maroon velvet chair she had carefully selected), 'it's a waste of time trying to fix the world. Louis
told me so.'

Herr Herrhausen grumbled, 'Well, the only place they need to
make changes is in Eastern Europe. And China. Isn't that all that
you fellows' – and he turned to Marx, Lenin and Tocqueville –
'are arguing about?'

Ariadne Meets Voltaire (Who Accuses Her of Plagiarism)

'No! No! No!' There was a sudden disturbance at the back of
the room. Voltaire, the skinny French *philosophe*, had arrived.
He rushed in, speaking agitatedly. 'I hear there is a woman going
round telling a story, how she and her dog came like two Innocents
to Earth, and what they saw there. That's my story: *Candide*! She
doesn't have any right to it! I thought of it first! I'll sue her for
plagiarism!'

'Yeah? Well just how do you think I feel?' Dante interrupted.
'All this stuff about travelling around the Cosmos – it *has* been
done before, you know!'

'And my part, taken by a DOG. How insulting!' Virgil turned
to Voltaire in disgust.

Ariadne looked alarmed, and contemplated immediate flight!
Everybody tried to tell Voltaire that that was two hundred years
ago, that he no longer had a copyright. And besides, Ariadne's
was her own story, a true story. Voltaire had never had a dog.
What about Leonard Bernstein using *Candide*? Shouldn't Voltaire
feel flattered?

Voltaire twitched with agitation. Then he realized that Ariadne
was *there*. He pointed his finger accusingly at her, declaiming dramatically, '*This* is the woman. She has stolen my story! And it's
not *Candida*, as she keeps calling it,' his face red with anger, 'it's
not a woman, it's *CANDIDE* – *C-A-N-D-I-D-E*!!!'

'I wish you'd stop drinking so much coffee,' Madame Du
Châtelet, his companion, cooed sweetly in his ear. 'It's making you
mervous, oh, I mean nervous. Now you're making *me* nervous!'
And she patted the scalloped ribbons on her very full pale

blue silk skirt with agitation, trying to get Voltaire to sit down.

A sultry voice wafted over Voltaire's other shoulder. It was Marie-Antoinette's modern counterpart, the ultra-femme Marlene Dietrich, who had come to caution Voltaire. 'Listen, fellow, the Enlightenment is dead. This is the Post-Modern World. Mythology and demagoguery are back in. And power! Strength is fascinating, after all. . . . And you know what they say: if the end doesn't justify the means, then what does???'

Voltaire didn't know whether to feel enraptured or beleaguered. He was torn between asking Marlene for her autograph and asking her to shut up, and the conflict made him twitch all the more until he screeched, 'Why are all of you picking on me? I shouldn't have to be defending my rights! I should get some respect around here!' He pulled a chocolate bar out of his pocket and started to eat it distractedly, but then stopped in surprise when Cleopatra began speaking to him.

'At least you and Ariadne are on the same political wave-length. Why don't you try being friends?' she suggested.

'You're just not used to women writers, or theorists and revolu-tionaries,' Charlotte Corday pointed out. 'Try it, you'll like it!'

Voltaire, sat down in shock. The interruption over, the debate resumed.

Ariadne's head was swimming. Her eyes blurred and suddenly she saw the whole scene as if in a dream. All of them – Marx, Lenin, Thomas Paine (just arriving), Tocqueville – formed part of a Giant Fantastico movie from the fifties. *The Greatest Story Ever Told*, in Technicolor! Hollywood kitsch, with Charlton Heston as the good guy, Peter Ustinov as the bad guy. Or was it Elizabeth Taylor as Cleopatra, with Peter Ustinov as her boyfriend?

Ariadne shook her head and blinked, trying to come back to reality. 'I'm feeling overwhelmed by all of you!' she cried. 'I agree with almost every new voice and then disagree. I still don't know exactly what is going on on Earth, who is attacking me, or why – and above all, I still don't know how the system could change. But I feel with everything in my being that it must be possible for things to be better, it must be possible to do something!'

Cleopatra, in a lime-green spandex dress and the reddest, longest

Lee's Press-On Nails known to woman, had arrived late and was lounging around on a plush pink velvet couch in the back of the room, with Jennifer, her pet asp, at her side. Fixing one of the Press-On Nails, she thought, It isn't worth getting heated up over these discussions, when I already know all the answers anyway – and there is something else so much nicer to get heated up about! But Ariadne seemed to need help. Cleopatra couldn't stand seeing her friend in distress. Putting her nail polish down with a flourish, she announced imperially, 'Look here, all of this talk about will the people understand how to unite for the Greater Good, how will they help themselves, and if they don't, why don't they – all this is wasting time. Ariadne, if you really want to *do* something, you just have to *do it*!'

There followed a Big Hubbub, some people saying yes, you can change society, you can make it better, you just need to change the ideology and the political system – others insisting that no, human nature is human nature and that's that. Jupiter and Fala yipped as loudly as they could that nobody had said even a word about the animals, but, as the canons of Western civilization had never included them before (the Church had even said that animals have no souls!), nobody paid any attention now either. In fact, one oversized man was so rude as to grip Jupiter's muzzle with his hand to shut him up! A quick bite from Fala to the seat of his pants resolved this problem quickly!

'Thanks, Fala,' Jupiter said, shaking his freed head with relief.

Just as Lenin was debating with himself whether to take on Cleopatra's remarks, or just tell her he was crazy about her spandex dress and the high-heeled leopard-skin print pumps she was wearing, there was an interruption. . . .

Time Out for a Dance

'Don't you hear music?' Jupiter asked Fala. Indeed, the sound of *Waltzes from the Vienna Woods* was coming closer and closer. The music was emanating from a tea trolley which now appeared at the door, piled high with mounds and mounds of sandwiches and scones. It was a creaky ancient silver cart with little multi-coloured Christmas lights inside, which merrily played one of six turn-of-the-century selections when you chose a dessert.

Everyone rushed up to the cart to choose their tart and get their treat – all except Tocqueville, who snuck off to watch reruns of *Dynasty* for a few glorious minutes. As they were munching and crunching, a second trolley appeared, followed by a gay café orchestra of strolling musicians, with the name 'Rock Czarda Melodies'. This time the cart was filled with champagne cocktails and vodka-stingers in oversized goblets. The race for these drinks set off an explosion of musical sounds. Everybody began dancing cheek to cheek a little later when the combo played 'Night and Day'. Some danced with partners, some without. Marx danced with Mao, the businessman danced with Marie-Antoinette, and Cleopatra decided to try Lenin.

Cleopatra Debates With Lenin

Lenin was such a political being that even though he was dancing with Cleopatra, the most fascinating woman in history, he couldn't restrain himself from haranguing her about the masses. Cleo thought to herself, Haven't I seen this in a movie somewhere? Maybe I'm Greta Garbo in *Ninotchka*, but, if so, shouldn't I be saying those things to him??? Smile, little father. . . .

Lenin, now on his fifth champagne, became sentimental as they danced round the floor. 'Ah, Russia, Russia! My Motherland. They love me there – although I feel like a big stiff, the way they installed me. You can't imagine what it's like, being on view like that all the time! I love them, too. I believe in the People, no matter what anyone says. Of course, most of the masses in Russia in my time were farmers – were they ever backward! They just loved the Tsar. I kept waiting for the factory workers to organize – they're the real proletariat. But before I got the chance to find out if they would carry on the People's Revolution after we gave it a shove, Stalin ruined everything and closed down debate. To this day I wonder, was I wrong about human nature? Aren't people rational, won't they operate in their own best interest?'

He suddenly started giggling hysterically, clutching his throat. Something was tickling him. . . . What . . . ? 'Oh blast! Gadzooks!**#?!' It was Jennifer, Cleopatra's pet asp, who had slithered down to entwine herself round his tie while he danced with Cleo, and was now working her way up around his neck, getting ready to give his ear a little love nip.

'Jumping Jehovah!' he let out, then looked round self-consciously, to see if anybody had noticed this staggeringly politically incorrect invective. . . . But they were all too busy drinking and dancing. So, while Cleopatra disentangled Jennifer ('Come to Mama, you silly asp . . .'), Lenin got hold of himself, and resumed his haranguing. 'Maybe most people really are basically conservative. Maybe the masses really do want to worship some idol. What do you think?'

'I think, Vlodya,' – Cleopatra finally got a word in edgewise – 'that if Ariadne wants to have a revolution, even just a simple little ideological one, you shouldn't tell her to wait for the People. You should tell her to get on with it!'

As the tea trollies and the musicians exited, the last refreshment having been chosen, the last tart devoured, in the sudden silence, Cleopatra's sentence rang crystal clear. Ariadne, who had been dancing blissfully with Jupiter and had forgotten about all of this, stopped when she heard them referring to her.

'I want to have a word with you, Mr Marx,' she spoke up clearly. He looked surprised. 'You were wondering – or I was – why, if people are capable of thinking for themselves, they don't always do the logical thing, to help themselves, or others? You wondered why they were "conservative", why they preferred a tsar to self-rule. . . .

'It seemed to me on Earth that the so-called conservative bent of the people was coming from the family structure, since the children are owned by the parents and have no choices – such as other homes, maybe like halfway houses, shelters where kids could go if things got rough at home say, if their parents abused them – they learn they must accept power in the end. Since they have no choices, they are legally owned, and they learn to adapt themselves psychologically to power. It becomes second nature to adjust to those in control of things.'

Ariadne was not sure anyone understood her, since no one

said anything. 'I mean, if you changed the family structure, you'd change "human nature"!' Still silence. 'You could end so much aggression on Earth . . . wouldn't that be good? Look at it this way: kids' food and housing comes from the parents, and so, even in good homes, they may learn to fear their parents' authority, that is, not to say too openly what they think around their parents. Eventually, this behaviour is transferred to other authority figures, such as governments. People learn to play it safe. This warps independent thinking for the rest of their lifetime, creating nations and centuries of conformists, masses of people who secretly worship power, even as they fear it.'

Thomas Paine started talking about how he had seen the cult film, *Rebel Without a Cause*, and he gave his James Dean impression: 'Ma'am, adolescence is a hard thing. We try to tell our parents what we think, but they never listen, they don't understand us. They just want us to be like everybody else, not to upset the goddam neighbours. They're afraid we won't fit in, and this will rub off on them. The trouble is, growing up, you have to make your peace with the world the way it is, and, hell, what do you wind up doing but fitting in too?'

Ariadne had one last thought as the laughter subsided. 'It's interesting to speculate that women may be more likely to think freely, as they have less to lose.'

Lenin, shaking the champagne bubbles out of his head, perked up. 'Interesting! If conservatism were something learned in the family structure, not a "natural" tendency to let others think for one, this would be very positive, hopeful for the future.' But he lost the train of her thought, and went back to his own refrain. 'Anyway, conservatism is dying. The People are good! They have risen up to end the Stalinist system! They will create something new, a Brand New World is possible. . . .'

'No, it's still the KGB in power,' Herr Herrhausen interjected.

Wellington couldn't contain himself any longer. 'What is this slavish romantic fixation on the idea of "revolution"? Don't you realize by now that "revolution", "progress", and the democratic greatness-of-the-people are all fictions of the Enlightenment? The *philosophes*, followed a few years later by Thomas Paine, and their disciples who set off the French Revolution, glorified the mob by calling them "the people"!'

There was a burst of applause from one quarter. Ariadne looked their way, 'Don't you like people?'

'My dear,' Wellington said, 'it's not a question of *liking*. You can't understand.' Then, thrusting out his chest in its neatly pressed (by whom?) uniform, Wellington became radiant. 'Now, Maggie Thatcher, she knows Revolution and Democracy don't really exist, they are just Romantic Fictions used to calm the masses. To let them think they are in charge, when, thank heavens, they are not, and never have been! And you, Karl, how you glorify the masses. Don't you see, my dear fellow, can't you accept that your ideology, Marxism, is now being seen through by everyone? It is rotting on the junkheap of history!'

'Hear, hear! The Enlightenment is a bankrupt dream!' some yelled while others called out 'Booo!!', 'Three Cheers for the Coming Counter-Reformation', and 'The Church Shall Rise Again!'

Jupiter, just waking up from a nap, informed Ariadne that he and Fala were going to go out for a swim – no reason to hang out here! 'Ciao!' he said, and with a jaunty wave of his tail, they set off.

Fala eyed him playfully, 'So, you speak Italian now? Been spending a lot of time with Rughetta, huh!'

Ariadne sat close to Cleopatra on a small pink brocade couch, her fuchsia jodhpurs contrasting spectacularly with Cleopatra's lime-green dress. 'Oh Cleo,' she confided, 'sometimes when Jupiter and I were on Earth, I wondered, *is* there a system here that truly represents Justice? Communism, people say, just didn't work – wherever they tried it, it turned into dictatorship. On the other hand, capitalism leaves a lot of people out: can it be fair for some to have money from birth, some not? Or for some to be born with white skin, when black skin is considered inferior? I can't understand, I can't find an answer. . . .'

Herr Herrhausen overheard her. 'You mean, where's the idealism for the twenty-first century? But you're asking the wrong question: peace isn't created by idealism and equality. Peace is created by power. And now, after perestroika, there will be peace: East – West is no longer the polarity; even nation-states are no longer the point.

International corporations will be more powerful than nation-states. In fact, they will *be* the new nation-states! There will be a Pax Fortuna 500.

'Each citizen will know his allegiance by the credit cards he – or she – carries.' He added the "she", remembering it was Ariadne he was addressing. 'The new nations will know their citizens via their credit card files. These growing files on each and every human being are better than the census – and people *pay* for these cards to take the information! Of course, some giant corporations, with millions of employees worldwide, also form new nations, with health, recreation and payment plans for their loyal citizens. These new nation-states will be the ones people increasingly turn to for help, because they are dependent on them for jobs, money, and stability. Some of them already give their citizens encoded name-tag-bars to wear at all times.

'As yet, the animals are exempt from this counting and penetration process.'

The Banking Chief continued naïvely, 'These corporations are crazy about the new rise of fundamentalist religion, with its authoritarian, you-must-obey-and-be-grateful mentality (the all-worship-one-central-god religion is the model for this). . . .' He would have gone on, but. . . .

Cleopatra interrupted him impatiently – her distaste had been growing for some time. 'Egyptian pantheon religion is so much better! Much more amusing, not to mention spiritually profound and appealing. But listen! Ariadne and all of you! You, Lenin! Look, forget all this worrying! You know what Justice is! The way to create a just state is to form an army of your own. Seize power! You know what is good for people, Ariadne! You know how to make women equal. You can find out what the agricultural policy should be (after all, you studied Balkan farming), and you'd be a whiz at finance! I could be your finance minister. . . . With power of your own, you could change policy, stop auto and factory emissions on the spot – no more "soon" double-talk. You could repair the hole in the ozone layer. . . .'

'What, with cling-film and sticky tape?' a voice remarked irreverently.

Cleopatra stood up, put her royal hands on her royal hips, and proclaimed as only she could, 'Ariadne, just get going and do it!

Don't wait around for some vague, amorphous mob, worrying how to convince them, or get into fights with these irrational guys here, or the media. They're not going to let some "girl", as they keep calling you, be a hero in a movement to change things. I'm telling you! Get an army. It's the Best of All Possible Ways, the only way you have a fighting chance to do something.'

Clausewitz couldn't agree more, and started sizing up the idea of asking Cleopatra for a date.

Ariadne's Manifesto: A New Vision of the World and the Causes of Aggression (An Alternative Analysis of Human Nature)

Tocqueville, irritated that two women had begun to "dominate" and lead the debate, fixed a resentful stare on Ariadne and said with biting sarcasm, 'By the way, Ms Rite . . . as to your notion that somehow women have a different, more egalitarian value system that needs only to be allowed to emerge, creating a new society – a value system that would work environmental and fiscal wonders for the Earth! – this is pure poppycock! Very idealistic, I'm sure, but nonsense nevertheless.'

Voltaire, consoling himself with chocolates in a corner, muttered, 'He's as dull as Dr Pangloss. An old fuddy-duddy before his time. What an apologist for the system!'

Tocqueville continued, strutting back and forth, his hands behind his back like a prosecuting attorney. 'And if the planet is in danger, the reason is clear: leaders aren't given sufficient power to take charge and run things. You, Ariadne, expect "the people" or "all the women" to rise up and stop the abuses, rule themselves. Ha! They never will. A great individual must come along and take charge.' Did he have himself in mind? Ariadne was sure he wasn't thinking of any women. And why was he so competitive with her?

Ariadne had had just about enough. As she listened to this barrage, everything became crystal clear in her mind. She stood up very tall, and with as much dignity and courtesy as she could muster under the circumstances, she began, 'My dear Mr de Tocqueville, feminist theory is not poppycock: it is the first significant advance on classical liberal political theory and on Marxist theory in a century. You and Lenin may think you are arguing two different points of view, but in reality you make essentially the same analysis: you simply prefer different classes, that's all. (You think you're Right and he's Left.) Neither of you has a plan for making human society less aggressive – or a realistic way to build a new society based on more beauty for all living things. Our theory does.' Her anger had made her quite fearless. Cleopatra noticed that Ariadne was growing up.

'Now,' Ariadne declaimed, more and more sure of herself, 'let me point out that neither the Western Enlightenment nor Marxist theory offered a credible explanation or historical analysis of why men have tried so indefatigably to dominate women. According to your theories, what are we to believe? That men's hormones make them do it, that men are "naturally" aggressive towards women? If this is so, why is there any need to *teach* men to fight, be warriors, raging Rambos? To distrust and disrespect women? (Please refer to my fourth red book report!) None of this seeking-for-dominance is biologically determined – even yours, right now! It's almost as if you and Marx *want* to believe male superiority is inevitable. But I, for one, do not believe that male attitudes taught on Earth are inevitable.

'My analysis is this: the problems are caused by the existence of a profoundly ingrained ancient mind-set, an ideology that continues to be culturally imprinted on humans. This mind-set gained dominance early in history because its adherents could conquer other, more peaceful groups. Archaeologists are unearthing cities that had no walls for defence. This shows that in prehistoric (pre-literate, not pre-civilized) times, aggressive invasions were not uppermost in people's minds. If it was possible once, it's possible again. Human nature, then, must not have been predominately aggressive. We could get back to this much more positive frame of mind. What I'm trying to work out, is – how?'

But very few of The Great Men of History were listening. How could they take the murmurings of a mere girl seriously? Especially as she was wearing the cutest ruby-red sparkly shoes they had ever seen? Ariadne paused for a moment, looked round in vain for a sign of recognition, sighed, and sat down feeling frustrated.

Chairman Mao, who had been sitting stonefaced and immobile

99

in a darkened corner, had eyes only for the 'greats' of the Western canons. Ignoring Ariadne, he challenged them. 'Your revolution didn't work and neither did mine. John Adams's opera *Nixon in China* helped me come to terms with this. If I could only reach my wife and tell her to give up – stop championing my mistakes. As a woman, she was punished much worse than I ever was, and used as a scapegoat by those in power.'

He sank back exhausted.

Simone de Beauvoir and John Stuart Mill Defend Ariadne

Ariadne was thinking maybe she *should* go out swimming with Jupiter and Fala after all, when Simone de Beauvoir, wearing her favourite 1950s Chanel suit and her ubiquitous turban, came breezing in. She had heard – what a miracle – that there was a woman holding forth in the Whist Club, and she came to stand next to Ariadne.

She glared at Mao. 'You always irritated me.' Then, surveying the room, she admonished, 'None of you are even listening to what she's saying! Don't any of you ever worry that women might have a revolution? If you never listen or have a dialogue, you're asking for it! I know what you think, you think we are so passive, we wouldn't do it. I'm here to tell you: don't take women for granted. That time has passed.'

A few jeers were heard.

'Oh, *really*? It's not out of weakness or stupidity that we haven't overturned men's system before – make no mistake about it. What Ariadne wrote about on Earth, women's ambivalent allegiance to, love and hate for, men and men's ideological system, is quite right: women now are thinking over their options, each one individually. I said women were "the Other", and Ariadne says that the Other is a Seer, a Doer – she's right! This personal ferment Ariadne's been documenting is highly political stuff, just as she points out. And of course, the powers that be recognize this. That's why she's being politically attacked.'

Ariadne looked inspired. 'Oh, Simone, you understand! *You*

believe the world can change. It's not inevitable that injustice reign supreme. . . .'

'No – though Jean-Paul and I used to argue about this – on a personal level! I said he was much more aggressive than I, though as a good Leftist he always denied it. But the fact is men learn they should be aggressive, and women learn they should accept it.'

The colour came back to Ariadne's cheeks. She only wished Jupiter were there; things were looking up.

Now the Little Father wanted a word with Ariadne. 'But, how are you saying anything different from what I said? I said if it weren't for industrial greed and ownership of the means of production by a few, Heaven would break out on Earth. . . .'

'You haven't been listening.' At the sound of John Stuart Mill's voice, Marx twirled around – a *man* now speaking in Ariadne's defence?!!? 'Feminist theory is the only analysis that offers a new understanding of the problems on Earth – problems neither Marxism nor capitalism solved.

'In my reading of it, feminist philosophy now analyses the fundamental problems in a new way. Feminism doesn't assume that a depraved human nature (no one knows what human nature is, all the human nature we've ever seen having been formed within a society) is responsible for suffering on Earth; nor does it pick out a Bad Group of people to blame (Marxism picked the rich guys, Hitler picked the Jews, some people in the West picked those on welfare). Feminism places the blame for the problem on an ingrained ideology, an ideology of aggression and hierarchy. This is the most hopeful social theory to come along in a long time.'

'In light years!' Ariadne smiled.

Simone was still focused on Marx, and said sympathetically, 'You and Engels never really got the subjugation of women figured out. That new archaeologist, Gimbutas, has you beat: she shows that domination-mentality could be a historical accident, the result of clash of two cultures early in history, not an inherent stage in the "civilization process".' Marx tried to scribble down the name.

Simone went on, 'As Ariadne wrote in her little red book, male aggression is a by-product of the family: if little boys learn that their fathers dominate their mothers, "big boys don't cry", and that

101

power is what counts (if you don't step on somebody, somebody else will step on you), then to call aggression and domination "natural" is wildly simplistic.'

Ariadne, inflamed with great spirit, stood up, raised her fist, quite carried away, and declared, 'And so, if it is only an ideology, it can be changed. The only question is, how?' Settling down, she reflected, " . . . how to reinstate a more spiritually beautiful culture on Earth – '

Martin Luther King, who had been sitting quietly nearby with Paul Robeson, boomed out in his melodious oratorical voice, 'The *same* arguments that are used to justify men's domination of women were used to justify whites' ownership of blacks just over a century ago.' What a beautiful face!

Darwin, who rarely spoke on political matters, joined in, 'The old ideological system is so entrenched that after I died, they distorted my theories and tried to apply them to justify racism and all kinds of things. The survival of the fittest! They wanted to show that those in power were in there because they were superior! And Freud used a similar rationale. He justified the status quo by proclaiming aggressive, competitive behaviour (especially in men) to be based on "instinct" – men were "by nature" aggressive and women passive – or even masochistic.

'But nobody has ever proved anything about what human nature is! They just look at what is going on, and argue backward from that, say that "what is" is therefore unchangeable, it must be inevitable! Hardly scientific!'

'Sounds like what Dr Pangloss told Candide,' Ariadne smiled. 'Whatever is must be, it is what should be, and this is the Best of All Possible Worlds!' She looked round nervously to see if Voltaire was going to protest against this citation – but all was calm on the Voltaire Front.

Martin Luther King was still considering what Ariadne had said. 'I've often wondered why the women's rights marches had so many fewer men than the black marches of the sixties had white people. During the Civil Rights movement, there were quite a few whites who took part in the great marches and donated money to black causes . . . but there are hardly any men at the women's rights marches. I hear men almost never make contributions to women's groups or the women's campaign funds.'

Straightening his tie, John F. Kennedy said, 'This reflects two things. One, most white men are even more threatened by women's rights than by black rights. There's a financial reason for this: since blacks are only about eleven percent of the population, to give equal pay to blacks wouldn't be as financially upsetting as to give it to women, who are about fifty-two percent of the population. And the second fact is that there is a decline of idealism in the US, especially on the part of men. They should have passed the Equal Rights Amendment; they look selfish otherwise.'

Marilyn Monroe stared at him in disbelief. 'Since when did you suddenly get all these ideas about women's rights???'

Pio Nono Encounters Hitler

A cold voice pierced the air from another part of the room. 'These women! Who do they think they are? They cannot shape the world, they cannot lead events – not to mention make a revolution. They are too weak!' It was Adolf Hitler in a grey business suit. Who would have recognized him?

But his manner changed, as he suddenly spotted Pope Pius IX. He rushed over, insisting that he had been longing to meet him, gushing his admiration for the Church. 'I was trying to copy it,' he said 'trying to put similar principles into effect. This could have led to the permanence of my Reich. Mass brainwashing techniques – they really work!'

'But yours didn't,' Pio Nono sniffed with superiority.

Hitler sputtered, surprised that Pio Nono did not admire him too. 'Well, haven't you looked at Earth lately? Who says they didn't work? My Reich took root in some people's minds. Now on Earth there's a resurgence. It was a formidable system I introduced – the system of the twenty-first century! Perfectly suited for massive states.'

Pio Nono remained aloof. 'What you don't see,' he waved his red-robed arm majestically, 'is that the Church is rising again. What the masses want, what they hunger for at the end of the twentieth century is Magic. They want a spiritual world, Beautiful and Mysterious Images, not a political world.'

Hitler, angry, was determined to win the argument. 'But you're no judge of anything! The Italian revolution overcame you and you hid in your castle. You're not up to date! People in Italy now are even in favour of abortion!'

Pio Nono flinched. 'Just wait. . . .' But then he grew assertive, waving a giant incense burner menacingly through the air. 'The secular world is over. We're showing them Maria in caves now. There's a major shift coming . . . the tide is turning! Why, we might even unite with the Islamic fundamentalists for a real twenty-first century grip on things!' He looked ecstatic at the thought.

'Hey!' Adolf asked 'Maria in the caves? Can you do those magic appearance tricks from up here? Maybe I can too. . . . Will you show me how?'

Ariadne was deep in thought, sitting in one of the yellow velvet, down-filled chairs, asking herself questions about Marilyn Monroe. Such an amazing creature. And her cleavage! How heavenly. . . . Ariadne reached for a glass of lemonade, about to take a sip, worrying she might not be taking Marilyn seriously enough, when she felt a tug at her elbow. It was Gertrude Stein.

'Ariadne, why don't you act your age?' Ariadne was stunned. Stein continued, whispering loudly in her ear, 'You seem to know a lot more than I thought, so why don't you act authoritative, in command (why mince words?). Ariadne! Serious Feminists look and act like *me*!!! Stop this Little-Girl-in-a-Big-World Act!'

'Well. . .' At first self-conscious, Ariadne gained courage. 'Because I think it is the ultimate smugness, such ego-trip, to take on mannerisms to show that one is "on top of it all" and has it all "under control". It goes against everything I stand for. I don't want to act like a know-it-all, one up on the hierarchical ladder.'

'But, at least you could stop asking questions, and start making statements. . . . What are you trying, a new version of the Socratic dialogues?!'

Ariadne paused, then continued, slowly and clearly. 'We are all wandering in a universe we little understand. As Jupiter says, people act smart, but they don't even know where they come from, what life and birth are, nor where they go when they die – whether their souls perish – or if this world came to be in someone's dream, or is only matter. And if only matter, then who created it? By asking my questions, prompting other people to ask themselves questions, I am trying to serve a more spiritual, more profound cause. By asking myself questions, I am making the ultimate voyage.'

This quieted Stein, who sat silently for a few moments, then uncharacteristically took Ariadne's hand and just held it, saying nothing.

It's Really Hard to Get Along With Freud

Pio Nono, in his papal robes, came towards Ariadne. He couldn't stand to see two women holding hands! 'My child, my child, I see that you are *tortured*. Come to the Church, the Holy Mother Church. *She is waiting for you*! If you would just accept our Great Religion, you could live in peace with all the inequality and contradictions on Earth, and be sure of yourself. Stop asking questions!'

'Not religion, but the Science of Psychology!' Freud butted in elatedly. 'This will calm you. . . .' Ariadne wondered why he thought she needed 'calming'. . .!? Clearly, this was just the opportunity Freud had been waiting for, and he was just getting warmed up.

'Ariadne, you've got to accept that the world is the best it can be, that humans are just innately aggressive!' He looked happy about this pronouncement, and continued, casting a glance at Voltaire. 'I don't care what Rousseau said about children being "clean slates" and all that – he had a strange childhood anyway, so he doesn't count! Now, my dear Ariadne, I didn't *want* to come to the conclusion that people are innately aggressive, that human nature has a dark side, but I couldn't escape it. Just like I couldn't escape the conclusion that male and female biology create their separate psychologies. Ariadne, once you accept These Immortal Truths, you will be able to adjust . . .!'

Freud sounded so self-righteous that Cleopatra rolled her eyes dramatically and yawned loudly. Meanwhile, Jennifer, who had been playfully curling round Cleopatra's toes (in platform Doc Martins), hissed in Freud's direction. He stared at the asp in disbelief. What!!! His symbol, come to life . . . ???

'But you were thinking of men anyway in your theories about aggression,' argued Ariadne – to a Freud who hardly heard anything right now. 'You labelled women (the three upper-class Viennese women you studied!) "masochistic" because they were not aggressive, and because they "chose" to live in a system that put them down. But the desire of women to have the same rights as men, you labelled "penis envy"! Women can't win, in your system. . . . I'm sorry, but you're confused. You left out the influence of culture and ideology on personality. You made up explanations and excuses for injustice, mumbo-jumboing this injustice away through supposed, never proven, "hidden drives" and "instincts", which you tried to claim were biologically determined and inevitable.'

Freud stroked his beard and regarded Ariadne condescendingly. He hadn't understood a word, or even tried. 'Poor Ariadne, you have to find out where your hidden anger comes from. You need to look into yourself, my dear.' (Should Ariadne let him have it?)

Ariadne shot right back: 'You, Freud! *J'accuse*! You are nothing but an apologist for the system! You took over in the suppression of women where the Church left off. Your theories were taken on by the Lords of Society early in the twentieth century, because they individualized social discontent. How do you explain that your system of thought replaced feminist theory around the turn of the century? Because yours was better? No, because feminism dared to ask society to change, to become truly just – whereas you safely put the blame for any problems (especially women's problems) back on the individual, relegating them to some obscure childhood 'abnormalities', as you labelled them. . . .'

'Yes,' Simone looked at him with loathing, 'your theories served to keep the middle classes from becoming too focused on social justice. Shulamith Firestone figured that out! Any individual who wanted to change things, improve things, was categorized as "angry", "maladjusted", suffering from "hidden anger" or "childhood problems" – all discontent was blamed on the individual, who had to figure out where his or her anger came from – anger being defined a priori as "unhealthy", because it

106

didn't fit in with the system! To be "mentally healthy" meant accepting the world as is and *fitting in*.'

Ariadne smiled broadly. 'Oh, it's Voltaire all over again, "this is the Best of All Possible Worlds", and don't you question it! As Proust put it, it's more forgivable to die than to be late for a dinner party!'

Cleopatra turned her attention to a bewildered Freud: 'You'd better watch out, old boy! Scare tactics won't work with women anymore!' Jennifer hissed in agreement: she was included! She was tired of him misrepresenting *her*!

Simone softened, 'Well, the one good thing you said was that people should talk through their problems, tell someone else, and increase their own self-knowledge. This has had a humanizing effect. But people *can* change the world, they shouldn't feel they have to try to fit in to a system which is not just. And they don't have to be psychologically perfect before they have the right to make changes!'

Thomas Jefferson lighted up: 'Yes! People around the world are envisioning new forms of society through which to express their rights. This is all part of the great idealistic belief that Something Better is possible. We cannot turn these dreams off now!'

'We should never have let them get started,' grumbled Clausewitz.

Beauvoir started to say something else – about liking Freud's book on dreams? – but there was An Important Interruption.

'I have to disagree that all this debating is leading anywhere!' Cleopatra stood up, banging her nail file down on the table. 'Talking, talking, endlessly talking – Ariadne, it's no change! Arguing politically, now that would be serious – if you had military backing. Every world leader from Queen Isabella to Winston Churchill has known this!'

Ariadne looked wounded. 'Then where does this leave the fight for women's rights? Is it hopeless? Do women have to take on aggressive characteristics to overcome the situation in which they find themselves? And what about blacks in America, for that matter? Cleo, can't women just continue their peaceful pressure and gradually change things?'

'More talking! Pooh!' Cleopatra looked disgusted.

Ariadne regarded her best friend, then broke into a big smile and laughed affectionately. 'Oh, Cleopatra, I adore you, you're wonderful!' Her smile faded, and she became serious, exclaiming passionately, 'But I can't help believing that the idea of democracy is right: there is a dream, a dream for all people to rule themselves. What fun would it be for me, leading my army, to make a revolution? I want a Revolution of Ideas, I want to change basic attitudes, to have a more loving, respectful, dignified society.'

'My dear,' drawled Peggy Guggenheim, super-sophisticate, 'the only place to have Perfection and Harmony is in art. That is where you should turn, that will satisfy you. Why don't you come by my office some time and we'll talk about it?'

Ariadne's head was swimming. She said goodbye to everyone; she needed time to think. She stepped out on the balcony of the Whist Club and sank down on a bench. Leaning her head back on the railing, she fell into a half-faint. Her head swirled with images. She dreamt that she was in a play entitled: *The Education of an Idealist: A Comedy. Or is it A Fiction?* In the play she asked everyone: 'Are people good? Can they change the world? Will they take action against injustice? Does true democracy work? Or will it be necessary to devise a new political system beyond it??'

Tocqueville appeared in the dream and chanted over and over in his perfect, snotty French, 'Vous voyez, je vous l'ai dit! La démocratie ne fonctionne pas! Les gens sont stupides, ils s'en moquent . . . s'en moquent . . . s'en moquent. . . . Je vous l'ai dit!!'

And Marx shouted simultaneously, 'No! The media Big Cheeses are the bad guys! The bad guys! The bad guys!' Ariadne put her fingers in her ears. 'Stop!!'

When she regained consciousness, Cleopatra was sitting next to her, looking worried. 'Ariadne, are you OK? I didn't mean to upset you in there. Are you angry at me? I do believe what I said, about getting an army, taking direct action and not just talking about change, so I had to say it. But I never want to lose your friendship!'

Ariadne leaned her head on Cleo's beautiful brown shoulder. 'Let's forget it! We'll be friends forever! Of course! I'm probably much too wound up with Earth anyway.'

'It's more than the politics, isn't it?' Cleo took her hand. 'Are you in love with someone down there? Is that it?' She grinned wickedly.

Ariadne lifted her head to look at her and laughed. 'You would think that! No! That's not why. Well ... as a matter of fact, I did meet someone at that costume ball.'

'Ah!' said Cleo. 'You mean the tall handsome man you talked to, the one with the chest?'

'Yes, that's The One. Oh, Cleo, I'm so happy with him! You should know him like I do!'

'Well, I could watch you two on TV from up here,' Cleo teased. 'We can see everything, you know.'

'Cleo! If you do, I will never speak to you again!'

George Orwell's New Predictions: The Ministry of Truth in the Twenty-first Century

Clausewitz, in a uniform straight out of Eric von Stroheim's dream wardrobe, and looking what he considered irresistible (i.e., affecting a cold and haughty elegance), came out onto the balcony to find Cleopatra. He was determined to ask her for a date. He clicked his heels and kissed Cleo's hand, giving her his sexiest look (no change in expression, just his idea of Meaningful Eye Contact). Ariadne took this opportunity to head for the stairs. She was ready to take leave of the Whist Club. She grinned at Cleo and vanished.

Travelling down a long, carpeted stairway which muffled the sounds of her feet – it was so quiet she could almost hear the building speak to her, could hear the sound of the centuries, the sound of time itself echoing in her ears – presently Ariadne came to a curve in the stairs, and discovered a wide and spacious landing she hadn't noticed before. On one side of it was a door with a small, discreet inscription: 'Media Room'.

Ariadne paused for a moment in the soft filtered light, and wondered what might be inside. Just then, the door opened a crack, and a thin man with round glasses and a British tweed jacket peered out at her, in a not unfriendly manner. Maybe he is shy, Ariadne thought to herself, but then she realized he was simply struggling to get her in focus through his thick spectacles.

'Ah, Ariadne! Come in! Look,' and he motioned behind him towards a giant TV screen. 'Can you see? It *is* 1984! I said this was what it would be like. Only, Big Brother is the media!'

Ariadne, her hand still hesitating on the banister, looked with curiosity at this unusual man.

'Oh – let me introduce myself: I'm Eric (everyone calls me George "Animal Farm" Orwell); Harry told me you'd be here. I was looking out for you, but I just couldn't bear to go upstairs and listen to all those heavy discussions. Ugh! I watch a lot of TV. I saw you on Earth TV the other night. Wow, what a mess! You may be suffering from the *rage des provinces*, but don't let it get to you. It's just the politics of the 1990s, don't you recognize them? It's double-speak! You say women are on the way to great changes, to being happier than ever. They say you say women are unhappy. What's black is white, what's white is black. That's how they win their arguments, now that Propaganda has taken over everything. By the way, it's TV that has caused the Revolutions in the East. . . .' He smiled shyly at Ariadne. 'Cheer up! We'll all go down together and the Scorpions will inherit the Earth!'

Ariadne couldn't help but smile back. At least he looked on the bright side. She followed Orwell into the room – a cross between the living-room of Aristotle Onassis's 1950s private yacht (with deep green plush overstuffed chairs and matching drapes), and a twenty-first century spy-electronics storeroom. Of course, the equipment wasn't made of chrome anymore, it was a new diamond-encrusted matte black plastic. Orwell turned off an episode of *Gilligan's Island* that he had been taping, so they could talk quietly.

'Look – here's what's happening.' George handed Ariadne a pencil so she could take notes. 'The Family is in. It's what, according to conservatives and big, bad reactionaries from every-where, the Western democracies to the Arab fundamentalists, is going to Save the World – or at the very least, the United States and Great Britain – from all the Big Bad Everythings: the deficit, other nations, AIDS, creeping demoralization of "the workers" and every other conceivable kind of creeping crud.

'Conformity is the order of the day. The Pledge of Allegiance to the Family and the Flag is going to become a mounting hysteria for the next few years. You saw it begin in some Arab countries in the 70s, and continue with the fundamentalists in the US in the 1980s. Remember the American presidential campaign of 1988, when all the candidates brought out their families and displayed them on TV like prize cattle? Well, you haven't seen anything yet! And you wanted to re-examine the family – in this climate! Tsk, tsk, my dear, what poor timing! Noble idea, but a suicide mission. . . . I tell you, you're lucky to have your hide still. . . .'

All this reminded Ariadne of the gruesome details of her media episodes on Earth, and she stopped writing and looked up at George. 'Earth is so bizarre. Whenever I got involved with the media, I always felt dizzy. An individual is so powerless in their clutches, and they are so manipulative – and blinded by stereotypes! I told Harry, I often felt like I had fallen down a long tunnel. . . .'

'Listen,' said Orwell, 'the media have become the most powerful shapers of ideology, more powerful even than religion. Their "stars" represent the post-modern archetypal mythological pantheon, equivalent in function to the Greek pantheon. TV personalities are more real to people than their next door neighbours. Thus the media giants who own/make these stars are the new rulers of the world. This is the new Ministry of Truth that presides over the world, even now.

'My Prediction is that there will be a Battle of Media Titans by the end of the century for Ideological Control of the World. And the world will become more reactionary as a result.'

Ariadne Introduces Cleopatra and George Orwell

While Orwell beamed at his own brilliance, Jupiter, Fala and Rughetta came bouncing in, excited and very wet from their swim. They jumped up on George and Ariadne, then shook themselves to get the water off, completely oblivious to the tracks they left all over the Media Room's wall-to-wall plush emerald carpet. In

111

their exuberance, they began playing catch with an old baseball they'd found.

Ariadne and George tried to continue their conversation. 'Do you think the media are *self-consciously* trying to tell the world how to think?' Ariadne wanted to know, 'Or do you think it's just that most journalists are so steeped in the Western tradition that they don't even see the stories that don't fit into their preconceived notions?

'Most reporters don't seem to understand or write about people and events except in terms of prototypical Western fairy-tales with stereotyped characters. They read everything through the eyes of this mythology, or the canons of their tradition. Everybody and everything is depicted in terms of these few basic stories, scenarios, or rudimentary plots.

'And if someone's life doesn't fit, if its meaning is different, well, it will just be made to fit the pre-set scenario anyway. Thus they "prove", over and over, that indeed these preconceived ideas are the only reality! But this is not true. . . .'

Rughetta began playing a coquettish hide-and-seek with Jupiter between Orwell's legs. Orwell, obligingly standing legs apart (nice man), tried to answer Ariadne. 'The media get their money from corporate advertisers . . . and I don't think those companies would be happy with new plots and characters. Unfortunately, most corporate heads lack the imagination to see how things could change for the better and benefit them!'

Cleopatra, finally escaped from her balconic encounter with Clausewitz, suddenly appeared in the doorway of the Media Room, quite a dish in her lime-green satin stretch gown, her glowing, deep bronze skin accentuated by the golden snake emblem jewellery she wore. (Where was Jennifer?) She just managed to catch Fala's baseball in mid-air as it whizzed past her head, and threw it back. Good right hook there! George looked at her in amazement.

Ariadne realized that they had never met. 'George, this is Cleopatra, the Queen of the Nile. Cleo, meet George Orwell,' – introductions are so awkward! she thought. How do I describe him? – 'writer, political wizard and soothsayer – fortune teller extraordinaire!' Ariadne smiled.

Cleopatra offered George her hand, obviously expecting it to be kissed. George, who had never kissed a hand before, was overcome, and did it – quite well, too! So well, in fact, that Cleo began to eye him with decidedly more interest. . . . She lay back on one of the Onassis-style plushy couches, the dogs on the floor in front of her, resting, the baseball between Jupiter's paws. A perfect portrait for a family album.

Seeing the provocative picture Cleopatra made, George was suddenly strangely inhibited; he began stammering, 'Uh, I was about to say – uh – a big part of the problem is those computer data bases the media have. When journalists write their articles, they do what *they* call "research" by reading old newspaper clippings by their cronies. They just push a button in their news corporation's computer, and get the computerized, media-created (or media-distorted) party line, and write that up as a "factual" intro to their articles. Repeated incessantly, this becomes the New Truth; once it's in the computer, you can't get it out.'

Cleopatra quipped, 'Rainer Maria Rilke once told me, "Fame is the sum total of the misconceptions gathered about a name".' George laughed, more loudly than necessary, because it was Cleopatra's joke.

For once in his life, George was on the verge of forgetting all about politics! Thinking of nothing except Cleopatra's charms, seemingly spellbound, George sat down next to Cleo on the couch, completely speechless. Cleopatra liked this . . . very much. . . .

Weekend in Paradise

One other human in Heaven had also given up thinking about politics. That night, after everyone else was asleep, Ariadne crept back to the Heaven Earth-Watch TV room to try to tune in Friedrich on the satellite dish Intergalactic TV ('Made in Heaven' model) operating from the roof of the Whist Club. She was desperate to see him. She wanted to be happy in Heaven, but she couldn't stop thinking about Friedrich.

After a few minutes of tuning, she had adjusted the set so she could see him in his Earth apartment. Friedrich! Her heart stopped. He was in his living-room. She longed intensely for him

– to feel him, touch him, see him look into her eyes. What was he doing? He was trying to get ready for his next concert. He played some of the Rachmaninoff *Third Piano Concerto*, then stopped, went over to his desk and looked at Ariadne's photo. He returned to practice, but then got up again and paced across the room.

He looked so dejected, Ariadne longed to speak to him, to tell him she loved him, and, most of all, to touch him, feel him, kiss him. She felt her body pulled as by some huge, irresistible undertow, as her eyes followed him. She felt ready to climb the walls if she didn't see him soon!

She clutched the TV set, trying to bring herself closer to him, wishing this would work as well as it had in her favourite film by Jean Cocteau. 'If only this were a Magic Mirror as in *Beauty and the Beast*, it would work,' she muttered to herself. . . .

But she had a Magic Jupiter, and now he came to her rescue. He felt so compassionate that his heart melted, and, in a flash, he whisked Adriadne back to Earth. . . .

The next thing Adriadne knew, she was in Friedrich's room. She rushed towards him, and he wrapped her in his arms, holding her, saying over and over, 'Oh, you are really here, you are really here! How wonderful it is to feel you! I dreamed you were far, far away. I couldn't find you. Oh, Ariadne, let's stay together for all our lives! Promise me you will be with me always! Promise!'

Then he kissed her, his lips and tongue all over her mouth. Tasting his beautiful lips and feeling his closeness, she forgot everything else in the world.

So did Friedrich, because an hour or so later he sat up with a start. 'My concert! Tonight is my concert! I have to go to the hall this morning to try out the piano! I almost forgot. Come with me, darling.'

'Oh, how exciting!' She spotted Jupiter lying at the foot of the bed (almost completely wrapped up in a sheet, which had somehow got twisted round him), and smiled, 'Can Jupiter come with us?'

'Of course! I'm the Star! At least for tonight. They can't say no to anything I request today!' he laughed.

While Friedrich took his bath, Ariadne sat next to him on the side of the tub. She took out a fuchsia nail polish and began applying it to her toes. She felt wonderfully sexy.

When she had finished her toes, she started washing Friedrich's back, then massaging every part of his body with the frothy white suds. Sitting in the large, white tub, he looked like one of the gods in the fountains at Fontainebleau, slightly larger than life. He was perfectly proportioned, majestic, regal. She ran her hands over his penis, back and forth, and as he came, his penis huge in the water, his ejaculation was like a spray of water on one of those pleasant summer days when all the water sprites in the fountain are laughing.

Friedrich, got out of the tub and dried himself off with a pink towel, smiling. Jupiter, who believed in mutual grooming as one of the social pleasures of life, began drying Friedrich's legs by licking them, just as he did to himself after a bath. Of course, there was considerably more surface to cover on Friedrich's legs!

Friedrich, laughing because Jupiter's tongue tickled, disappeared into the next room to get dressed. Ariadne showered, then stood in front of the old Venetian mirror with its pink and blue glass flowers, letting her hair down. She liked the colour of her skin and her hair. She liked her face, and her breasts, the way they curved, the colour of her nipples. Friedrich, man of good taste, said he liked them too. She decided to paint her fingernails. While she was waiting for them to dry, she kissed Jupiter on the head. 'Oh my darling, how happy I am! And I love to spend time with you like this.'

Friedrich wanted to be kissed too; one thing led to another, and when they looked at the clock again – ouch! – an hour later already. They decided Friedrich should go to the Concert Hall on his own: it would be less distracting!

Could Ariadne Betray Feminism by the Clothes She Wears?

Lounging around the apartment that afternoon, Ariadne tried to decide what to wear to the concert. First she tried on a leopard-skin print dress. It was very tight and short and made her feel excited. It was made out of a plushy material, with a low neck, long tight sleeves that closed with a zipper, and a pegged shirt.

It's funny, she thought, I feel so exhilarated when I dress like this, so powerful. Why?

She took it off and tried on an old, tattered, brown silk velvet skirt from the twenties and a flowing Victorian blouse. She liked herself more this way – or did she? As she slipped on a pair of maroon shoes she thought that no matter how many of her friends, feminists she loved and admired, were embarrassed by her high heels, she still loved to wear them. She had them in different colours, especially in velvet – she liked the softness – magenta, olive-green, black, purple, red.

Ariadne's affection for old clothes grew out of her love for history. She liked the soft fabrics of earlier times with their subtle textures. They seemed to represent the last great stages of Western culture, a time before industrialization had blighted the environment beyond repair. People had assumed the natural resources of the globe would last forever. Now, here on Earth were these artefacts of nature. The worms had made this silk, women's loving hands had sewn these small stitches, late into the night – perhaps for a sister or a daughter. And the cotton. Well, it may have been picked by abused sharecroppers and that wasn't such a nice idea, but still, it wasn't like the manufacture of polyester with its chemical by-products that were sending fumes up to Canada and creating acid rain, killing the forests and wildlife so beautiful there, and filling the workers' lungs.

Swifty, her agent, was always complaining about her clothes. 'Why do you dress like that?' he would chide her. 'You should wear plain black dresses. Can't you buy some Calvin Klein or something? And another thing: your jewellery should be bigger, much bigger. It doesn't make a Statement. Always make a Statement! And your hair! Why don't you pull it back tight to your head, something sophisticated? Then you'll look chic, smart!'

One night Ariadne had a dream about feminist politics and sex. Everywhere she turned she was told she was wrong: either she was not sexy enough (Cleopatra), or she was not feminist enough (Gertrude Stein), or not professional enough (Swifty), or not realistic enough (Wellington and Tocqueville), or not something enough.

Oh, dear, Ariadne thought in her dream. Do I have to choose between having fun and being serious? Can't politics be fun? Can't I be a feminist and be sexy too?

As she lay tossing and turning, trying to reconcile these feelings, she remembered that day in Heaven when Gertrude Stein had warned her, 'How do you expect to get credit for being a feminist philosopher and theoretician, not to mention strategist, if you insist on wearing clothes like that? And your hair! Now, if you'd only listen to me, I could help you consolidate your position, get your name firmly located in History. Otherwise, my dear, like so many others, I'm afraid you and your contribution will be wiped out.'

'What can I do?' Ariadne had asked, feeling stupid.

'Well, if you would join a university, or try teaching for a while, that might increase your respectability.'

'Ms Stein, *you* never taught at university. Anyway, I've been asked to lecture at almost every major university and scholarly association, and I've talked at lots of them. Isn't that enough? When do I become "respectable"?'

'As soon as you cut your hair and stop wearing make-up and high heels.'

'Oh, help!' Ariadne cried, waking to find herself clutching a surprised and sleepy Jupiter.

But the press made everything an issue: instead of writing about the issue Ariadne had raised of emotional violence to women, they ran headlines like 'Long Red Nails'!

She remembered how, when she wore inexpensive thrift-shop clothes, the press wrote that she was messy, that she had no taste. Then, when she wore a designer suit, they wrote she was money-obsessed!

But, her sleepy mind wandered on, maybe dressing in frilly feminine clothes is a sign of being male-defined, trying to suck up to men, to get power through them. And isn't it a sign of competing with your sisters? Trying to outdress them to win the attention of men?

But it's such a pleasure to enjoy your body, your skin, the colours and textures. . . . Ariadne thought about how she liked to get dressed, how she liked to arrange her clothes sometimes, and play around with colours and fabrics, and how she liked to brush her hair and look at the colour of her skin next to her nails and toenails after she painted them vivid colours. Was this wrong?

With a start, she looked at the clock. 'Oh!' She decided to wear the leopard-skin dress after all. She threw it over her head, zipped it up, put on some heavy oil perfume with a strange, exotic smell (Cleo had given it to her in an antique Egyptian bottle), and some long gold earrings. She grabbed her old black velvet purse, her long fuchsia fingernails and white skin a beautiful contrast with the deep black velour, and raced from the room – followed by Jupiter.

A Glorious Concert

Friedrich was waiting outside, ready to go.

'Am I late? Oh, your tails are fantastic!' Jupiter wondered what kind of tails these could be. Friedrich leaned back against the dark grey plush seat, in the limousine provided by the Concert Hall, happy and excited. 'Well, this isn't like the old Philadelphia Orchestra limousine. That one has more character. They've had the same limousine with the same driver for years. You really feel like you're riding in a piece of history. And you are!' Friedrich tended to get hyper before a concert. Jupiter joined in, jumping on and off the seat.

'By the way,' Friedrich chattered on, 'I really like the way Isaac Stern did the hall. I don't agree that the acoustics are ruined. Well, I never actually played in the hall before, but it really feels good in there now. The stage just welcomes you somehow, it almost has a personality. It feels right.'

Jupiter had come to love taxicabs, limousines and cars of all kinds. At first he thought he preferred flying, but with the congestion of the city, you really needed that steel case around you. And it wasn't bad, either, to sit right up there on the long, deep seat and have someone drive you around – especially in a limousine! Wait until the dogs back in Heaven heard about this!

When they arrived at the Concert Hall, they smuggled Jupiter backstage, where he stayed in the wings with Friedrich's friend Clarence, the guard, while Ariadne went to her seat in the orchestra stalls. Jupiter could just see her through a little hole in the curtain. There really were a lot of people! Why did almost everybody wear black? he wondered.

The lights went down and the concert began. Jupiter felt very much at home, and he lay down and closed his eyes, listening. The arching music lifted his thoughts to another level – there was Rachmaninoff and Prokofiev, then came the waltzes, the *Liebesleider* and *Liebesfreud* transcriptions.

Too soon, it was over, and Friedrich stood with Jupiter, behind the curtain, drenched in sweat. It was a great physical labour playing the piano! Friedrich went back out and bowed in that elegant European way that made you feel you had just been transported to some fabulous nineteenth-century evening.

The excited audience rose to their feet shouting. 'Bravo! Bravo!' Jupiter was impressed too – he had come to love the Tchaikovsky, Scriabin and Prokofiev that flooded the apartment all the time now when Friedrich played. And Jupiter loved Friedrich's friends; of the other musicians he invited to the apartment Jupiter particularly liked Alexander, since Alexander's mother owned an Indian restaurant and often brought Jupiter Indian dinners. He loved curry!

Ariadne rushed backstage and found Friedrich already surrounded by admirers. Pushing through them, she whispered in his ear, 'Darling, you're a genius. Listening to you play makes me feel I am living in a greater reality than daily life. It's like a heroic poem, bringing home to me the meaning of life, who I am, why I am here. Your playing will make people reflect, remember there is Beauty, remember what is important.' Friedrich beamed with pleasure.

More of Friedrich's friends joined them. Gediminas Taranda, the dancer, who was dressed from head to toe in a stretchy silver bodysuit, swept his cape over Friedrich's shoulders, and bowed to him, bending to his knees, making great fanciful swirls in the air with his hands in tribute.

'Is he giving you his cape?' Nikolai, Friedrich's manager, asked, jealously.

'Well, one of them,' Gediminas's friend, Tercheskaya answered in his deep bass voice. 'He has so many! To play it safe, he has fourteen – you know, in case one gets too sweaty!' He made a face and held his nose theatrically.

Out on the street, Friedrich, elated by the evening, struck heroic poses in his new purple silk cloak and began orating dramatically *à la* Demosthenes (or the Gallic Wars?) 'And I will come in my purple robe, out onto the stage, fling it down onto the floor and bare-breasted stand there to take the slings and arrows of my villainous critics.'

At the nearby Ritzy Bar, with blue and gold swirls overhead and Jupiter under foot, they drank champagne and vodka alternately while Friedrich laughed, told jokes and grinned unstoppably. Ariadne guided his hand under the table to reveal that she was wearing a pair of crotchless tights.

They made out on the way home in the cab, and as soon as they got in the door (Jupiter made himself scarce), Friedrich rudely pushed up her dress and began kissing her crotch. 'You smell really sexy . . . I love to breathe in when I smell you.'

'Listen, darling, that Medtner piano concerto, it would have been good tonight too!'

'Shut up! Did I ever tell you that you have a beautiful ass?' He started to feel her.

'What! Not now! We have to go to bed. To sleep. It's 3 a.m. and if we start this. . . .'

'Who cares?!'

Memories of Ariadne's Childhood

When Ariadne awoke next morning, Friedrich was looking at her intently. She put her arms round him. 'Darling, there's something I want to tell you, something about me. When we first had sex, it was so magical, just like when I first discovered my own sexuality, long ago in a little bedroom, with white curtains blowing in the warm spring air.

'I have such a strong memory of that room. It was a small, simple, beautiful room. It was so simple as to be almost austere, but it had a special atmosphere. I remember it most intensely in spring. The room was square, with a high ceiling and the walls were covered with soft, patterned paper. The furniture was blond wood: there was a small desk for homework, a dressing-table, a little chest of drawers and a full-size bed with a blond headboard. The bed had a white chenille spread. Just next to my bed there was a window, with sheer white ruffled curtains.

'During school terms, I usually went to bed quite early. As I wasn't yet sleepy, I would lie in bed listening to the sounds of the trains passing by in the distance, or the last birds singing, or the crickets, and once in a while a dog barking somewhere. Sometimes I got up to go to the open window, where the curtains moved gently in the breeze. If I sat on my knees, the window was just the right height for resting my arms, so I could sit there to look out and smell the fresh grass, and dream.

'The house was white outside, too, a white wooden frame house. Beneath the window was a large, lush patch of dark green plants that came up every spring. For a few weeks, the most delicate flowers would bloom – lots of lilies of the valley. The soil was dark and rich and moist, and the green shoots came up full and strong. The hundreds of tiny white blossoms gave off the most intense, luscious perfume, and it mixed with the night air and filtered through the open window. I would sit by the window and let the moist, magical fragrance completely cover me in the darkness. It was intoxicating.

'I remember nights when the moon shone down on that little garden spot beneath my window, while I sat watching, wondering that the world could be so divinely beautiful. The moonlight shone brilliantly on the moist green leaves, as if specially for me. I sat there for indeterminate amounts of time – maybe hours, maybe years, maybe eternity. And a shaft of moonlight touched the side of the house, making patterns as it filtered through the branches of the young tree we had planted there.

'Later, when summer came, and I was still put early to bed, it would be light for a while outside and I wished I was still out playing ball with some of the other kids in the neighbourhood. Sometimes I could even hear one or two of them shouting and saying good night to each other as I lay in bed.

One of those evenings, a strange desire began to creep over me, a deep craving that seemed to be coming from inside my body, or all around, somewhere I could not reach. I learned the sensations could be increased by moving my legs around, with my body pressed against the bed. If I grasped my pillow, facing down, I could get the best feeling. I began to pull my body against the bed until, instead of ending the feeling, the feeling grew and grew and became more and more demanding. I pulled and twisted against the bed, gripping the mattress with one hand, but no matter how hard I pressed myself against the bed, my body cried out for more. It was a sweet torture. I did not know what it was.

'One day, doing this, I felt a wonderful explosion deep inside my body. The pleasure was like an electric shock between my hot, writhing legs. I loved it. I wanted to do it over and over, and I did, again and again.

'Soon I did it every day. But I began to worry: had I broken something inside my body? What was it I was doing? Since no one had ever told me anything about their having such an experience or such a physical feeling, or loving to rub themselves, maybe it was unnatural. I began to wonder if God (he, as I thought of him) could see me. I was sure he could, as he could see everything. And if it wasn't right, would he stop me, would he punish me somehow?

'But he never did.

'These first ecstatic sexual feelings, in that white room with the moist fragrant air, me lying in the bed, the white voile curtains swaying in the breeze at the open window, and the soft summer sounds drifting in, the room's pale colours contrasting with the intense green of the leaves and the grass outside, are beautiful in my memory. It was a wonderful way to discover my sexuality – not hearing about it first through pornography or seeing women's naked bodies displayed for profit on every newsstand, but just alone in my room, in my own bed, finding my self.'

Earth: Act III

Does Free Speech Live on Live TV?

The next day, Swifty called. 'Hi, honey! Have I got a great deal for you! The best chat show on TV – yeah, you bet your life, I take good care of you! The Honest Frank Talk Show wants *you*!'

Silence. Ariadne couldn't reply because Jupiter was wildly shaking his head, No, no, no! Don't do it!

She exhaled. She hadn't thought about all this for quite a while.

'Speak up, speak up. How's about it? Oh yeah, and they want you there in two hours.'

Friedrich walked into the room and saw the expression on both of their faces. 'What's going on?'

'Uhhh. . . .'

'Ariadne, have you gone in for deep breathing?'

No reply. No movement. No change of expression.

'Are you pregnant?'

Silence.

'Darling, speak to me!'

Swifty screamed down the phone, 'Yeah, darling, speak to me too! *Are* you pregnant??? That'll make a great story. Just think what I can do with that??!!'

Ariadne found her voice. 'I'll call you back.'

Jupiter looked worried.

'Oh, Friedrich, they want me to go on The Honest Frank Talk Show.'

'I forbid it. You can't do that to yourself.'

A question mark hung over Jupiter's head as he looked from one to the other.

'Sweetheart, I know it's a risk, maybe a long shot, but it's live TV, it's not edited. I can say anything I want, it doesn't matter what the questions are. By now, people must have such a distorted idea of who I am and what I'm trying to say, maybe I should try. . . .'

Friedrich looked pained, and stood silently regarding her. Finally he said, 'If you're going, I'm going with you.'

'Really?' Tears of happiness sprang to her eyes.

Miraculously, Honest Frank agreed to let Friedrich come on the show with Ariadne, as well as a professor of philosophy familiar with her work. He drew the line at Jupiter.

Two hours later, right on schedule, they sat down on the set in their black vinyl seats, and were being miked, a veritable portrait of optimism. After all, Honest Frank Talk had a reputation for fairness and, so far, he was being genial.

The music started – that peppy, everything's fine, oh-the-excitement-of-showbiz music. Ariadne laughed, thinking Jupiter was probably in front of the set putting his paws over his ears at the sound of it, and rolling his eyes heavenward.

The show began. Frank turned on Ariadne, smiling menacingly, as the camera did a close-up.

'Mizzz Rite,' Frank began with a flourish, 'you have been running around the country, doing what?' He looked at his notes covertly. 'You have been talking to people, lots and lots of people. Why did you do that?'

'Well, I'm interested in what people think about things.'

'What makes you think you're so good at finding out? Who appointed you anyway?'

'I've been told this is a democracy and that what people think is important.'

'Who told you that?' Frank said before he could catch himself. He carried on immediately, 'Well, tell us why you think what you've done is so important.'

'Well, I have here a statement,' and Ariadne took out a letter, surprised to have to defend herself so early on, 'signed by twelve feminist writers.'

124

Frank scanned the paper briefly. ' . . . Rite's work is a very important social document, with testimony by thousands of women. . . .' He threw it on the table. 'This is all very well and good, but, I mean, what can you expect from a bunch of egghead feminists? Now let's get down to cases, I think you have a lot of explaining to do.

'You've been accused of talking to the media by using another name on the telephone. You claim you are using a secretary by the name of Bookfinder. The newspaper says that its conversation with Ms Bookfinder, "whose voice bore a strong resemblance to Ms Rite's . . ."'

Friedrich interrupted, 'I spoke to that reporter and he had never talked to Ariadne. So how would he know if the secretary's voice resembled Ariadne's . . . and what if it did, frankly, Frank?'

'They called my secretary's tape,' Ariadne added, 'late at night and left messages like, "Oh Kate, good Kate, call us back so we can record your voice! Are you really there, Kate? Oh, Kate?" It felt like a horrible kind of harassment, Kate was so upset.'

'But,' Friedrich spoke up, 'what kind of show is this? Is Ariadne going to have the chance to speak about her book? Or are you setting another agenda? Don't you think your audience would be interested in knowing about the real issues? Why this attack on Ariadne's character? What point do you want to make?'

'You want the issues? OK, I'll give you the issues.' And Frank blasted in a prosecutorial voice: 'Mizz Rite, you have said in your book that seventy percent of all women married more than five years have had an extramarital affair. I'm here to tell you that's not true!'

What's up with him? Ariadne wondered. Is his wife having an affair? She decided, politely, not to say this. Good ole Frank didn't know how lucky he was that Ariadne had her principles! Instead she said, 'Where did you get your information? Did you interview 4,500 women too?'

'OK, OK, I can't prove it,' Frank grumbled. 'Let's get on with it.' He looked at his notes again. 'You've been accused of storming off television programmes.' He pointed his finger at her. 'You have behaved terribly!'

Ariadne, looking at his finger, could only think of the first time she was on TV, when other fingers were pointed at her – 'You're going to be in Big Trouble, My Pretty.' Hadn't she seen this on some late-night movie on TV? Then she thought, No, no, I must be losing my grip, maybe my mind is going!

Frank went on, 'Well? Well? What do you have to say?'

Ariadne laughed, 'Frank, you can't be serious? Am I on trial? Or don't you. . .' she took a deep breath and turned towards the audience, remembering her vow to speak to the audience and not the host, if necessary. 'What I'm here to talk about is not gossip, but very real and important issues – women's issues, and environmental issues.

'The value system that keeps women paid half of what men make is the value system that's sending gases into the air, making holes in the ozone layer – maybe killing us all. The emotional violence women describe getting at home is part of the same value system, and the greed that carelessly exterminates entire animal species, that rapes and ravages nature. . . . All this, so tragic, is coming from the same place.'

'Oh, brother,' said Frank, rolling his eyes theatrically. 'Are you a do-gooder!'

'And what's wrong with doing good in this world?' Friedrich challenged Frank.

Ariadne spoke up, hopefully, 'Frank please – I came on your show not to get embroiled in petty personal gossip, but –'

'You're afraid to discuss gossip, as you call it, because you're really intolerant of any criticism whatsoever!'

'How can you say that? I live with it every day of my life!' She suddenly realized she was holding Friedrich's hand.

'You say that everyone who criticizes you is a sexist.'

'No, I don't say that,' Ariadne responded, amazed.

'I'll tell you what is off-putting,' Frank said, desperately trying to provoke Ariadne. 'It's the male-bashing in your book.'

Ariadne's eyes opened even wider. This man was astounding!

'I'd like to respond to that, Mr Talkie,' Professor Linda Emeritus finally got a word in edgewise. (Being an academic, she wasn't used to all this aggressive to and fro.) 'This book is not about men; it's about women, women in love – not only in love with men, but also loving women. It's a beautiful book, with women describing all the kinds of love there are – it's almost poetry – but some reporters have taken it out of context. They seem to think there's a threat.

'Perhaps there is: there is real anxiety surrounding these issues in our culture, since love is supposed to be Power. But for many women it involves violence against them, both emotional and physical. And so, many women are refusing to remain in "the family"; the majority of the divorces in this country are initiated by women.

'As the culture gets progressively more anxious and beleaguered with economic and race-relations problems, it places an even greater premium on love. It becomes hysterical in its insistence that the family is fine, women should stop complaining. . . .'

'Don't you like the family, Professor?' Frank snipped.

'Yes – but what difference does that make? I like love, most women like love – it's a great way to feel free, spontaneous and human. What women are saying in Ms Rite's excellent research is that love doesn't work out the way it's supposed to half the time. We're trying to explain why it doesn't.'

'That sounds reasonable.'

'Why couldn't you hear it when Ariadne said it?'

Frank looked nonplussed. 'Right, well, let's hear what our viewers at home have to say. The phone lines are now open for your calls.'

Female Caller 1 [*with great enthusiasm*]: Ariadne Rite is right. I'm living what she's writing about. I'm unhappy with my relationship. My friends are unhappy with their relationships. Even my mother is unhappy with her relationship.

[*Audience laughter*]

Female Caller 1: I mean, Rite is right, so why are you badgering her like that?

Frank Talk: You mean, men are –

Female Caller 1: Yeah, men are women bashers! I mean, they say things like 'You're hysterical. I'll talk to you when you've calmed down, dear', or 'What's the matter, got your period?' if you try to bring up even one little thing they don't like, like Ariadne is doing now.

Frank Talk [*charmingly*]: Oh, come on. You don't think all men are like that, do you?

Female Caller 1: I sure do!

[*Audience laughter*]

Frank Talk: Go ahead, next caller.

Female Caller 2: Listen, Rite did a study, right? Why do you dispute what she found just because you don't like it? The people she talked to have their opinions, whether you like them or not. So why can't you just accept that?

Frank Talk [*hoping to get the audience back on his side*]: Uh-huh. Well, Rite claims that seventy percent of all women married over five years have had an extramarital affair. Do you accept that?

Female Caller 2: It's possible. The people she interviewed weren't forced to answer her questions. If seven out of ten of my friends are having affairs, it's not only because of sex, but the whole relationship with their husbands is unfulfilling emotionally.

Frank Talk: You mean, their husbands don't talk to them, so they go have an affair? That's great, isn't it?

Professor Emeritus: Let me ask you a question, Frank. You seem to be really disturbed by the prospect that the extramarital statistic is true. You want to say it can't be true, but what if it is? Suppose another study showed that the figure is only six out of ten – would that really make a difference? The trend is still clear. And what does that trend mean? Does it mean Western civilization is falling apart? If you think it does, surely that's something to discuss, not a reason to stick you head in the sand.

Frank Talk: Next caller!!!

Male Caller: Why can't anybody talk about anything but this one statistic? I've read the book and there's a lot more in it than that. I bet if you interviewed all the people who are criticizing Ariadne Rite, maybe ten percent at the most would have even read the book.

Frank Talk: We've got another caller on the line. Go ahead.

Female Caller 3: I want to say thank you to Ms Rite! I felt really alone until I read her book. It helped me to know that there are a lot of other women out there who feel the way I do. I've read every book I could find on how to improve my marriage, but my husband won't read one. Instead of criticizing her, it would be nice if men would read her book, go home and talk to their wives.

Frank Talk: Oh, I give up. Ariadne Rite has obviously tapped

128

into a hornet's nest of what ails this country – men! We men are doing the opposite of what brave men are supposed to do.

Friedrich: I'm certainly glad to hear you say this, but why didn't you say anything like this before? Your attack on Ariadne during this show has been unremitting. Now you want to sound like a good guy. Do you believe anything you're saying?'

But the music was playing again, that razzmatazz music, so no one heard what Friedrich said. Frank Talk waved (tossing his wadded up notes in the waste-basket with relief) and smiled at his cheering audience (a sign above his head said 'APPLAUD NOW'), and the commercial for lavatory cleaner came on screen.

Professor Emeritus was heard to say as she walked off, so disoriented that her pen went in one direction and her pad in the other. 'That's it! I'm never doing this again. TV's a real dangerous place. I'm going back to academia – even that's safer.'

The Aftermath

On the way home in the car Friedrich held Ariadne, both his arms tight around her. Ariadne had kept up a brave front on TV, but now she was shaking all over, feeling humiliated and upset. She hid her face in his rough wool jacket, and let out a sob. He shuddered, and held her all the more tightly, then whispered, his mouth against her hair, 'Listen sweetheart, did you hear those callers today? They heard you – and you've got hundreds of letters of support. . . .'

Ariadne looked up into his face. 'Oh, Friedrich, sometimes I just want to go away and hide in a hole, somewhere where nobody knows my name. I know it's all not true, but they're saying such horrible things everywhere. I don't want to go through life like this! It's too painful! I don't like public humiliation.' And she cried as she nestled against him.

As soon as they got home, the phone rang. It was Honest Frank's competition, Sally Bright. She wanted Ariadne on her *Today is Tomorrow* show. Her brisk and bouncy voice filled Ariadne's ear: 'Ariadne! I want *you*! Will you go on alone with two hundred angry men?'

'Two hundred men? What are they angry about?'

'Don't worry, Ariadne,' cooed Sally, 'I'll be there with you! No tricks, no gimmicks. How about it?' Her voice was soft and velvety now. Could Ariadne trust her?

A Midnight Conversation With Jupiter

Ariadne tossed and turned in bed, mumbling in her sleep. 'She's out for money. She hates men. She's hysterical. She can't handle it. Discredited, you're discredited!'

'Ariadne, wake up! Wake up!' Jupiter nuzzled her gently with his sweet head.

Rubbing her sleepy eyes, Ariadne told him, 'Oh, Jupiter, I was having the worst nightmare. All about TV. . .'

'Ariadne, remember how we thought about all this in the beginning? We never took any of it too seriously. You're getting needlessly Earth-bound. Remember, we can leave any time you want! Don't lose your heart over it.'

'You're right,' Ariadne smiled, encouraged. 'I was losing my perspective.'

So they had a midnight snack of cheese sandwiches, and went back to sleep.

By the next morning Ariadne had decided it was either fight back or give up, and the only way to fight back was to keep going on live TV. She decided to trust Sally.

Going Live, One More Time: The Heavenly Gazette Sees the Hilarious Side

Fortunately, Dorothy Parker was the Heaven-to-Earth correspondent for the ultra-snob (but feminist) *Wellesley Review of Books* (an insert in the prestigious *Heavenly Gazette*). Here is how she summed up the scene that week:

> November 6. It is a mindless moment for me between phone interviews. I click on the TV to catch up with reality.

It is halfway through the Sally Bright show and there is — Ariadne Rite, surrounded, as though engulfed, even imprisoned, by men seated on her left, men seated on her right, men seated behind her. Stringy men, rangy men, big men, fat men, little men, white men, black men. Men in the audience thrust towards the aisle microphone to ejaculate venom.

My God! It's as if it's 1972! What has happened to the veneer of the 'new man'? Where is his tenderness? His compassion? His nurturing? The scene gives 'surrounded by hostility' a whole new meaning. Ariadne Rite is being held personally accountable for not just the entire Women's Movement but for these men's wives' and girlfriends', for their own mothers' betrayals and for everything else they can throw in the fracas.

'You're always blaming men.' 'Your trouble is you want to be the man.' 'A father can't even get custody of his child.' The whole caboodle. And following each man's righteous accusation — applause, jeers, whistles, roars. It's a Roman circus and there are moments when it seems like Sally is mainly engaged in crowd control.

Whatever insights the careful reader of these 922 pages might carry away, a thorough discussion of the merits and meaning of the book is not what is in progress on the show. What these guys know is that this book bears copious testimony from women who are emotionally dissatisfied, unfulfilled, unlistened to in their relationships with men. There is certainly potential irony to be found in the fact that *New York Women* was at that very moment carrying an article, 'Desperately Seeking a Date', and that in mid-November the *New York Times Magazine* would carry a feature story on the sorry and worrisome phenomenon of an increasing number of 'available fellas' stoically committed to bachelorhood. Irony, however, is lost in this stampede of passion without reason.

I do not mean to be snippy. What I mean to suggest is that the explosiveness of this report is that it punctures the media-created truce that had supposedly been reached. Men had changed. Relationships had changed. Fatherhood had changed. All that talk about women's issues in the Seventies had given rise to exhaustion and peace in the Eighties. The assumption was that as long as women weren't complaining, everything had been fixed.

And Ariadne Rite has the nerve to come along and say, 'You're still not listening to us.' And men explode, 'But we listened, dammit.' The degree of passion and vitriol Rite's study has brought down must be taken very seriously indeed. It is as though to men's minds Rite stands for every woman in their lives who has ever instigated 'that' conversation about wanting more — house money, closeness, communication, whatever.

It's as if for that decade when they were forced to listen to women natter on about how men and the media had kept them down, men now feel justified to leap to their feet as a mob and to holler back, 'Bitch! We already talked about that!'

An Afternoon in Paradise

Ariadne and Friedrich drove through the countryside, headed for another TV show (he had insisted on accompanying her: 'At the rate you're going, you need not only emotional support, you need a bodyguard!') in a big black limousine the show had sent to pick them up. It was a peaceful ride through rolling hills with green lawns, to the small studio where the show was filmed. For once, the programme was uneventful — informative and honest. The media were doing what they should do, or at least what they could do — informing their millions of listeners of new ideas.

Ariadne and Friedrich were elated and, coming home, they relaxed in the back seat of the limousine. They felt like they had been given time off for good behaviour. As relief settled in, they became happier and happier: they were in love, the sun was shining, and they had a whole afternoon together ahead of them. Most of it would be in the limousine, but the driver *did* have his back turned. And there *was* a sort of a curtain.

Ariadne tried to return two urgent calls from the limousine's telephone, but in the midst of this, Friedrich decided he wanted to have sex. He began very erotic advances, driving Ariadne crazy while she was trying to talk. He kissed her neck, trailing down to open her blouse, then kissed her nipples. He got down on the floor of the limousine, pushed up her skirt, thrusting his head between her legs. She shrieked with laughter, squirming around, and trying to get away while she talked.

'Stop it! Oh, Friedrich, stop! Now *look*! I'm on hold, this person is going to come on the line any minute! How can I talk? And it's Toby Duel, that fellow from the *Storybook Times*!' Friedrich nuzzled deeper. 'You don't care? You won't stop? OK, you asked for it. Here, *you* talk to him!' And she thrust the phone next to Friedrich's ear just as Duel came on the line.

Friedrich, still on the floor of the limousine, straightened up, cleared his throat, and just managed to say 'Hello? Hello! This is Friedrich Paeschke. I am returning your call to Ariadne Rite.' Friedrich and Ariadne tried to control their laugher. 'Ariadne? Yes, she's here. But she's tied up right at the moment.' He grinned, pinning her to the seat. 'Yes, of course. I'll be glad to pass on to her any question you have.' Friedrich camped it up in his most supercilious, official, la-de-da voice.

Duel sounded querulous. 'Tell me, does Ms Rite think that all this negative publicity will hinder sales of her book?' Friedrich repeated the question for Ariadne, crossing his eyeballs and making idiotic faces.

'If he can answer that, I know a lot of authors who will come to him to read their palms!' Ariadne laughed as Friedrich repeated her answer to Duel.

Duel was surprised. 'Why, Ms Rite is laughing! You two sound in great spirits! We thought you were depressed.' The phone went down.

After the call, Friedrich and Ariadne giggled, laughed, then roared so hard their eyes watered, thinking how everyone was trying to make them gloomy with absurd, off-the-point questions. It could be depressing, no doubt about that. On the other hand, so much of it seemed ludicrous that one just couldn't take it seriously all the time. At least not today.

Friedrich and Ariadne were in a party mood. The limousine was stocked with champagne and cocktail glasses, canapés and linen napkins. Ariadne donned a napkin folded like a hat. 'There. Do I look like a nurse?'

'God, it's sexy. Let's play doctor.'

'OK, take down your pants, be a good boy.' There was complete memory loss of the Revolution in Progress. . . .

The Driver Loses His Cool

The next morning Ariadne was getting dressed when she heard Kate come in. Walking out to say hello, she saw that Kate was on the verge of tears.

'Darling! What is it?' Ariadne was alarmed for her friend. They hadn't had a chance to talk to each other about anything other than business lately and Ariadne couldn't imagine what had hurt Kate.

'Oh, it's so awful,' Kate began to cry. 'Roger and I broke up. I know it's over now. I'm so unhappy, I just can't bear it. I don't know what to do. But we can't live together – he's always mad at me because I have to go to work. He usually wants to have sex in the morning, and this makes me late. He doesn't have any pressure to be anywhere, he just sits around and expects something to happen – Well, he's supposed to be studying, it's his last year at university. . . . Oh, I know he's not going to be this way always, but I feel so destroyed when we fight, I can't stand it. . . . God, what should I do?'

The doorbell interrupted her. The doorman's voice crackled over the intercom, 'Ms Rite, there's a car here to pick you up.'

Ariadne was surprised. She was booked to go to a neighbouring city to appear on a local TV show, but she had been told the car would come at 11:30, over an hour later. 'The car's very early. Could you please ask the driver to wait and just charge me for the time? I'll be out in a while.'

Kate clutched the mug of coffee Ariadne handed her, and lit a cigarette, shaking. 'I know this is just a phase he's going through, but last night I got mad and told him he wasn't good for anything except sex and that I was tired of carrying the whole weight of our relationship. Alone. So he got even by calling Margo, one of

134

my best friends, and asking her to go to bed with him! Luckily, she is a great friend and wouldn't have any part of it, even over the telephone, but it was so awful. So humiliating . . . painful. I feel like someone scorched my brain. I can't stand it. I don't know what to do.'

'Oh, Kate, my love,' said Ariadne, holding her friend in her arms. 'You don't deserve this. This is awful. You are a lovely woman, and a very valuable person. I hate to see you going through this much pain. Listen, don't worry about work today. Stay here, take it easy, call your friends, relax. Then when I come back from the TV show, we can talk some more if you want. You don't deserve any abuse. . . .'

The bell rang again. 'The driver says you *must* come now.' The doorman's disembodied voice was insistent.

Ariadne checked her printed schedule again. 'It's only a one-hour drive, and even allowing an extra half hour leeway, we still have plenty of time,' she told the doorman. Ariadne wanted to be with Kate, who needed her, as long as she could – to help Kate in any way she could.

But the doorman kept calling, buzzing every few minutes, explaining that the driver kept pressuring him, until Ariadne finally said, 'Alright, I'll come down and go, even though I think we're early.' But when she got outside, the driver stood on the steps in front of her, refusing to go. He informed her, vindictively (triumphantly?), 'You're too late! You can't make it now. It's a long ride, y'know. Women! Ha! Always late!' He winked broadly at the doorman. 'Just can't get themselves organized, can they?'

Ariadne was irritated by his patronizing manner, but ignored his personality problem. 'Well, let's just go now!' she said.

'I don't think we're going to make it,' the driver gleefully repeated, with exaggerated slowness, refusing to move.

'Well, we won't if we don't leave. Let's at least try. Come on!'

The driver turned to the doorman again. 'Women! What would we do without them! One thing one minute, another the next.'

Ariadne was fuming now, worried that indeed she *would* be late, if they didn't go soon. 'Are you going to move or not?'

'No sense getting yourself steamed up, my dear. You can't tell me what to do, I'm the man in charge here. Now why don't you just calm down like a good little girl, heh, heh.'

Ariadne slapped him. Stunned silence. The driver grabbed his nose and hurried to his car muttering 'lawyer', 'lawsuit', and 'You'll hear more about this!' And thus was another career launched.

Ariadne stood there, feeling rotten.

Swifty Hopes to Make Hay

The following day, all the papers carried stories of how Ariadne had hit the limousine driver. Ariadne, Friedrich and Kate were shocked.

'Listen to this one,' Ariadne read aloud. 'Rite Retort: Pow!' And, '"Dear" Earns Driver a Punch in the Nose'. They looked at one another in amazement. Friedrich said, 'It's on every news station in the country. They're making it the event of the century.'

The phone rang. Friedrich grabbed it. He turned to Ariadne, 'Darling, it's Swifty calling from his suite at the George V in Paris.'

Ariadne took the phone.

Swifty's irrepressible spirit zinged down the line. 'Listen, you! I'm getting offers from all over the world for you to write a book about the fight you had with that driver. Will you do it?'

'*What*? You bet I won't! That's crazy! No!'

'Oh, come on. Plee-ze,' he pleaded.

'No, absolutely not!' Ariadne was adamant.

'OK,' Swifty sighed in defeat. 'I don't know what you think you're going to gain by it, but if that's the way you are, that's just it. Goodbye.'

Using Another Name: Ariadne Tries to Avoid the Press

The phone rang again a minute later. Ariadne, thinking it was Swifty again, picked it up – but heard a new voice . . . .

'Hello, may I speak to Ariadne Rite?'

'I'm sorry, Ms Rite's not available. May I help you?'

'Who are you?' the voice of a male reporter demanded.

'I'm Anne Star. May I help you?'

'Do you work for Rite? Are you a temp? Are you permanent there? How long have you been there?' It was a prosecuting attorney, badgering her.

'Yes, I work here for Ms Rite. Who are you?'

'John Pizzaprofit of the *Power Press*. You've probably seen my byline. Now, what I'd like to know about Rite – '

'Of course I've seen your byline,' Ariadne said sweetly. 'By the way, have you read *The Meaning of It All*?'

'What? No, I didn't get a chance, and there's no point in doing it now that the story's broken. So, tell me – '

'But how can you write a news story without reading the material yourself?'

'Well, this isn't exactly what you'd call a news story, you see; it's for the Style-Trend section.'

'Really? Well, you know that the *Pompous Oracle* and the *Serious Press* both covered it in their news sections. I feel that what the women are saying in the report, and the statistics based on their statements, is more than "style" – it's Hard News.'

'Oh, right, yeah, well, I would have reported it as news too.'

'I see, so you write for both the news and the Style section?'

'Uh, no, we put that kind of news in the Style section.'

What could she say! Counting to ten, Ariadne-Anne managed to say evenly, 'Of course, lifestyle issues are extremely important, but don't you think there's still a tendency in the press to treat everything women say and do only in terms of "style"? Isn't what women do and think "hard" news?'

'Yeah, well, I guess it might jazz up the front section of *Power Press* if they put in some of these kinds of stories.'

Ariadne, realizing that this conversation was about as purposeful as talking to a heavy breather, said she was sorry she couldn't help him and hung up the phone. Freedom of speech in the hands of the Bad Boys of this world, Ariadne thought, was a lost cause and not so great for the survival of the democratic process, either!

At the special request of her publisher, Ariadne went to the capital to do an hour of interviews by satellite television.

Suddenly, Ariadne heard the voice of a well-known sports announcer.

'Hello out there. It's a fine sunny day here in the stadium – '

'No! NO!' his producer whispered frantically. 'This isn't sports!'

'Yes, uh, today we have Ariadne Rite with us. She thinks she knows what men think about women, and what women think about men – in bed and out. She's in the headlines today for packing quite a punch, so let's find out what she has to say.

'Well, Ms Rite, it's been quite a week for you. First there was the poll that came out with findings quite different from yours. How do you interpret this?'

There was no monitor, so Ariadne couldn't even see who was asking the questions. She simply had to address her remarks to the blank camera lens. 'I'm trying to describe a kind of emotional violence and abuse which is endemic to the system, a violence often directed at women, but also at all "weaker" groups – '

'Now, let's get back to the topic. About yesterday: what happened?'

Ariadne was getting frustrated. 'Listen, I've been trying everything to say what I discovered when I went around the country and interviewed thousands of people. I was told this is a great democracy, the greatest democracy on Earth. But dealing with the media, it's come to seem more like The Greatest Show on Earth, Barnum and Bailey all the way! Please – can't I say what I came here to say?'

'Now, about yesterday, when you were supposed to appear on a television show and didn't. What happened with the driver?'

'Well,' Ariadne began, 'he waited for a long time; I thought we could make it and he didn't.' Then, she thought: it's now or never, I've got ten seconds, what can I say before they cut me off? And she blurted out, 'The ideology here on Earth must change or the planet will be destroyed!'

'That's quite a diversion, Ms Rite. In fact, I'd say you're hitting the ball right out of the ball park!' sniggered the interviewer. 'Now, let's get back to those headlines. We just happen to have the driver here with us.'

'If I had known this was your reason for interviewing me,' Ariadne was furious, 'I would never have come here. I shouldn't have lost my temper, but I don't want to continue this discussion.'

'Why so angry?' the interviewer tried to sound truly puzzled. 'This is a good story! Whatever the subject, it's great PR! You're a headline in just about every paper in the country, Ms Rite, and – '

'And I will not continue this interview,' Ariadne interrupted him. She got up and tried to walk away. A studio man tried to restrain her physically. 'Stop it!' she cried. 'You don't have the right to hold me here! I have the right to get up and walk off camera.'

The interviewer was still trying to get her attention. 'We have the driver here and he wants – Where is she? She's gone? Well, guess I've got a home run on that one! Good night, folks.'

Off the set, Ariadne was amazed to find that the people there were still trying to restrain her physically. They attempted to block her way through the door, prevent her from going into the dressing room to pick up her briefcase, and generally intimidate her into doing the three more interviews they had lined up. Ariadne only wanted to get away.

Breaking Down and Crying in an Airport

Out on the street, having kept up a proud front all the way down in the elevator, Ariadne began sobbing uncontrollably, shedding all the pain of weeks and weeks of anguish through her tears. 'I just can't take any more, I just can't take it,' she said over and over. 'All my idealism – and it's turned into this!'

It was almost dark, and she was standing alone in the middle of a deserted square. The tall, dark buildings on every side seemed to hate her and impose even more isolation on her. There was no phone box or café in sight, nowhere to get a cab, and her briefcase filled with books seemed to weigh a thousand pounds.

She walked down street after street, searching for a phone that was working. Her head was hot and she felt faint. Shaking, she finally found a phone, only to discover she didn't have the right change. Near despair, Ariadne asked the only person in sight if he had any change. He did. The world wasn't all bad. Ariadne called a cab and waited for it in the street.

When she finally crawled into her hotel room, Ariadne fell onto the bed, totally drained. She didn't care anymore if she never moved again. She felt very strongly that she did not want to go on with this. Exhaustion made every limb as heavy as concrete. She lay there, immobile. After a long time – thirty minutes? one hour? two hours? – she heard the telephone ringing, as if in the distance. Slowly she came back to consciousness and answered, 'Hello. . .'

'How do you feel, darling?'

Friedrich! She was so glad to hear from him. But she could hardly find the strength to reply. She didn't have the energy to tell him in detail all that had happened; that would be for another time. She just said, very faintly, 'Do you know, I found out today that just one plane flying from New York to Washington can kill a hundred birds? It's common for them to get caught in the engine. Last year in Denver, there were so many birds tangled in an engine that it caused a plane crash, killing several people. Masses of birds in the engines, ripped to shreds.'

'Darling, I saw that horrible show on television.'

'Oh, Friedrich, is it worth all this? I feel my soul is ripped to shreds too.'

'Listen, you are speaking about emotional violence. Just as ten years ago, no one wanted to acknowledge the extent of wife battering, now no one wants to hear how widespread emotional violence and condescension are. But women are glad you are speaking out. There are hundreds of letters here, all encouraging you. They want you to know it means a lot to them. What you are doing is valuable. There is no question.'

'Part of me dies with the birds.'

'Come home, Jupiter misses you and I miss you. We'll cheer you up. We'll take you to the park, we'll give you a bath. We'll go around town and play. I'm going to go with you when you travel from now on. I'll go on all the shows too, if you think it's all

140

right. You shouldn't have to stand up by yourself all the time.'

Ariadne managed to make the last shuttle flight home. All the way through the airport, she sobbed, keeping her head lowered and wearing sunglasses, so that no one could see.

At home, Jupiter, Friedrich and Ariadne walked in the park under the night sky. A bird sang. Friedrich took Ariadne's hand and said, 'Do you hear that bird? It's an amsel, called the composer of all the birds, because he or she never sings the same song twice. They don't have the most brilliant plumage, but they sing better than all the rest.'

They stopped to listen to the song. The simplicity of it, its sweetness, took some of the week's pain away. If she could just remember what was really important, Ariadne thought to herself, maybe she'd be all right.

Tenderly, Friedrich whispered, 'And, darling, did you know that bees communicate through dancing? Some of the bees are sent out from the hive to investigate where new flowers are blooming, and when they come back, they do a dance. The different turns and patterns tell all the others where the flowers are in bloom. The honey they make is one of the only kinds of food where no other life is killed. They make it without hurting anything.' He held her. 'You see, there are beautiful things in this world.'

'Oh, Friedrich,' Ariadne broke down. 'I started out trying to describe how a more caring system could work, how life doesn't have to be so harsh. But the whole process has turned into something crazy. No matter what I say, they twist it around. It's so painful, so frustrating. Why do they want to do this?'

'Sweetheart, sweetheart.' He stroked her hair, tears in his own eyes.

As the three of them stood together, looking up at the stars, Ariadne said, 'I heard a lovely poem, by Stephen Hawking. Do you want to hear his idea? It goes something like this:

'We live in a major spiral galaxy that we call the Milky Way. . . . If the starlight were all collected to look forward in time, we could see billions of years of cosmic history. But we can only collect the starlight of the past. . . . We are now, at this moment, creating the starlight of the future, each one of us an energy cell giving off light and radiance into the future. . . .

'The universe has no boundary, there is no centre to the beginning. All matter is a stage in the ongoing dance of energy.' Jupiter rubbed against her legs. Friedrich held her more closely and with great tenderness, and Ariadne began to feel safe again. 'Darling, do you know what I want?' She looked up at Friedrich. 'To be as much like the trees, like the leaves in the wind as possible. This is all. To be there for my friends like these trees. To feel no pain.'

Private Moments at Home

Ariadne needed a day or two of quiet, time at home alone with Jupiter to regain her equilibrium. So after telling Kate and Friedrich her plan, she turned off the telephone, and put on some classical music – Mahler, then Jascha Heifetz. She and Jupiter sat with only their own sounds, quietly.

In the silence, Ariadne confided in Jupiter's soft ear, 'The stillness is so good. I love to listen to all the sounds that come to you when it is quiet. Many thoughts, feelings, come clearly to your mind if you wait, don't you think? An inner rhythm seems to emerge when I stop talking – or even listening or speaking – a different world.' Then she smiled, realizing she was only telling Jupiter what he already knew.

They passed the day together quietly, pottering around the apartment, looking at books of paintings and enjoying the soft colours of their rooms.

Towards evening, they looked out of the window. In the long twilight, the birds were drowsing in the large leafy trees, the setting sun's half-light still filtering its soft golden haze through the branches, refracting a million fragments of light onto the shiny russet and gold oak leaves – a shimmering moment in time, wherein there was no present and no past, a last moment of expectation before the soft veil of night descended.

A small crescent moon soon appeared, even while the birds fluffed out their feathers in a final arrangement, nestling down into their twig-nests, searching for a soft spot where the tiny sticks were cushioned by dried grasses, their eyes already half closed.

It was so peaceful.

Ariadne whispered to Jupiter: 'I love to be with you. I am so happy with you. Just doing little things around the house together is so much fun. Or playing together, sitting and feeling you next to me, your solid little body so much like your soul, your spirit shining through . . . or looking at you and seeing you looking back at me, your eyes shining. Do you know you have the cutest little teeth? And the prettiest, most adorable pink tongue I have ever seen? And you move with such grace. . . .'

Jupiter stretched and nuzzled his head in her lap. She sat with him, happy to think of nothing but running her hands through his soft warm fur.

Next morning, feeling renewed, Ariadne made the big mistake of looking through the mail and listening to the messages on her answering machine. The first message was, 'This is Stan from Station SXQ. We think you're a real hot lady, and we wonder if you'd do us the honour of being on our show, up here in Wyoming. We're going to have a bunch of guys on with you, just so you can hear what they think of the ladies around here. We thought it would be kinda nice to have it real personal, you know, like just folks, you can all talk to each other about what you like to do on dates, and so on. Now, we don't plan anything hostile! So just give us a call, at –'

'Oh!' she screamed. 'Why did I turn it on! I've got to escape all this! I need to get out of here!'

And putting her hands to her head, she cried out, 'Jupiter! Jupiter! Friedrich! Cleopatra! Cleopatra! Oh – someone – help!'

Sailing Aboard a Yacht
on an Emerald Green Sea

Quick as a flash, a strange sensation invaded Ariadne's limbs, a kind of peace, and with it a tremendous desire to close her eyes. 'Maybe I am still tired,' she thought vaguely. She began to imagine she was floating somewhere, with cool breezes blowing all around her, and the smell of the sea. But she couldn't open her heavy eyes to look. This lovely state lasted for some time, until . . .

She became aware of the sound of waves lapping against a boat and the smell of – could it be? – glazed doughnuts! Where *was* she?

A familiar voice commanded, 'Open your eyes, adorable nut!' Now, Ariadne *knew* that voice. She opened her eyes and saw Her Royal and Divine Highness Cleopatra standing in front of her with hands on her hips. 'Wake up!'

Ariadne opened her eyes wider. She was on Cleopatra's yacht! There was a brilliant sea, the sun was shining and a *huge* mountain of glazed doughnuts sat on the coffee-table in front of them. Yachting in The South of Heaven was going to be fantastic!

'Wow!' Ariadne came to life. 'What a great place!'

'I thought it would be fun to spend the afternoon on deck,' Cleopatra said. 'You could use a little colour.' Cleopatra sat down in an old-fashioned striped canvas deck chair, and put her legs (what great ankles!) up on the table. 'What on Earth has been happening to you now on that wild planet?' Cleo asked. 'With all your idealism! Tsk, tsk. Well, stay here for a while and relax. Have a doughnut.' She waved one tantalizingly under Ariadne's nose. 'Come on! What are you waiting for? Try it!'

Ariadne couldn't resist, and immediately sat up and took a

large bite out of the one Cleopatra was holding. She chewed contentedly, beaming at Cleo. She even listened happily as Cleo went on complaining: 'Wow, you are in such a mess down on Earth. I wasn't surprised when I heard you yelling for help!'

The sun glinted off Cleopatra's ripe-tomato-coloured toenail polish, which matched her orange-red sunhat and red Scotch plaid swimming suit. Her lovely brown legs, stretched out on the little white table contrasted appealingly with all the red.

Ariadne swallowed the last mouthful of her doughnut and felt her strength returning. She sat up and looked around, her turquoise silk skirt brilliant in the sun against the white deck, her long red-gold hair blowing lightly in the breeze. 'Wait. Where's Jupiter?'

Cleopatra looked up suddenly. 'Oh, zoot! You're right. I knew I forgot something. Not a strong enough spell. Just a minute.' She closed her eyes, murmured a mysterious incantation and – poof! presto! Jupiter appeared on deck! He shook himself like he did after a swim to get the water off, blinking his adorable big brown eyes.

'Where am I?' he said groggily. 'I was home asleep, minding my own business, napping, waiting to go for a walk.' Then he saw Ariadne. . . . Now he got the picture – a surprise vacation! He yelped with excitement, doing somersaults in the air to celebrate this sudden turn of events. Cleopatra and Ariadne laughed, delighted. 'This is the life!' they all agreed.

They began a game of charades. Jupiter impersonated Lassie; they guessed that very quickly when Jupiter waved goodbye with a terribly sentimental look on his face, gazing sadly into the distance. Then Cleopatra became Delilah – also not too hard to figure out, but exciting to watch. Finally, Ariadne was Greta Garbo in *Ninotchka*, drunk on champagne, giving a speech in the ladies room of a fancy night club about the benefits of socialism. So they whiled away the hours, eating all the doughnuts, and Jupiter finished off the remains of a watermelon Cleopatra had produced, having a good time hearing the sloshing sounds he made as he chewed.

When the sun set, they made dinner, corn on the cob and fried zucchini, and brought it up on deck, where they ate contentedly.

'Let's never go back!' Jupiter barked. 'This is Heaven!'

'You said a mouthful, Dog!' laughed Cleopatra.

'I wish we could stay here,' Ariadne mused, 'but what about my project on Earth? Maybe even I don't care. But Friedrich is back there.'

'Getting used to making love, huh, Ariadne?' Cleo teased. Ariadne blushed.

'You could say she doesn't mind it!' Jupiter interjected.

'But have you seen how Friedrich has been defending me on television?'

Cleo laughed. 'Yeah, I heard about that! What a he-man. He must be fun, Ariadne.'

Jupiter felt a little jealous, hearing all this praise for Friedrich. Seeing the moonlight shining on the water, he dived in for a quick swim. Ariadne took a big gulp of lemonade, while Cleopatra poured herself a drink from a tiny bottle with an Ancient Egyptian label on it.

'By the way,' Cleo said, 'Voltaire has been bugging me and everybody up here again, running around complaining that you stole his story.'

'What? Still?'

'He is constantly complaining that you got Candida, some friend of yours, mixed up with *Candide*, or something like that. Oh yes, and he's looking all over for a lawyer to sue you. Roy Cohn turned him down. At any rate, Voltaire sits in the Whist Club for hours, drinking hundreds of cups of coffee, eating a seemingly inexhaustible supply of chocolate bars, and talking about it. He even told Diderot (I couldn't help overhearing), "Well! If anybody, just anybody – and a woman, with no family name, nothing – can now use our philosophical tradition, well! The world is not what it used to be!" Diderot replied, "Anyway, what's wrong with women playing around with ideas? I thought you said that the only difference between women and men is that women are more amiable?" And then Diderot admitted that Madame de Staël had actually helped him with the *Dictionary*!

'Finally, it was Madame de Pompadour who set Voltaire straight. When she heard him saying that "some woman" had stolen his plot, she managed to mention, very politely, that Voltaire had really gotten his idea for *Candide* from her, when she was still Madame Poisson. After all, she had been an innocent in society and he had known her in those early days, before she joined the Court. They had talked about it a lot, how she saw everything when she was still a raw recruit.

'When Voltaire heard that, he went very quiet, reached into his pocket for another piece of chocolate, and sat down munching it distractedly. Madame de Pompadour lowered her voice and said to him, "Listen, so much chocolate isn't good for you, even Frederick told you so. By the way, is it true that he cut your chocolate ration, so you stole all his candles and sold them to buy more chocolate? Anyway, about this *Candide* plot, you and Ariadne ought to get together. You are both on the same side."'

Ariadne and Cleopatra roared with laughter. Jupiter, just returning from his swim, was glad to hear them on a new topic. They all shared a swig from Cleopatra's ancient black bottle. Then Cleopatra remembered another piece of news. 'Oh yes, Ariadne! I ran into your other best friend, Gertrude Stein, the other day. She was terribly worried I would be a bad influence on you. That you would follow my side of your nature and not hers, and go overboard sexually!' They laughed uproariously. 'She says you simply *must* change the kind of shoes you wear; in fact, she was even ready to lend you hers!'

Ariadne liked Gertrude despite everything, but she laughed until tears came.

The three of them were tipsy now from the 'drink me' concoction; they laughed at the slightest thing.

'The funniest thing was when she described your hair and what you ought to do with it. Get this, she says you should dye it *brown!*'

They were wiped out by the sun, the food, the drink, the laughter, and finally agreed to go downstairs and get settled for the night. Jupiter's paws sounded friendly as he bounced them two at a time on the narrow wooden steps. Cleopatra's bedroom and the guest sleeping quarters – smaller than those at home in her flying saucer, but interesting – were situated in the deepest part of the yacht.

Cleopatra's bed was a large, full moon covered with white satin. Overhead a green velvet canopy glimmered with pale golden stars. At the foot of the bed was a mauve taffeta coverlet. Jupiter hopped onto the bed, then Ariadne and Cleopatra made themselves comfortable too – thinking of watching TV together (maybe an old movie) as a bedtime story.

In bed with Cleopatra, Ariadne began chatting, while half-watching a Bolshoi Ballet performance of Prokofiev's *Romeo and Juliet* featuring their favourite dancer, Galina Ullanova. Ariadne's head rested drowsily on Cleopatra's shoulder, and Cleo played with her hair.

Lying on the warm bed, with its canopy and drapes, was like being inside a beautiful, multicoloured tent – or womb – with very soft colours and a warm light filtering through onto them. Ariadne absentmindedly mumbled on about whatever passed through her head. 'Do you think Stein's right? That if I dyed my hair brown and wore orthopaedic shoes, I'd be taken more seriously? My work would be recognized as "scientific"? I guess the more I look like a man, the more scientific I can be ... or, maybe that's not true – Kinsey's secretary told me he had the same trouble, that even despite the gall wasps, they claimed he wasn't scientific ... oh, what does it really take on Earth? I wonder....'

'What *are* you talking about?' Cleopatra asked.

'Oh, who knows? But if I dressed like that, people could just say that I only wrote about women's problems with men because of sour grapes – "she couldn't get a man".' Her voice drifted off, and her head rested even more heavily on Cleopatra's breast: those problems seemed so far away now, and here she felt safe ... in Cleopatra's arms, with Jupiter's warm furry body snuggled next to her, the boat gently rocking them like a cradle.

Ariadne was very happy, alive and full of love. She felt a warm glow rise in her own body and ignite all of her senses, as love radiated from the soul-bodies of her two beloved friends. Cleopatra's skin was radiant and warm; her breasts vibrated as she breathed in and out in a sort of triumphant paean to life: her body trembled ever so slightly as she lay there, full of wondrous scents, lights and shadows. A flood of happiness swept over Ariadne. Cleopatra's careless seductiveness was inspiring.

'Oh, Cleo, what am I going to do about Friedrich? I love him, I feel in Paradise when I'm with him – but can he accept me? Do you know,' she said, lowering her voice, 'the other day when we

148

had sex, I was so carried away I didn't know what I was doing! I pushed myself down over him again and again. Sometimes I come so many times when he touches my clitoris, I think I will explode! I have such extreme feelings! Do you ever feel things like that?'

The camaraderie of the day, coupled with the flickering candle-light, gave an intimate feeling to the room and put them all in the mood to reveal their personal thoughts to each other.

'Did I ever feel like that?' Cleopatra asked rhetorically, letting her hand glide slowly and sensuously over Ariadne's arm, then down over Ariadne's entire body. 'Yes, of course I've felt *all* those things – and more.' Cleopatra fell silent, and Ariadne began to experience a strange tension. 'Ariadne . . . Ariadne, when I feel you near me like this, I . . .' Cleopatra placed one hand gently on Ariadne's heart, and with the other, she held Ariadne's head and pulled it to her. Then, she kissed Ariadne on the lips. The kiss reached deep inside Ariadne.

Cleopatra tossed her head, breaking the spell. 'Ariadne! How can you wonder if I've ever felt so much passion! What an insult! Remember my telling you about Antony? Well, dear Antony, the last I heard, he was off on Sirius. He had that "I-must-conquer-the-Universe" look in his eyes when he left. I wish he were here, but that's the way it is. Anyway, who knows what he's doing? Playing around with some other Queen, no doubt. But I miss him, I really do. Part of the reason I have affairs is that I don't want to be angry with him when he gets back. I don't want to feel so deprived and vengeful. It's the worst, the hardest, when I'm going to sleep at night. . . .'

Her voice trailed off, and Ariadne, sensing her sadness, put her arms round Cleopatra, softly singing her to sleep with a lullaby about how True Love Never Dies.

In the morning they made a huge plate of pecan-blueberry pan-cakes and sat on deck to eat them in the sun. Cleopatra told them the stories her friend Gyula used to tell her about the bears on the street corners in Budapest who danced to music for coins. And how Gyula once risked his life during the war to steal the most valuable cigarette collection in all of Europe, so that he could have a smoke!

After many more stories and many glasses of lemonade,

Cleopatra stood up, brushed the crumbs off her lap, and announced, 'Oh, I almost forgot. I brought you some newspapers that should make you very happy.'

Ariadne looked doubtful.

'No, really! Don't worry!' Cleopatra reassured her.

'But, this is a beautiful day,' Ariadne protested. 'Do we have to see those?'

Jupiter moved closer to Ariadne, protectively.

Cleopatra sighed, exasperated with the two of them. 'Oh, for Heaven's sake! Here.' And she thrust the newspapers into their hands (and paws). 'Look! Your publisher has put a big ad in that powerful paper, with all kinds of famous people supporting you. *Look*!'

Ariadne Rite's New Report

'A study of major importance' – *Library Journal*

'The *Rite Report* on women and love is an authoritative and scholarly book that will prove extremely valuable as we re-evaluate our culture'
– Dr Max Siegal, Former President, American Psychological Association
– Dr Bonnie Strickland, Former President, APA, Department of Psychology, University of Massachusetts, Amherst

'A landmark redefinition of the female psyche by women'
– Dr Frank Sommers, Department of Psychiatry, University of Toronto

'The *Rite Report* trilogy will long be regarded as a landmark in the literature of human behaviour'
– Richard P. Halgin, Ph.D., Department of Psychology, University of Massachusetts, Amherst

'A classic. Read Rite's book for a brilliant new understanding of American society today – or read it simply for the supportive company of Rite and her 4,500 respondents – but read it'
– Barbara Ehrenreich, New York Institute for the Humanities

'Ms Rite adds [an] incredibly important new question: Now that the role of the house-wife is fading into history, will woman continue to play her emotional role? Will men take it up? Or will we do without it? . . .

In *The Second Sex* Simone de Beauvoir saw woman as a passive object of history, the Other. Ms Rite calls for the Other to become a seer, a namer, a sayer of how things should be. The world would be better off, she says, if men could love more like women. This is a bold and brilliant claim'

— *The New York Times Book Review*

'Even *The Times* in London is supporting you!' Cleopatra continued. 'Listen: under the heading "Is It Genius?" they say, "The internationally recognized cultural historian and researcher is reeling from the controversy that has surrounded her report, *The Meaning of It All*. The attacks on her methods have been launched almost entirely by men in order to conjure up a smoke screen to obscure the "real" issues raised by her book.'

'And the *British Bastion* even says right out that it thinks the *Power Press* article is biased! "Her enemies do not like what she has to say . . . nothing explains the sheer malevolence and brute aggression displayed against this book . . . . *The Meaning of It All*, Rite's report, is a milestone of a book, powerful and moving . . . . Rite has a vision of how life might be in a society where women were genuinely equal . . . . The attacks on her certainly smack of the backlash.'

Cleopatra looked up to find Ariadne and Jupiter doing handsprings and cartwheels – so elated and amazed were they! Ariadne picked Jupiter up, twirling him and dancing round the deck with him, kissing him over and over on his schnozzle – while he laughed and beamed radiantly.

Swimming With the Rhinemaidens

Crisped by the sun, Jupiter suggested that they all go swimming. Cleopatra preferred to take a sunbath, so Jupiter and Ariadne dived in together, and swam out to a rock, where they met with three fish – porpoises – whose names were Wellgunde, Flosshilde and Woglinde.

They were preparing for a performance of *Das Rheingold*

151

the next day. One of them was terrifically worried about her hair, or lack of it. 'Because, you know, Wagner wrote that the Rhinemaidens' hair was flowing down their backs. But he should have known, when you live in the water, you don't have lots of long hair on your head!'

'But Flosshilde,' Woglinde countered, 'as long as you can portray passion, that's all that matters. Quit worrying about your hair.'

'She has such nice hair,' Flosshilde enthused, swimming up close to Ariadne to inspect her hair more carefully.

Wellgunde, interested in higher things, seemed embarrassed by Flosshilde. 'I think Wagner was very noble to write about love and to give women such heroic parts – especially, Brunhilde in that other opera. She rides into a ring of fire on a white horse, for love!'

Woglinde interrupted. 'But that's so macho! We women don't have to die for love, do we? Isn't that like all the old stereotypes? How was Wagner so noble? I think women should be independent. I'm taking part in this performance only to show my artistic skill, not to glorify Wagner!'

'What's wrong with being crazy about love?' Flosshilde wanted to know. 'I think it's very sexy.' She dipped into the water, and continued when she resurfaced. 'You just don't like love, because you had that rotten experience with Wolfgang.'

'Well, what about you and Stefan? I remember you crying your eyes out.'

While Flosshilde and Woglinde continued to argue, Ariadne wondered whether she had any right to be so happy when so many women – including these porpoises, for Heaven's sake – were so unhappy. How can I be so fortunate? she thought to herself, to find what most women are not finding? And can I trust and allow myself to be happy? Should I surrender to my feelings? Or should I hold a part of myself back? Oh no, whatever happens, I will love him without reservation, without saving any part of myself. I will be true to him and to myself, always and forever.

A spray of water brought her back to reality – if reality meant playing with three talking porpoises, one talking dog and Cleopatra. She put her arm round Jupiter, they said goodbye to the three sisters, then raced to the yacht. Jupiter won, naturally. He could do everything faster – run faster, swim faster, leap faster, see things sooner (he had marvellous eyesight) and, oh yes, fly faster!

When they had dried one another off, Ariadne sat in a white deck-chair and started worrying that Friedrich would be wondering where she was. What would he think? They had grown so close, he was with her most of the time, and now? He must be wondering.

Ariadne's moody reverie was interrupted by the distant sound of Cleopatra's voice. 'You haven't heard a word I've been saying! Look, Ariadne, you'd better go back and get Friedrich. My oh my, what love will do . . . I'll see you when you get back!'

Ariadne began to object, but before she got even one sentence out of her mouth, she and Jupiter felt that drowsy spell of Cleopatra's coming over them again, the same sensation of droopy eyelids and torpor that had brought them here. Once again, they were transported together across the seas, over the islands and clouds, until they arrived safely back on Earth. They landed with a bump to find themselves behind some little bushes in the park, jolted abruptly out of their languor.

'Ouch! Oh, well, here we are.'

Return to Earth

Paradise Strained: An Argument With Friedrich

They headed straight for Friedrich's house, where he was watching
the soccer game on TV (yes, even concert pianists watch soccer
games), and getting drunk because he didn't know where Ariadne
was and he was upset. When Ariadne walked in, he didn't even
get up to greet her, he just scowled.

'Oh, darling! Don't be mad!' She rushed over and put her arms
round him. 'I've missed you so! I've been off with Jupiter at a
meeting about animal rights. It was in – uh – Vermont! Very
beautiful place. Do you like my tan?'

Apparently not. He wouldn't talk to her. Not even a small
welcome-home kiss. Ariadne had come full of hope, resolved to
tell Friedrich all the great love she felt for him, wanting to make
him happy.

'Aren't you glad to see me?' she tried again, her eyes downcast.
The silence was interminable. Finally Friedrich put his glass down
on the table and got up.

'Listen, I never get any rehearsal time anymore, there's always
something to do with you – go on some TV show or console
you about some newspaper mess. It's always something – and
always you first. And you never have time for me, you're always
working, writing late into the night, making speeches. You eat
dinner at your desk – '

Oh, a fine romance this was. While she was out on the road,
sometimes a week at a time, doing interviews about how women
and men needed to really talk to each other, to really listen to
each other – well, she was out on the road; she wasn't talking

or listening to Friedrich. And to make matters worse, when she did come home she was often too exhausted to be interested in him. So while she was out helping the rest of the world with their relationships, her own relationship was going down the tubes. Wonderful irony.

'Let's go to the café and talk this over.'

They walked all the way without speaking a word. They sat down at a table by the window and ordered. Still silence. The waiter brought their food. Just when Friedrich thought he had Ariadne's full attention and opened his mouth to speak, Swifty spotted them from the sidewalk and came bouncing in, hoping to convince Ariadne that she was crazy not to turn that limousine-driver incident into a best-selling book.

It was the last straw for Friedrich. He stood up, shoved his chair aside violently, threw something on the table (it landed in his glass of Coke) and announced, 'I'm leaving!'

Ariadne sat paralysed, watching him walk out of the busy café. The waiter came over, picked up Friedrich's drink and asked, 'Something wrong? This no good? I take away?' Ariadne nodded absentmindedly, yes, you can take it, focusing not on the glass, but on Friedrich disappearing down the street. Surely he would turn round and come back.

But he didn't. She tried to stay calm, she tried to swallow a little bit. Swifty said maybe she should write about her breakup. Ariadne paid the bill and went home as fast as possible.

As she walked into the apartment Friedrich said, 'Where is my ring?'

'What ring?'

'My ring. Give it to me.'

Ariadne was confused.

'My ring! I threw my ring in the Coke!'

'Oh no! Not the ring I gave you? The waiter threw it out! It must be in the garbage in the restaurant.'

Friedrich threw himself into a chair, holding his hands to his head.

Ariadne went to Friedrich and stood with her arms round him, her head next to his. He looked like he could cry. He reached up to put his arms round her, and she sat in his lap. They held each other for a long time.

'The most important thing,' Friedrich said in the voice she had fallen in love with, 'is to remember we love each other. Nothing else matters. I just missed you so much, that's all! Let's never be apart again!'

'Darling do you mean it? Oh, I love you too – so much.'

Paradise for Eternity

Despite Monumental Efforts, they never found the ring. 'Let's call the restaurant and ask them to look for it.' Ariadne dialled the number. Of course they remembered them being there and of course they would look for the ring, but no, they hadn't seen it. It was probably all mixed up with the mounds of food scraped off dirty plates, mashed potatoes and gravy, and heaven knows what else. No, they really didn't want them to come over and conduct their own search through the garbage bags . . . but if they insisted. . . .

But what did last from that evening was their vow to love each other and never be apart again.

It was now December, with a cozy expectation of snow outside and a warm feeling of closeness inside. On a long, especially beautiful weekend together – almost never going out, spending hours and hours rolled up together in a world of their own – Friedrich and Ariadne talked about getting married.

For months, Friedrich had repeated, 'Ariadne, I want to be with you, forever, forever my darling. I love you. Never leave me! I want us always to be together.' Tonight, when he said this, they suddenly looked at each other, the same question on both their lips: 'Does this mean we want to get married?' They had been standing together, no more than a foot apart (they often seemed to be doing a sort of perpetual dance, weaving in and out and around each other, so happy were they together – and this weaving involved quite a bit of physical contact) – and now they stood very still.

Ariadne was awakened early by Friedrich's tossing and turning.

She noticed he was awake, and staring intensely at the ceiling. But she was so sleepy, she drowsed off again, holding his hand. Later, she was vaguely aware that he had got up and was pacing around the bedroom, up and down the hall, then back around the room again. She had no idea what time it was.

Sometime later, she woke up with a start to find Friedrich lying directly on top of her, looking down into her face. As she opened her eyes, trying to get his face to come into focus, she heard him saying, 'Well? Do you still want to do it?' Sleepy as she was, Ariadne knew almost immediately what he meant. Her first impulse was to play coy, to say naïvely, 'Do what?' hoping to hear him say it again; she loved knowing what he wanted. But on second thought, she realized that if he was afraid to say the word – and he was – and she loved him, how could she make it more difficult? She resolved to say what she really meant, what she really felt. She caught herself and, still half asleep said, 'Yes! Of course!'

In a strangely uncharacteristic, businesslike way, Friedrich replied tersely, 'Good!' and got up again. Ariadne was deliriously happy and lay there dreaming. She assumed they would talk about it more during the day, or when the alarm went off and they really got up.

But the next thing she heard was Friedrich asking her, 'Have you ever had rubella?'

'What is rubella?'

'A form of measles.'

'I'm not sure. I mean, I had something when I was little, but I don't know if it was measles or chicken-pox. I think it was measles. Why?'

'Because they want to know if we have ever had it.'

'Who?'

'The marriage licence people.'

She sat bolt upright. 'Are you thinking of going there?'

'Well, yes, here we would have to wait two days. I don't want to wait two days.'

'You mean you want to get married *today*????!'

Friedrich looked crestfallen.

'That is the most exciting idea I have ever heard!' Ariadne beamed.

Friedrich's face shone as bright as a thousand light bulbs. 'I called Kate and she suggested Rhode Island. We could fly up there this afternoon. But that's where they demand the rubella tests. Connecticut and New Jersey, I found out, are worse. . . . '

Ariadne sat up on the edge of the bed, her favourite pink bathrobe sliding off one shoulder, petting Jupiter. Both of them smiled, watching Friedrich walk excitedly back and forth across the room; he stopped occasionally to kiss both of them.

Ariadne still couldn't get over it. 'You mean, all the time I've been sleeping here, you were in the other room calling these states to find out about their marriage licence requirements?'

'Yes.' He continued talking about the various requirements, debating which state they should go to – Pennsylvania, Connecticut, New Jersey, New York, Rhode Island. All Ariadne could think of was how wonderful this man was! 'Here he is, surely as sleepy as I am, but getting up, doing all this work, trying to organize a way for us to get married this very day!'

Then Friedrich had a brainstorm. Not only was Washington D.C. very close by air, but Virginia was right across the river. He phoned Virginia. There were absolutely no requirements! The decision was made! But was there time? Their marriage registration closed at 5 p.m. It was now noon. If they caught the two o'clock plane, they could be in Washington by three, at the marriage bureau by four, go to the local justice of the peace before it closed – and be married!

'Ariadne, get dressed! We have only forty-five minutes!' He kissed her.

'What should I wear!' But who cared? There was no time! She had to just grab the plain skirt and white blouse she had been wearing the day before, and GO! They raced out the door.

Everyone smiled at them as they came in. The people in the office seemed actually to be waiting for them. Up some pale-green-carpeted stairs, into the small, airy office of the attorney who would perform the ceremony. He was a friendly, calm man of about forty, who radiated a quiet pleasure in life. Perfect. Without a word of preparation, they repeated after him the most perfectly worded marriage ceremony they could have devised. No one was asked to 'obey' or anything remotely resembling that. Instead, the words described the beauty of love, how love between two people should last forever, how they should help each other in sickness and in health, 'till death us do part'. They were now husband and wife, wife and husband.

In bed together that evening in the small hotel, while Ariadne was sleeping, Friedrich leaned over her and gently kissed her. She woke up for a moment. 'Friedrich, my love,' she murmured, 'I love you with all my heart and soul. I adore you. I never want anyone but you — ever, ever. I will love you always.'

New Hassles and Objections

Soon, Friedrich's family began taking an interest in his personal life. They heard that he was growing more and more serious about Ariadne — they were reading about her in the papers — and they hit the roof, warning him of 'the mistakes young men make', telling him not to take love 'so seriously' and predicting that if he were rash, he could make 'a decision that you will regret for the rest of your life!'

Friedrich loved his family; he had never really quarrelled with them before. But now he was furious. They hadn't even met Ariadne, and they had already closed their minds. They mistrusted his judgement, and tried to control him. 'How unusual she must be,' his mother told Friedrich, with raised eyebrows — adding, 'How do you think I felt when my friends heard? I was just humiliated! And then,' she continued, 'a few weeks ago, you sent me to the store to buy her book. You said that would be a good way to get to know her. Well, it was full of filth. Full of sex! Do you think that was nice? To make fun of me? I was so upset!'

Meanwhile, in the true newsroom tradition of never letting a good story die, *Power Press* ran a new attack on Ariadne in its sister newsweekly, *The Truth of the Week*, a full-page story headlined 'A Bad Week for Ariadne Rite'. It was accompanied by a picture of Ariadne looking worried, dug up someplace to 'match' the article. The whole thing read like a Victorian thriller, full of old-fashioned myths of female psychological 'instability', and the like. And it ran next to a review of *Fatal Attraction*.

Friedrich's mother phoned again. 'I read the article! Friedrich, you are making a terrible mistake. This woman may ruin your life! You don't know a thing about her, really. Who is she? Where does she come from? You'd better watch out. She just wants to use you!'

'Oh yeah? Well, what opportunity will she get with me? It seems like she's a lot more famous than I am. Maybe it's me who looks like the opportunist! Mama, we're in love. Try to understand. It's like my life meant nothing until I met her. I want to be with her always. I want her to be my wife, I want to be her husband. For always, forever. I never knew happiness until I met her.'

'You think you are all grown up, my boy!' His mother was furious. 'But just you wait! You will see I am right. All these things in the paper cannot be conjured out of thin air. She has a History and a Past. What about your loyalty to me, to your background – all the training we have given you?'

'But give her a chance! You can't imagine from the papers how wonderful, how sweet and charming she is. She is exceptionally gifted and well educated and, Mama, she's polite. She's nothing like they say! She's shy, she's almost too sensitive. She lives for music and poetry, and her friends. And her companion is Jupiter, her dog – he's always with her. We will make a wonderful family. You can come and visit us anytime. Mama, I need her. Try to accept us.'

Thanks to the article, a new spate of reporters phoned Ariadne, leaving hundreds of weird, off-the-wall messages. 'This sounds like a bad novel entitled *My Terroristic Diary*,' Ariadne tried to laugh them off. But the final message was chilling: 'Ms Rite, I see you are listed to speak at the upcoming meeting of the American Culture Association. Are you *really* going to appear? Would you *really* try to make a speech? You can't be serious! We'll be there, if you do. . . .'

'All this controversy,' Ariadne cried out. 'It's not what I want my life to be about! This is somebody else's definition of my life! It's a nightmare! How do I get out of it?'

The phone rang again. It was Friedrich's mother – again. Now she was actually trying to persuade Friedrich to leave Ariadne. 'Come home!'

Friedrich exploded! 'Well, come to our wedding next week if you want to see me!' He slammed down the phone. Ariadne looked at Friedrich, confused but happy.

'Ariadne! Let's have a big church wedding and announce to everybody that we're married! Let's invite all our friends!'

Ariadne loved the idea. It would be a giant celebration, a great day!

'What's a wedding?' asked Jupiter, looking puzzled.

The press, ever vigilant, heard about the upcoming wedding. A woman from the Style section of the *Power Press* called, gaily announcing, 'Oh, dearest Ariadne, we have just decided to *do* your wedding! Isn't that marvellous – just too divine?'

Ariadne was flabbergasted. 'What do you mean, "do my wedding"?' After a pause, the woman replied archly, 'Well. If you don't want us to do it . . .' Her brittle voice implied that Ariadne should simply be grateful.

'That's right! I don't want the press invading my wedding!' Ariadne hung up before she could stop herself. It was a visceral decision, taken even before her brain could think it through – and never regretted.

The Defence Committee Strikes Back

'Good news!' Kate shouted out. 'I just got a call from a Nona Weisstein, one of the brilliant women who wrote the statement defending you. She says so many people are talking about the unfair press attack on you that their committee is growing like wildfire. She said, "It's like Ariadne is being made to pay for all of feminism! But she won't be alone from now on!" When I filled her in on what's happening, and told her you were getting threatening messages from two reporters, daring you to give your speech next week, she hung up, then called right back, saying that all the co-organizers had decided to hold a press conference the very day you speak, present their statement to the press and scholars right there at the conference. How about that?!' Kate danced around the room, clutching a surprised Jupiter in her arms. 'How about them bananas! That should stop the "reporters" – if that's what they call themselves – from harassing you and disrupting the panel!' How adorable Kate was!

'Oh,' Kate put Jupiter down (he was relieved!). 'She also wanted to know how you are doing financially, whether all this is causing any money hardships or financial disruptions? She said you could tell her, she'd be discreet about it. What a Woman!' Ariadne agreed. How splendid to know women like this on Earth.

Several hundred people were waiting at the American Culture Association to hear the panel discussion by Ariadne and three distinguished women. The press conference organized by the Defence Committee began first.

Grace Atkinson, representing the Committee, read a statement signed by many women:

'Terribly important issues that concern women's lives and health, in particular the emotional, psychological and physical abuse of women, are being obscured and trivialized by the media's assault on Ariadne Rite's book, *The Meaning of It All*. This is tragic at a time when the cases of Hedda Nussbaum and Charlotte Fedder, among others, are before us. There is a clear need to explore the hidden emotional dynamics between women and men. The attack on Rite's work is part of the current conservative backlash. These attacks are not so much directed against a single woman as they are directed against the rights of women everywhere.'

The two reporters who had called Ariadne were in the front row, shouting, heckling and jeering. 'Why are you defending her? You're all man-haters!'

'You weirdos! Those male-bashing statistics are too high! Maybe you're just not satisfied! My woman is! Our women are satisfied! You betcha!' The first man turned to his buddy with a macho leer.

Another committee member, the refined Babs Seaman, then took the podium, looking disdainfully at the "reporters". 'You in the press are carrying on the worst kind of methodological mystification to attack Rite. Rite has become the condensation point of what other women are saying and doing, and her reporting has hit a nerve – your nerves.'

Germaine Steinem added, 'The truth is, these matters are something women *did* want to write about and *do* want to talk about. The statistics, if anything, are too low.'

Ruby, a distinguished professor, observed wryly at this point, 'If Freud were reincarnated, I imagine you would criticize him! All your garbage about methodology is just meant to keep people from reading what she says!' The scholars in the audience applauded in solidarity and agreement.

C. Smyth-Rosenburg introduced Ariadne, along with Janice Wolfe and Betty Ehrenreich, and the panel began. Ariadne stood to give her speech, but the "reporters" shouted too loudly for her to be heard, and she remained silent, until someone forcibly escorted them out.

As she delivered her speech, she began to feel confident and strong, noting that most of the audience was truly interested in hearing and understanding what she had to say: 'For a very long time women have been defined by love, told their job is to take care of others, both emotionally and physically. Frau Loretz called loving "emotional housework". Now, however, women are questioning what "love" means, whether it means sacrifice and serving, caring, or passion – and whether men sacrifice for love too. Many women feel that love with men is not equal, they feel that they are giving more emotionally to keep the relationship going. Therefore, they question – with regret – whether they want to continue giving love such an important place in their lives, making love such a priority. Also, many describe experiencing what I call "emotional violence" in the name of love – both married women and single women. Encouraging this cultural revolution is the fact that the vast majority of women today work outside the home. Even though they earn one-third less money than most men, they are increasingly in a position to question or leave relationships which they feel are not right. The question is, will women today continue to believe in nurturing if they are not being nurtured by men in return?'

When her speech was over, there was a huge round of

163

applause. As Ariadne stepped down from the platform, a journalist approached her. 'My name is Laura Chillingham, I'd like to do an exposé of the reporting on you.'

Ariadne hesitated. How could she trust *any* reporter? 'I'd like that,' she said quietly.

Chillingham wasn't just another crank. A scholar herself, she had done her research. Her article cited the praise for Ariadne's work, then interviewed the two reporters, skinny Elvis Trouble and his twin at the *Storybook Times*, chubby Buddy Butterfield, about why they hadn't even mentioned any of this praise – in fact, claimed there was no praise, only condemnation.

'Why didn't you use any of the positive statements from the scholars who have supported Rite's work – even those on the book's cover?'

Buddy replied, 'Because none of them were in on the afternoon I called.' Trouble stalled, then admitted that the people he talked to had said mostly positive things, but 'that wasn't what I was interested in'. Trouble, "off the record", tried to convince Chillingham not to defend Ariadne since "he had heard" that Ariadne was going to 'have a mental breakdown!' So much for Objective Journalism!

Ariadne also learned that the Major Glam Celeb Interviewer, 'Liz', had printed the entire statement of defence in her column: wonderful woman!

All this was more than Ariadne had hoped for – and now, even though the attacks in the 'majors' continued, more strident than ever, and very few people saw the two (relatively small) articles in her defence, she was happy. She was in love, she had Jupiter and she had *friends*.

How could she worry about anything? Except, of course, the wedding. . . .

Jupiter Attends a Wedding

The night before the wedding, Ariadne chatted to Jupiter as she got her clothes ready. 'Tomorrow is the day! Jupiter, should I wear this veil? Should I put my hair up or down? How about these shoes? Oh, I want the day to be beautiful! But I'm still worried about meeting Friedrich's mother. . . .'

Jupiter wasn't thrilled about the prospect of meeting Friedrich's mother either. 'But I can't wait to go to the church in that wooden carriage drawn by two white horses!' he said eagerly, his ears at attention.

In the morning Ariadne, Friedrich and Jupiter stepped into the elegant carriage that Friedrich had chosen. He knew the names of the beautiful white horses and said good morning to them. Ariadne was dressed in ivory with a lovely long veil flowing over her hair, down her back, and trailing on the ground. She looked beautiful.

They arrived at the church to find all their friends, lots of women from the Defence Committee, Kate and her friends, the grocer, the 'owners' of Jupiter's friends on the block, the dancers from the ballet, Robert, and many more. But Ariadne was stunned to see near the door a group dressed entirely in black. Who were they? Protesters? Reporters in disguise? One had a long black feather sticking straight up out of her black hat. Then Ariadne realized. . . . It was Friedrich's mother! The whole group in black was Friedrich's family!

His mother stood silently in the corner, surrounded by all the other black-clothed members of the clan. Ariande thought of the raven in Edgar Allan Poe, who chanted 'Nevermore, nevermore!' She shivered, but vowed to herself, No matter what, nothing can bring a curse down on my wedding! This is something that not even the *Power Press* can do!

With that, the Wedding March began. Ariadne and Friedrich stood arm in arm, smiling at each other. Together, they walked down the aisle. Jupiter smiled as he trotted along happily behind them, bearing the ring in a little satchel round his neck. This is a totally new experience, he thought, his brown eyes sparkling, as he wondered what would happen next.

All he knew was that soon, everyone was smiling. Ariadne and Friedrich exchanged emotional words, asked him for the ring, kissed, and wonderful music began to play. They turned round and headed back down the aisle. Ariadne threw her bouquet to her friends as she went. At the end of the aisle, they were sur-rounded by congratulating friends, all happy for them.

165

But there was a Commotion. They all looked round. Friedrich's mother marched towards them. 'No, no, it just won't do! You're not really married! You're not Right for Each Other! I don't accept this!' She waved her black umbrella, and behind her stalked the others, all in black, all looking wrathful. . . .

The three of them, Aridane, Jupiter and Friedrich, grabbed each other and started to run. They headed for the door. . . .

Heavenly Ascension for Three:
Friedrich, Ariadne and Jupiter Fly to Heaven

★

Coming out into the bright sunlight with blue skies overhead, Ariadne had only one thing in mind: Heaven. As her lovely creamy tulle veil and satin skirts danced and billowed in the breeze, she could only think how much fun it would be to fly! The black-hatted ones were coming closer and closer. . . .

She turned to Friedrich. 'Darling, now that we are married, really married, there's something I want to tell you. . . .' But there was no time to finish.

'Ariadne! *Not now!*' Jupiter bounced up and down, yelping with growing urgency. 'Let's take off, hurry up! Friedrich will like it too!'

'I didn't know Jupiter could talk. Did you just say something?' Friedrich looked at Jupiter peculiarly.

Ariadne's face lit up. 'Right! Jupiter, let's go!' Jupiter always had the best ideas.

Standing on the church's steps, Ariadne held on to Friedrich and Jupiter, one with each hand, and suddenly they began ascending, floating up into the sky, Ariadne's beautiful dress and veil flowing out all around them against the glorious blue of the Heavens.

Friedrich was stunned to find himself flying. 'Don't be afraid! Don't worry! You'll love it!' Ariadne reassured him. Rising farther, they saw the people in the street below pointing up at them, wondering whether to believe their eyes. At first, Friedrich felt nervous about their weightlessness, but soon, his wild nature took over and he started playing.

'Flying!' he shouted, 'Look at me, I'm flying!' And he began singing, 'Volare, *Vo-la-re!*' – the same song he had sung to Ariadne on the night they first met, the night they went to the

Plastique Bertrand. To accompany his singing, he struck various flamboyant poses in the air, experimenting with different movements like swimming, then dancing. . . . Ariadne and Jupiter began trying to explain it all to Friedrich, but he was no longer interested in explanations. 'Why bother? Who cares?!' They all laughed: he was right!

'Isn't there a scene like this in a movie by Jean Cocteau? But it sure didn't have a dog in it!' Friedrich wondered.

'Well, it would have been better if it did!' Jupiter shot back.

Ariadne began to wonder if she could keep peace between Friedrich and Jupiter for the duration of the trip, but they settled down to a little nap, and in no time, Heaven was in sight.

At last, all three together!

Landing slightly away from the Centre of Things, Ariadne hoped to have a moment now to explain everything to Friedrich. She was so excited, she tried to tell him everything about Heaven all at once: 'You see, it all started one day a long time ago when I was playing baseball with Jupiter, and . . . well, later, Cleopatra became my best friend, and then I met you and . . . . Oh, how do I start?'

As it happened, there were big posters everywhere announcing that tonight was a special night – the occasion of the annual Celestial Cocktail Ball. 'The Biggest Bash in Heaven! Everybody will be there, just everybody!' Ariadne chattered on nervously. 'I can introduce you all around! I hear this year's charity is new jerseys for the baseball team.'

To Friedrich, this sounded very strange! (Baseball in Heaven? Did they serve hot dogs and beer too?!) But it sounded good, and he liked parties. Most of all, he liked Ariadne.

Jupiter announced he had special plans for the evening, and said mysteriously, 'I have to meet Fala to arrange things, so see you later!' And he was off!

Ariadne couldn't wait to introduce Cleopatra to Friedrich – and to fill Cleopatra in on everything that had been going on – so they headed right over to her place. At the door, Friedrich turned to Ariadne, 'Why does her house look like a spaceship? Isn't she Egyptian?'

Before Ariadne could answer, George Orwell opened the door. 'George!' Ariadne was surprised.

'Hi, Ariadne! Come in. Cleopatra is getting dressed for the Heaven Ball.'

'George, I want to you meet Friedrich!'

'Oh – you're the one Cleopatra calls "The Chest". Well, well, come in! Come in!' Grinning, George offered Friedrich a drink that looked like molten volcano lava.

Friedrich settled in right away, and he and George launched into A Big Discussion about politics and history. When George learned that Friedrich knew classical Greek and Latin, he commented, 'Well, you've come to the right place. This is about the only place you'll be able to use those things! Tonight there'll be a lot of those old codgers there to see Cleopatra's floor show, though they'd never admit it. They have a club here – can you believe it, called the Whist Club? I never joined – well, they never invited me. Of course, anyone can go there, it's just that if you're a member, you can go there any evening, no tie, in just your socks.'

Ariadne wandered down the long chamber of secret rooms with their pale brocades and burnished golden antiques, looking for Cleopatra. After a while, she heard happy splashing sounds, and felt warm, humid air scented with perfume enveloping her. Cleopatra was in her salon-bath. Nearing the room she heard Cleopatra singing along with a new Madonna CD, 'Down There'. Ariadne called out, 'Cleopatra! Hello! Can I come in? It's me, Ariadne!'

'Ariadne! I thought you'd miss the Ball tonight!'

Ariadne peeked round the door. Cleopatra was submerged in the lime marble pool, her black hair floating out around her on the water like a lotus pad. By her side was a large lemonade topped with a bright red cherry – and also, Cleopatra's personally engraved golden-plated Tampax case with the royal seal. Jennifer, curled up nearby, snoozed contentedly. Ariadne couldn't stop staring. 'What style!'

'Come and sit down over here.' Cleopatra smiled in her direction. 'Say, my pet, what is that you're wearing? Fab Dress! But – why the veil?'

'Cleopatra . . . Can't you tell?'

'You got married!'

'Yes! And Friedrich's here! He's with George now. Oh, Cleopatra, we're married!'

'So . . . tonight will be quite a celebration!' Cleopatra blew Ariadne a kiss from the bath, sending foam in her direction. 'But – I insist – get out of that Sweet But Totally Unsexy Dress. Virginity is OK up to a point, but basically boring. How about a black lace bodysuit? And big hanging diamond earrings to match?'

'That would suit me perfectly!' Ariadne began stripping off her clothes. 'But what's up with you and George? He's answering your door. Does he live here now? Are you in love?'

'What can I say? He's an adorable man. I love him.'

Finding Cleopatra's tone somewhat less than convincing, Ariadne probed deeper, 'Do you still miss Antony, Cleopatra?'

'Well . . .' Cleopatra snapped, 'I found out he's got himself reincarnated as some politician in the United States. And he's married. Oh, Ariadne, it's really getting to me. . . .' She stifled a sob.

'Oh, Cleo, don't cry! I can't bear to see you cry. He'll be back. No woman in history could be as beautiful as you. I'm sure he misses you.'

Cleopatra put a brave front on it. 'You're right. It's only a matter of time until I see him again. We aren't parted forever. Meanwhile, I love being with George, really I do. Anyway,' she looked at Ariadne and smiled determinedly, 'I can't cry! I'm giving a performance tonight!' She took a deep breath, stood up, and let the water run off her statuesque bronze body in rivulets – happy little rivulets, proud to adorn such a strong and noble form.

She was so regal! Ariadne felt the same sense of awe that she had on the first day she met Cleopatra, the day they had exchanged make-up.

Cleopatra stepped out of the tub, and reached towards the golden Tampax tube. Ariadne jumped and spun round the other way – was Cleopatra going to insert it? Ariadne might be bold, but not *that* bold! She didn't look.

'Shy?' Cleopatra chided Ariadne affectionately, noticing her about-face, then continued. (What is she doing while she is talking? Ariadne wondered. . . .) 'By the way, my sweet, I was thinking about you the other day when I was looking at the red thread –

you know, the beautiful blood-red string that hangs down from the Tampax when it's inside you? Such a superb colour, crimson with blood like that.... And it reminded me, Ariadne, of *your* red thread, of the answers that are inside you ....'

'Why?' Ariadne was puzzled, but intrigued (who wouldn't be?!), her back still turned.

'You know about the other Ariadne, don't you?' Cleopatra continued. 'She was trying to find her way out of a labyrinth too, by unravelling a red thread (was it red?) which she had brought along with her. Just like you – you believe feminist philosophical theory holds an answer for the world's problems – it's just necessary to unravel the arguments logically, and debate the options, from the new perspectives you and others are developing. Ah, Ariadne, this will keep you very busy! Wouldn't you rather be out vacationing with me on the yacht? Anyway, if you insist, you can try....

'Your goal, your red thread, is to unravel the mysteries of the universe and human nature, twenty-first-century style – *and* work out the best political system to fit human nature. What an agenda! But don't forget to take your vacations – and your vitamins!'

Ariadne blushed with pleasure at Cleopatra's compliments. And – like shy people everywhere – she rushed to hide her pleasure, and change the subject.

'Let me fix your hair, okay?' Ariadne said tenderly. Cleopatra sat down at the little dressing-table with the pale yellow and mauve silk tapestry skirt, and looked in the mirror. Ariadne kissed the top of Cleo's head, before starting to comb her lovely black hair with the ornate eighteenth-century engraved silver comb.

Back in the living-room, Friedrich, feeling no pain, had got over his initial shock with the help of several well-mixed volcanic cocktails, and was now playing lounge-lizard with George in front of the plastic zebra-skin bar. They were finding their own 'in' jokes about nineteenth-century politics Terribly Amusing.

Cleopatra and Ariadne arrived, ready for the Big Event. Friedrich was stunned to encounter Cleopatra. He bowed to her, then kissed her hand (encased in an iridescent lavender glove) in the extravagant way that only classically trained Earth Europeans know how to do.

Friedrich had decided he quite liked Heaven. He liked it even more when he saw Aridane's black lace body, fishnet stockings and Remarkably Politically Incorrect High Heels, with laces going up all around the ankles. She was smiling at him, her red golden hair cascading down around her shoulders. This Visual inspired him to drag her over to the lime-green chaise, fondling her . . . .

'Come on! Later with that! Let's go!' Cleopatra and George laughed from the doorway.

Arriving at the Heavenly Ball

They arrived at the top of the stairs of the Grand Ballroom. Looking below, they saw a fabulous hall filled with hundreds of people milling about in all kinds of outfits – some in tails, some dressed as sultans, some as animals; others had on masks and wigs. Every kind of imaginative costume was there, from twenty-first-century hip to classical Cretan.

The room was a rococo vision, a set done by Heaven's Blockbuster Entertainment (all the old MGM team were on the committee). There were pink Venetian glass sconces lining the walls, filled with glowing candles, and chandeliers of pink and gold. The walls were painted the blue of the afternoon sky, with fluffy white clouds gracefully floating across them – the symbols of Heaven. As the evening continued, the walls gradually changed until they assumed the colour of the evening sky, and then deepened into the blue-violet velvet of night. Little gold stars on the walls and ceiling blinked on and off, giving the whole room the fantastic appearance of a rococo spaceship ready for take-off.

As the four of them began to descend the stairs, they heard a set of chimes ring, like those heard at the end of intermission on the Texaco Metropolitan Opera Saturday Afternoon broadcasts. Cleopatra picked up her skirt and rushed off. 'Oh! I'm late! My floor show is the Opening Event! Such an honour and I'm about to miss it!' *Sans* Cleo, the three of them followed the rest of the crowd out onto the terrace where The Queen of the Nile's Glorious Event was to take place.

Most of the guests were already seated in anticipation under the yellow-and-white-striped umbrellas that shaded tables out on the balcony. Drinks were being served in small golden 'Queen of the Nile' glasses, complete with straws bearing the royal seal – the asp in gold. Cleopatra hoped her logo would bring attention to the important place animals had in her imperial court – the place they should still have. Inspired by Jupiter and Fala, this was her contribution to ecology.

A Fashion Show of Cleopatra's Sunfrocks

Seventeen miniature Cleopatras, all in short yellow resort frocks (just perfect for tennis, or for frolicking on the beach), paraded around, smiling and carrying big striped beach balls in Cleopatra's signature colours – luminescent lime-green, sun-yellow and pulse-pink. They were accompanied by the music of 1930s American cartoons. Each represented one of the stars in the Heavens. As they moved round the galaxy, and each little sunbeam came to the centre of the stage, she moved to the footlights and recited a tiny two-line poem about her last vacation there. Then the music changed to Fred Astaire singing 'Night and Day' by Cole Porter, and they all broke into soft-shoe tap-dancing.

Cleopatra herself appeared at the top of the stage, hovering over the seventeen sunbeams. Dressed in gold, she represented 'the golden sun of evening'. (Busby Berkeley had nothing on Cleopatra!) The crowd went wild as Cleopatra made her royal descent through the air, and the golden-umber curtain came down. All the little sunbeams came out for a bow, and the cartoon music resumed.

Amidst the applause, Ariadne, Friedrich and George raced to find Cleopatra backstage and congratulate her on her success. She was in a state of elation with all the little sunbeams dancing round her – and her old friend, Elizabeth Arden, by her side (wearing Red Door Red). Cleopatra proposed a toast to 'Women Friends Forever' – the old Egyptian toast – and gave a special salute to Ariadne.

Then they all went to mix with the guests in the ballroom.

In the fantastical room, the party atmosphere was heating up. People and animals were talking excitedly, the music – a combination of Strauss waltzes and Latin disco – was taking off and lava cocktails were flowing everywhere.

On the programme was a brief history of the Heaven Ball:

History of the Heaven Ball

The Heaven Ball has a long and glorious tradition. It was founded by Aurora de Chaumont and her fabulously charming brother, Lapin II, in the forefront of Heaven Society for many years.

It was originally a type of Venetian Ball at which people wore masks covering their entire heads, often animal masks. In fact, the choreography of the opening Ball scene of the 1942 Bolshoi Ballet production of *Romeo and Juliet* was influenced by a Heaven Ball held some years earlier. And most of the animal sequences in *Sleeping Beauty*, too, were inspired by previous Heaven Balls. So one can see that the Balls go back quite a way and were very influential.

Aurora and Lapin originally gave each of the Balls a special theme: The *Bal de la Mer*, the *Bal des Rois et des Reines*, and similar fêtes of froth and glitter were attended by one and all. Bores found no welcome – although even they became unboring under the magical spell of the beautiful evenings. Valentine Dumas, Aurora's best friend, once attended dressed as a carnival merry-go-round: fastened to her voluminous skirts were cutouts of a horse, a cow, a sleigh and so on, and she had also attached a mechanized music box which told fortunes.

Sometimes the Balls opened the social season, and sometimes they closed them, but almost always, they came complete with fireworks which ended the evening's festivities.

Eventually, some years back – no one knows exactly how many; this has been lost in the mists of time – the Ball became a permanent annual Event, and now every year in Heaven it becomes bigger and more popular. It seems safe to predict that this is an institution that is here to stay.

174

Ariadne and Friedrich joined the swirling disco crowd pounding the floor of the rococo room. Hundreds of creatures in exotic outfits milled around drinking champagne, lava cocktails, and eating Frito-Lays.

Eavesdropping on various party conversations, they learned that the topic of the day among former Earthites seemed to be politics.

Two Democrats Discuss Why Democracy is Such a Mess (and How They Long for a Great Big Dictator)

Two Congressmen recently arrived from the States, both Democrats, were talking over the Situation At Home.

'Like that stewardess said on the way here, if we can't even make one perfect ice-cube anymore in the US – the country that *invented* the refrigerator – well, where are we???' In rumpled blue suit, this Democrat looked disgusted and morally outraged.

'Yes, democracy is so damned inefficient,' the other Democrat (in rumpled brown), fretted. 'When you think of all the time and energy thousands of people put in to get a candidate elected... And then, his hands are tied anyway once he gets there ... you wonder if the system works at all. It would be worse if he never got there at all, you tell yourself – but would it?'

The Democrat-in-Blue looked nervously around him, 'Well, this is something I would never have said at home, so don't spread it around – but I would give anything to see everything great again – even if that meant less democracy!' He looked relieved to have got this out, but anxious lest he be called Politically Correct.

His companion shocked him by going even further. 'Yes, democracy is *the most* Frustrating, Inefficient System! It's painful! I'm sure the most efficient, rational system is Benevolent Dictatorship!' He rushed to qualify his remark, lest anyone think him a Royalist. 'Of course, not an inherited dictatorship!'

175

Amazed to have found a fellow-traveller, the Democrat-in-Blue opened his heart, declaring expansively, 'I long for the nineteenth-century, don't you? What a civilized time it must have been! I mean, your shirts really came back white in those days!' He smiled with brotherly love at the thought, then stopped dead in his tracks. 'On the other hand, what if I were reborn as a servant?' He blanched. 'Or,' – oh horror! – 'a woman?!!'

Ariadne couldn't resist listening in on this one!

'Yes,' his friend picked up the theme, 'Oswald Spengler may have been right about The Decline of the West. The US could be in its last days of Empire and Decline, like the Roman Empire.' He struck a heroic expression.

Ariadne burst in, 'Not necessarily! There is a lot of talent around! For example, feminist women! They might bring about a Renewal of the Nation's Spirit, if they had a chance.... By following the basic ideals of democracy they could make the system really work, but in a quite new way....'

The Democrat-in-Brown was intrigued. Deciding (contrary to first impression) Ariadne wouldn't bite, he asked, 'Are you saying that Western democracy has become too much of a closed shop, a class, race and gender system – that's why it's declining, not because democracy doesn't work? *That what's needed is more democracy, not less?*'

The rumpled Blue looked thoughtful. 'Yes . . . maybe our Lost Idealism is the problem.... Our sense of direction as a nation was eroded and cynicism set in when President Kennedy, Martin Luther King, and Robert Kennedy, all three were shot. Was it a *coup d'état*? How could it happen in America? We didn't know what to believe.

'It got worse when Nixon was pardoned – no Afro-American or blue-collar worker would have been! "It's all in who you know, the class system is in America too", was the message. Thus were produced a whole generation of selfish Airhead Yuppies and Yuppettes.'

Just then, Jupiter and Fala came running up: Jupiter in an adorable yellow party-hat and Fala in a jaunty checkered racing outfit. They had been trying on things backstage in Cleopatra's costume closet. Chattering animatedly about their plans, Jupiter confided in Aridane that later that evening, he and the other animals would present a divine floor show. . . .

Seeing these two dogs talking, the ex-Democrats gulped down the rest of their Scotches. They saw they still had a lot to learn here in Heaven!

They were further astounded when Fala began to inform them, 'FDR told me recently that he is terribly worried that the American Dream has gone off track. Otherwise, Americans would change their attitude to the animals, and environmental problems could be solved. (Yes, yes, I *know* he said that thing about "a chicken in every pot", but that was a long time ago. . . . And he's sorry, he's apologized to the chicken's rights lobby, OK?)'

Fala continued relating what he had heard at home, and taking on the FDR radio-chat drawl, 'How many Americans still believe the American Dream is for dignity and freedom for all, an Equal Chance? Too many now think it is just the right of every American to Have Things, make all the money they can, no matter who they hurt. Jefferson warned that once the frontier had been used up – so that the endlessly expanding promise of prosperity came to an end – this would mean an identity crisis for the country. This crisis was avoided after the end of the frontier, when America and the West bought time by extending the frontier into the ground, under the ground, and. into the "third world" – taking out minerals and oil and creating more "prosperity". But this borrowed time is up – now what?'

Friedrich, heretofore more interested in the lava bubbles than in Congressmen's banalities, speculated, 'Could the US, fearing it is no longer the Number One Nation, in control of the rest of the world, try to start a war – like Germany did after World War I, when it felt it was no longer "the greatest"? There does seem to be a spiritual malaise there. . . . The only large-scale reaction yet to this spiritual void is fundamentalist religion: now, through religion, some Americans demand to be special, God's chosen – no matter what!'

'Yes, democracy seems to be very fragile,' Ariadne knew what she was talking about. . . .

'Just look at Germany,' Friedrich went on. 'No country was more open and democratic than Germany in the 1930s. There was great freedom of speech, a strong, diverse culture and art.

Then all of a sudden, the country turned round and did the most barbaric, heinous things.'

'Civil rights, the labour movement, the women's movement – what did they really achieve?' Democrat-in-Blue asserted cynically. 'The sixties may have changed some people's thinking, but overall, what did they really achieve? Fun and euphoria, but few concrete gains.'

'You're too pessimistic! Some things did change. I remember during the civil rights period, when Faulkner said force can't change hearts; it turned out he was wrong. Forced integration did work. And the government's action was a response to people protesting.' Democrat-in-Brown's enthusiasm was building. 'Look, we stopped the war in Vietnam in the sixties. Of course the military defeats were a factor, but the government might have just gone on to bomb those people into oblivion, back into the Stone Age, if public protest hadn't stopped it. We the people *can* make a difference.'

'Yes, but it never lasts.' His colleague's cynicism was implacable. 'People always get tired, and have to go back to work. *And* – you can't count on idealism to get re-elected. Not term after term!'

It was clear that neither Democrat would ever become Enlightened, so Jupiter asked Ariadne to dance: smart Jupiter!

Aimable and his Combo (of 'Aimable and His Café Orchestra') were just then playing some of Ariadne's and Jupiter's favourite 1930s tangos on their accordions, smiling ever so amiably.

Cheek to cheek, Jupiter and Ariadne performed the most complicated steps, oblivious to all else. Democrats, Friedrich and Fala, all applauded and tapped their toes in time to the music.

A tall white cat gracefully approached with a tray of fresh lava cocktails – some in peach, some in banana – so foamy, frothy and bubbly that everyone stopped and raced to get one, afraid to miss their chance! As the tray moved on, a group of men in Seriously Elegant Business Suits (Savile Row) followed, determined to get their own goblets of lava before they disappeared. Meanwhile, the conversation continued. . . .

'Why is the dollar falling?'

'Someone wants it lower, obviously.'

'Who?'
'I hear the Russians are dumping gold on the market. . . .'

Men in Suits Discuss the Investment Possibilities of the Coming Battle of Media Titans for Mind Control of the World

'What are they talking about?' Ariadne, ever curious, listened in. A group of Ex-Businessmen were debating the Business-future of the World. They planned to keep on playing the market from Heaven, keep their fingers in the pie.

'Listen, you want a hot tip?' Friedrich burst in on their conversation with mock intensity, 'I suggest you try the technology and engineering of dikes – because when the ice caps start melting, all the world's major cities will be flooded!'

The Savile Row suits all turned to look at Friedrich. Was he for real? Seeing his nice square shoulders and his impeccable Earthmade tails, they decided he must be One of Them – despite his weird sense of humour. (Ariadne was probably 'the wife', they decided, since she was listening dutifully, saying nothing.)

'Oh, that ozone-hole thing,' sighed one Business-Man. 'That's too slow. We want Big Deals now. Currently, we're placing bets on which media magnates will win in the Sweepstakes for Control over the World. . . .'

'That's *your* game, Aristotle,' a Business-Player in grey remarked. 'Mine is War. My latest hit was providing governments with Do-It-Yourself War Kits – "Everything you could ever need to start a war". Went over big. A shame they don't have a War Index Page in the financial papers, it would help tremendously. War is a Sure Bet Business – maybe not as exciting as yours, but there's Security in it.' He smiled contentedly.

'But, Giscard, it won't be sure for long. Investments are changing for the twenty-first century. Nations won't even need wars anymore, they're *passé*, it's only economic warfare that's in now. Odd areas may still have real fighting (like the former Yugoslavia, Afghanistan or Iraq), so we can still sell them weapons, of course, but media technology has made True World Domination possible for the first time! Oh, it's so exciting!' He became rapturous,

'Just think, Giscard, now we can have One World Culture, one dominant cultural hegemony, by Ideological Brainwashing through international, global television. . . . So forget making weapons!'

'Absolutely correct,' another of the Savile Suits enthused. 'Soon we'll be the greatest society yet! Of course, wealth will dominate. But so what? Just because the peasants were downtrodden didn't make late nineteenth-century Russian culture any less great; the Enlightenment wasn't less great because so many people were poor in eighteenth-century France. And we, the owners of the New World Media State, will subtly and carefully manage the world – and the world will be a better place for it!'

'Maybe I'll try your investment strategy in a few years, but for the moment it strikes me as premature.' Sergei stood firm. 'I'll stick with the good old Arab fight, because they have all that money from oil. The Africans don't have any money, so there's no point if they fight. . . .'

'But wait!' Ariadne asked. 'Isn't it important for Business Stability that there be some kind of a just, stable democratic order? That the environment be protected so that life can continue?'

'How naïve!' They all gave 'the wife' simultaneously withering looks.

'Aren't you afraid,' the wife continued, 'that if the under-privileged nations and people are kept waiting too long to participate equally in your wealth, they will become very angry and have a revolution against you?'

'We're talking about how to make money – not some moony, blue-eyed idealism. . . .'

'But lack of idealism *will* cause the West to collapse. If it can't face its problems . . . if it can't find a creative way to have equality, democracy and justice, decline is inevitable. A more open system would lead to stability – even a stable business climate!' Ariadne laughed at her own joke, even though it went right past them.

'My dear young woman, people aren't so rational. You're still part of that old Enlightenment crowd. "Politically correct", in up-to-date terminology. Get with it: liberalism is out. There can't be equality – we saw that in Russia; democracy, Jeffersonian demo-cracy, was a Utopian Notion which sent turmoil around the world. It kept causing revolutions, revolutions that never improved any-thing, by the way. . . .'

'But you can't put the lid back on all of people's hopes now. . . .'

'No, but we'll give them Consumer Goods, and that will quiet them. And pleasant stories on TV. It will be generations, if ever, before they realize they are soul-starved. . . .'

'Are you sure? Look at the fundamentalist religious resurgence everywhere from Moscow to Poland to Iran to the US and France. Don't you think this is an attempt to find some values? Not that I agree with these values. . .'

'You young people are always Idealists. . . . I used to be too. Now my son – too radical for his own good, but that's another story – talked a lot about El Salvador. He said that the media only reported what the Republican administration wanted: I do feel a little ambivalent about helping to finance some of my businesses, under these circumstances. . . . But anyway, with the Death of Communism, the West and its media have been vindicated. It's probably the Best of All Free Presses there could ever be, so why should I worry? Yes, why should I worry!'

'I wonder . . .' Ariadne and Friedrich were holding hands. 'Somehow I think that idealism and equality are important. . . .'

The third Super Tycoon changed the subject abruptly, turning to Friedrich in an attempt, no doubt, to be 'fatherly' and get this lad back on a more solid track. He announced, 'I am in Gold. As a Swiss banker (we Swiss always understand global politics, that's how we play the market so well), I may be able to explain. She,' he gestured disdainfully towards Ariadne, 'may be right that a moral idea like freedom has the potential to lead the world. But now that communism has shown that it only produces dictators, US joy-in-consumerism and colourful hyper-commercialism – run by fast-track types like me – have become the symbols of what people around the world really want!

'Idealism made them poor. It was no fun. They want the new Bravura Commercialism – it's fun!'

At this point, Jupiter whispered to Ariadne that he and Fala were decidedly not having any fun, and felt they must be trotting off. 'Besides,' Jupiter added, 'Rughetta is waiting for us to help us put the finishing touches on the floor show. Ciao, ciao, bambina!'

'I can't wait to see it, Jupiter!'

Friedrich was answering Super-Business: 'But what if Ariadne is right? What if Eastern Europe – or even the West itself – comes up with a new philosophy? Not materialism, not communism, but a New Spiritual Imperative? One in which money could be made, but which considered the mind and the soul more important?'

'You're talking pie in the sky, my son,' the Swiss gold man looked worried about Friedrich's future. 'Get practical!'

Queen Elizabeth I suddenly appeared, looking very much like Bette Davis: 'Why not our European Community as the New World Number One? As Madame Thatcher says, it will have a population of 350 million. Think of it, 350 million! (Why couldn't I get them to produce like that when I was around?) With that, we can steamroll the USA and all those other upstart trading blocs!'

'With no disrespect,' Friedrich bowed to Her Majesty, 'While it used to be that the great nations were Great Britain, France the US and Japan, now I fear, the new nations are really IBM, US Steel, Boeing and all the other multi-nationals.'

Ah! How sweet it is! Friedrich's statement made the Savile Suits deliriously happy, and they began whispering new secret insider mega-trades to one another, calling Earth on their portable telephone headsets.

After a few blissful uninterrupted minutes of this, they became happier and happier with their plans . . . so happy, in fact, that they sprang onto the stage and burst into song. . . .

The Businessmen's Floor Show

Dressed in their look-alike business clothes, and pleased as punch, the Men-in-Suits stood in a row together on stage, singing in unison:

> *Oh ho ho!*
> *What a jolly good thing it is to know*
> *That all will be well,*
> *That all will be well!*
> *Why? Because . . .*

We are the men who run the world!
We love everybody – just
As long as they are good,
As long are they are good.
So whatever you do, just
Mind that you take your cue
From Dow, GE, and don't forget
Abbott Laboratories too!
(Send s.a.s.e. for complete list)
And know: We love you! No matter how it
May seem to you!

Oh! We are the happy men who own the world!
Without us, just what would life be?
Things would not be so happ-eee
Just watch us and you'll soon seeee!

They disappeared in a puff of cigar smoke, while the audience clapped and cheered wildly. Confetti swirled down to cover everybody.

Famous Women Argue About Whether Women Are Getting Anywhere

Friedrich had gone in search of some further peach and banana-prune lava cocktails. Ariadne was drawn by the increasingly animated sound of female voices nearby. In fact, a rather heated conversation was taking place between some quite Famous and Notorious Women.

As Ariadne approached, she heard Eva Braun saying, 'If women are oppressed, it's their own fault!'

Simone de Beauvoir shot her a scathing look of contempt. 'That's like saying it was the Jews' fault they were gassed, it is the blacks' fault they are oppressed. Really, how absurd!' She reached up to adjust her turban.

'Just like some Jews were nervous when others spoke out,' Hannah Arendt nodded, 'They said, "Just keep quiet, we're doing fine, don't be a troublemaker, don't protest the ghettos." Some

183

women are doing the same thing. It's fear that makes women quiet. It's not that women don't know about their situation.'

Gertrude Stein stepped forward. 'Eva, you're just like all those other women who fall in love with men. You're an apologist for the system.'

'What do you mean?' Margaret Mead glared at Stein. 'I had several husbands and lovers!'

Stein persisted, unperturbed. 'And, you might have gone to university. Hitler would have paid for it,' she sniffed.

Dorothy Parker took notes, finding it all too, *too* hilarious.

'Let's not pick on each other! Let's think about what we can do to help the women on Earth,' Eleanor Roosevelt *was* always intelligent. 'Don't you see how the ideology of "the family" is being used right now in the US, the UK, Germany – everywhere – as a political weapon against women? There's fundamentalism not only in the Arab world, but right there at home in the West. . . .

'In this climate of family-hysteria a woman must be either for or against "the family". Whether she's married is a "test" – almost like membership of the communist party was in the fifties. . . .'

Ariadne smiled hello to everyone, but especially to Eleanor, for whom she had a special fondness. 'What I saw on Earth was an attempt at a New Counter-Reformation, turning back all the individual rights won over the last two hundred years. It is a Backlash against all the rights women worked so hard to achieve. The situation is at a real turning point. Women are questioning their allegiance to the patriarchal family in a great cultural revolution – one overlooked or not understood by the major press political analysts – and reformulating, democratizing the family. Women still want love, of course – to love and be loved – but they want a love that is equal and real, not a love that is draining them emotionally, or one that is psychologically or physically violent.

'Women are still pressured to feel that to be a "normal woman", she should always have a man; a "real woman" should be married! ("What's a pretty girl like you doing without a man?") Statistically, the fact is that adult women now live half of their lives on their own: this includes the years they are not married, sometimes the years after a divorce, or years when they are widows. But the question is, why must everything but "good old marriage" be branded as "abnormal"? They're using the family as a device for social control, to make women feel they must fit in, to point out that this is the only way that women *do* fit in! As reproductive models, not people in their own right. . . . '

Hannah Arendt had a chilling analysis: 'Hitler too made a big point of the fact that women's primary function must be to bear children for men and the state. Support the family! Now it's the same thing all over again! Totalitarian thinking always pushes women back into the home – or tries to.'

'The climate in the film industry is something awful too! Did you see the movie *Fatal Attraction*? The star was like a medieval witch who had to be burned, because she tried (supposedly) to break up a family. Talk about pro-family propaganda! We never had such dreary scenarios in our movies in the thirties,' a sultry Carole Lombard declared. 'We would never have done them!'

Mme de Beauvoir observed astutely, 'The current glorification of the hierarchical family is the Counter-Reformation. It is against all that the sixties and seventies stood for, people's right to think for themselves.'

'We used to be able to critique the family,' Margaret Mead rapped her walking stick on the floor for emphasis. 'But now it sounds "un-American". (I do, however, remember a few knocks they gave me for Children of Samoa – those kids had too much freedom for their taste!)'

'Women on Earth are calling for the democratization of the family,' Ariadne said with pride. 'They want a new emotional contract, a new emotional equality.'

Amelia Earhart arrived in her chic aviator's hat and flight pants: 'Well, girls, from what I can see, now women on Earth have got Power Dressing and Power Lunches, but they still don't have Power!'

In a nutshell – yes. 'Is this why you decided to leave and not come back?' Ariadne asked her. But it was too late; everyone was talking at once, and before Ariadne could hear her answer, Amelia was swept away by a group of dancers discoing right through the middle of their group. Just like trying to talk to a friend anyplace, Ariadne thought. I should have said, Let's have lunch!

Ariadne went in search of Friedrich, and soon saw him leaning against a tall baroque column, holding one giant (de-fizzed) lava

185

goblet in each hand. She rushed over to him. 'Darling! I'm *sorry* you were waiting! You won't believe who I ran into. . . .' He stopped her from talking by pouring one lava cocktail into her mouth, simultaneously downing the other himself in one gulp. Ariadne's mood changed abruptly. . . .

'Kiss me . . . mmmmmmm, oh, yes, like that!' And she pressed herself against Friedrich and the column, feeling his wide chest and his strong hips against her breasts and clitoris, and his penis bulging against her. . . .

'Let's go out on the balcony – '

Soon they were outside in the dark. 'Oh, darling – ' Ariadne sighed, and they left the balcony to walk under some shady bushes. Now, wrapped in the cool night air and in each other's arms, Ariadne twisted and squirmed with pleasure against Friedrich's hard body, then moaned as he undid his zipper and brought his penis out of his pants. She took it in her mouth, into her throat, she was all over it – then she lay down on the ground, inviting Friedrich to come inside her. . . . Soon she felt his hard penis touching her wet and swollen lips, then in, in, deeper, and finally, all the closeness she longed for – it wasn't enough – now, each time he thrust into her body, she could feel the strangest, sweetest sensations, a vast ache and longing, almost a fever, to have more, more . . . until they lay entwined in each other's arms, repeating over and over, 'I love you, I love you. Oh, my darling, my sweetest. . . .'

A little later (maybe much later) they returned to the ballroom. . . .

Jupiter's Cirque Fantastique

Hundreds of animals and people sat in the ballroom, watching the stage expectantly: Jupiter's floor show – 'In Celebration of the Animals of the Galaxy' – was about to begin. 'So this is his surprise!' Ariadne sat forward in her seat.

The curtain rose and the audience was treated to a luscious glowing salmon-coloured shell with matching Austrian taffeta drapes circling round it, and a second tier of creamy white satin drapes above those. The drapes were like hundreds of *marrons glacés*, the white fudge poured out in ribbons and dried there in mouth-watering, shiny, sensuous folds. In the centre, a small magenta silk curtain opened slightly to reveal a midnight-blue landscape, illuminated by twinkling stars.

Suddenly, out of the opening, people and animals flew onto the stage, as the *Boutique Fantastique* music started to play. First, clowns came out with a large Easter egg wrapped in shiny red paper, followed by several yellow chicks and ducks. In the Chicks' Dance, four chicks danced together in a row, while the lights they wore on their heads and wrists twinkled and blinked in time to the music. Two horses stood elegantly on each side of the stage while the chicks danced, holding old-fashioned blue and gold banners saying 'Cirque'.

Then bears of all sizes appeared, waltzing onto the stage to the strains of 'Babes in Toyland'. They lay on their backs and twirled giant yellow eggs on their feet in the air, while others transported to the front of the stage a giant Easter basket with a single shining scarlet egg. To the roll of drums, it hatched, and out popped three white baby panda bears with a scooter.

The stage lights changed to deep blue, and large white birds flew onto the stage. Quietly, other shadowy figures in animal masks formed a chorus at the back of the stage. Gradually the lights deepened to purple, and the stage became a mysterious grotto. Small votive lights flickered to a popular Italian version of 'Ave Maria' and the whole audience began to sing. For the finale, Rughetta carried in a blazing candelabra in the form of a star, and presented it in tribute to all the animals.

The curtain fell with the muffled rustle of taffeta, and the entire cast danced together before the curtain for the final number – Jupiter and Rughetta, Fala and Silvia Rea, all the bears and chicks, the two elegant horses with the blue and gold banners saying 'Cirque', and the bears and pandas on their scooters.

Now, all together, they formed the lost symbolic Crest of the Ancient World, wherein animals and humans shared power and lived together equally.

Moved by the display, Cleopatra whispered to Friedrich, 'This is why animals surrounded me always on my Ancient Throne; the

187

prehistoric legacy was that we humans should always be accompanied and protected by animal consorts. We revered them and their spirits, as they revered us. To this day, you will still see on royal crests a king or queen flanked by a pair of animals, one on each side of the throne.'

Tumultuous applause greeted this finale of the Animal Circus. No one wanted it to be over, so the animals repeated the final scene several times, forming an even larger Crest, standing proudly on each others' shoulders in formation, while the lights alternated from magenta to yellow to blue-mauve, then back again, faster and faster.

The Invitation

As the lights intensified and the crowd's clapping became louder and ever more ecstatic, Ariadne felt a light tap on her shoulder. Turning round in her seat, she saw a tall, serious-looking white Persian cat reaching across the others in her row to hand her a small, understated white envelope.

Taking it in her hand, Ariadne opened it to find inside an engraved invitation:

Invitation for Ariadne Rite
Ceremonial Celebration and Debate

Topic: The World Before History
Time: Midnight
Place: The Far Side of Heaven
Transportation: The Swan

– Admit One –

Ariadne looked at the card, wondering, What can it mean? Then, she remembered Cleopatra had told her there was *another* side of Heaven ... a time before history. 'I'll be right back,' she told Friedrich, 'I'm going to see what this is all about.'

188

Outside, Ariadne walked down a shadowy lane, where every-thing was still. Suddenly, she heard the flapping of wings. A beautiful white bird came towards her. As the swan swooped down, stopping in front of Ariadne, it spoke, offering to guide Ariadne through the secret passageways to the Far Side of Heaven. Ariadne quickly accepted the swan's offer.

Dense fog surrounded the hidden passages through which the swan transported Ariadne. In the half light, the swan delivered a message: 'There are two parallel worlds. All beauty is there. You have only to see for it to be real. Time is an illusion.' Just as Ariadne was going to ask the swan more about this riddle, she bade Ariadne farewell, and left her on the Far Shore.

The Herstory of the World Before Patriarchy

On the shore, Ariadne was met by Athena, who took her hand and led her along a leafy path until they reached a stone door hidden by underbrush. At a signal, the door opened, and Ariadne passed through it to step out into an open-air proscenium. Many women were seated around a small circular stage. Ariadne was struck by the posture and dignity of the women, their nobility and the directness of their gaze. Their faces were unselfconscious: they seemed not to feel they must be amusing or decorative – the hallmark of many women in the late twentieth century, Ariadne had observed. These women, with their serene expressions, did not look under pressure to prove their right to existence – either by being mothers or by being beautiful, 'desirable'. They *are* beautiful, Ariadne thought, but this is a different kind of beauty.

Many were wearing clothes of ancient design, some markedly different, as if they had travelled a long distance, or from many places. Their emblems were flowers, deer, dogs and bears.

A tall woman rose. 'I am Isis. Today we, the peaceful Seal Ring Matrilineates of Old Europe, will discuss the possibility of battle with dominant negative forces on Earth.'

Hypatia began the opening ceremony. 'Much of what was beautiful in Earth's past has been obliterated from memory. Here, once a year, we commemorate the truly great societies, now unrecorded, which flourished for thousands of years.'

Two women in long full skirts, with thin, narrow waists, their shoulders, midriffs and breasts bare – and with fantastically ornate jewellery – took centre stage: 'We were two priestesses living on Earth in the time of Old Europe. . . .'

Diktynna and Kallisto continued in unison.

'The story of our civilization goes back beyond, far beyond, the Greeks. Our culture endured for three thousand years, from the seventh to the fourth millennium BC. It was the society from which classical Greek culture took many of its roots.

'Our religion had its centre in goddess worship – the worship of creation, pregnancy, rebirth, and the cycle of life. The art and traditions of this sacred religion continued in an unbroken line for over twenty thousand years, going back much further than our culture, and stretching from the Russian steppes all the way to Romania and the Greek islands.

'Agriculture was developed during our time, with the combination of certain grasses to make wheat. This made the first stable settlements possible – the first towns.

'But all this came to a sad end, when our civilization was overrun. Our cities were peaceful, they contained no walls for defence – notably different from the groups that conquered us, the Indo-Europeans from the Eastern steppes. Their culture was authoritarian, highly stratified, pastoral, mobile and war-oriented. This group eventually superimposed itself on all Europe and the Middle East. We, however, prevailed at the southern and western fringes of Europe until the end.

'These Indo-Europeans came in three waves. From beyond the Russian steppes they travelled westward to India and the Mediterranean, between 4500 and 2500 BC. During this period, the female deities, or more accurately, the Goddess Creatrix in her many aspects, was largely replaced by predominantly male divinities.

'Our culture's mythical imagery and religious practices were continued in the latest historical period on an island, Crete. The Minoan culture on Crete mirrored our earlier life, depicting the same glorification of the virgin beauty of life in all its aspects.'

Reflecting on what she had just seen and heard, Ariadne told herself that if the world before history were anywhere near as sophisticated and witty as these two women appeared (she marvelled at Kallisto's earrings!), then Earth historians had a totally fallacious idea of pre-history! Why, they seemed to think everybody before 'The Rise of the West' was running around nude, living in caves, with mud stuck in their hair: cave men dragging around 'their' women. Earth historians said history was only two or three thousand years old; these women declared it to be twenty-five to thirty thousand years old! Of course, the animals could probably tell an even greater story. . . .

Diktynna and Kallisto now passed around a famous statue, the (later named) *Venus of Willendorf*, only a few inches high. 'Our religion made many of these small statues (this one is an original, made centuries before we were on Earth), which emphasized the mysterious elements of the cycle of life: the miracle of childbearing anatomy, the changes during pregnancy. Later, during the sixth millennium, the period of early agriculture (which is our period!), the goddess image was transformed; she became more vigorous and less obese.'

Kallisto held up a ring. 'Look at this! It's an elegant onyx gem from Knossos on Crete, with an engraving portraying the goddess as a bee, flanked by winged dogs. The dogs seem to like her a lot – one looks like he's barking in friendliness, sort of talking to her.'

Laphria, who was sitting next to Ariadne, and looked to Ariadne like a young demigoddess, leaned closer to Ariadne to explain: 'As a Supreme Creator who created from her own substance, the Great Goddess was the primary deity of the Old European pantheon. She was not the same as the later Indo-European Earth-Mother (though she is often confused with her). The Earth-Mother was not in herself a creative principle, as it was the male sky-god who was dominant. The Great Goddess of the earlier traditions was independent: she represented Nature with all its brilliance and wildness, its purity and strangeness.'

Ariadne had been spellbound ever since the ceremony began. Her mind was racing. 'Does this mean that the real symbolism of Mary's virginity is not that she didn't have "impure" sex – but that she had the ability to create life? That she was magical?

Does Mary's symbolism go back to the time of the early Great Goddess?'

Ariadne remembered Cleo's explanation of the pyramids, how they were created with their secret underground passageways to resemble a woman's uterus, so that the dead could return there and be reborn. As Cleopatra had said, 'First, Aridane, to go into the pyramid, you have to travel through a small, narrow opening until you come to a bigger room – just like going through the vaginal canal to reach a woman's uterus – then you come to the larger room, the hidden room inside the pyramid: this is the hidden life-producing chamber inside women's bodies. Do you see??!'

Ariadne's mind raced on, 'But this could mean that the pyramids are also related to Creation worship. . . . .'

The ceremony over, the women left the stage. They proceeded down a path to sit under the trees, and turn their attention to the state of things to come.

Heaven's Wrath

'We have been watching Earth,' Artemis spoke. 'Some of our favourite animals are dying. This has aroused our Royal Wrath.' Silence. Fumes seemed to rise out of her lovely head, and her bows quivered in their brace.

She regained her composure. 'We must stop those who are creating this mischief. They are followers of the very same archaic culture that destroyed our civilization 2,500 years ago. Our culture is 20,000 years old! Theirs is only 2,500. We can rise again!'

Ariadne stood up bravely, and said simply: 'How?'

Jeanne d'Arc Debates the Nature of Post-Modern Revolution with the Ancient Matrilineal Goddesses

Isis, Cleopatra's favourite goddess, restated the issue: 'The condition of the planet Earth is worsening: more and more women are living in poverty. Forest animals are faced with savage death. We are asking, "What would a revolution under current conditions be like? Could people overthrow patriarchal thinking and heal the natural and emotional environment in time to save the Earth? Should this be a revolution in thinking, an ideological revolution – or a physical taking of power?"'

Rachel Carson spoke up. 'I don't think the change needed is a revolution; I think reforms will come incrementally and often because someone has changed her life – perhaps a husband will get the message or a child will be raised differently, or one small company will change its policy.'

Jeanne d'Arc stood scowling, dressed in full armour. 'I'm not in favour of ideological revolution. The twentieth-century women's movement lacks force. It has only done what Marx did: shown what's wrong. It has meticulously documented women's lowly position, over and over. Now, the ecologists are documenting the environmental problems. But what will anyone do? And we here? What will we do?'

The atmosphere was electric, intense. Elizabeth Cady Stanton was first to respond. 'Yes, the twentieth-century movement was naïve. Women thought, especially in the early seventies, that if they presented their case, and it was moral and just, then those in power would simply roll over. But no one in history has yet given up power voluntarily. In a way, some of them were like four-year-olds, stomping their feet and saying, "But it's not fair!" Uncovering the ills is not enough. We have to do something more.'

'Maybe it's a lot to expect in one's lifetime not only to name the problem, but also to solve it,' George Sand smoked quietly in a corner.

Rosa Luxemburg quickly cut in: 'We don't expect to solve it, but why not try?'

'Does slow ideological change really work?' Hypatia queried philosophically. 'I wonder if the twentieth-century truism – "things will be better for our children" – represents reality or fear. Women, from myself in the classical world, to Christine de Pisan in the fifteenth-century, to Simone de Beauvoir in the twentieth, have been using persuasion, discussion, debate, in favour of a more peaceful philosophy. Wave after wave of women have tried to create change of this kind through the centuries, women

193

such as the beguines in Holland. But has any of this discussion changed the basic situation?'

Jeanne d'Arc challenged them: 'If there hasn't been much progress, why aren't you more impatient? Why aren't you prepared to do something?'

Ariadne asked the obvious question: 'How can we change the system without becoming aggressive and warlike – taking on the very values we dislike?'

'You can only change the ideology if you take power. Rulers control ideology. We must fight for this!' This was Jeanne d'Arc's final answer.

Ariadne reflected, 'I don't think military revolution works. I agree, thinking must change, there must be an ideological revolution – but I'm not sure how to achieve that. . . .'

Speaking in her dense, poetic voice, Sappho observed, 'Being an idealist is frustrating. It's frustrating to live with the belief that things can be improved. Throughout the centuries, I have watched people who stood for higher ideals try to enlighten or wake up others. But their work didn't always take effect. So often, the stronger dominant society just adapted to the changes, turning them to their own advantage. . . .'

The fiery Empress Theodora of Byzantia leapt to her feet. 'For just this reason, something different must be done *now*!' Aphrodite stood at her side in support.

'Should we form a revolutionary ideological brigade ourselves?' Ariadne was ablaze with excitement.

'It's tempting to think in terms of old-fashioned force – revolution,' said Athena (such grace and serenity in her strong body!).

Hypatia, queen of Greek philosophers, stressed, 'No other oppressed group besides women has been expected to educate their oppressors.'

'We Spanish (and the British too) didn't give up our colonies to be *nice*,' Queen Isabella of Spain entered the discussion forcefully. 'It was only when people decided to kill our soldiers that we gave in – only when the colonies fought back.'

'Yes,' Alice Paul spoke up. 'Women weren't "given" the vote, they *took* it. Just ask Emmeline Pankhurst!'

'Conquer them!' Jeanne d'Arc urged. 'Then it'll be easy to change their minds! Otherwise, you will have little choice.'

'I do not believe most women want a revolution.' Karen Horney forcefully opposed this line of argument. 'Men's revolutions usually don't work, they are just change-of-male-dictator events that result in the deaths of many people. They are "revolution" with a small "r". What we want is Real Revolution – ideological revolution. It's slower, but it works.'

Ariadne suggested, 'Maybe it's happening. I believe people on Earth now, especially women, want a change. The statistics on physical and emotional violence against women are staggering, women are becoming more and more alienated from the dominant culture – yet at the same time, strangely free and happy. They form the backbone of the ecology movement.'

Yet even as she spoke, she sensed that she might be wrong . . . pictures of otters lying dead on the banks of rivers and streams flashed before her eyes, and she gasped, 'But this is too slow!'

A heated discussion ensued, in which many voices were heard: Can there be a revolution? And against what? Should there be one? What kind of revolution – a military revolution, or an ideological one? Do women have the right to take back their own rights by force?

'Yes,' Catharine the Great of Russia was heard to affirm. 'Otherwise we will never get them.'

Rosa Luxemburg offered, 'While being patient is a good quality, if people are too patient, there is a real danger that the situation will just go on and on. I say some women should talk and explain, others should boycott manufacturers of poisons, others should join the activists of Greenpeace, some should enter government – and some should follow in my steps.'

Gertrude Stein had been sitting quietly on the Left Bank, but she rose to announce amid the hubbub, 'There's one thing you all seem to overlook. You say the world can change through ideological revolution, yet you forget that today the media control the ideology, an ideology they don't want to change.'

Silence.

'If the media control opinion,' Joan Scott thought aloud, 'then "the masses" will never get a chance to make a decision based on the facts. Perhaps there can never be a bottom-up re-thinking process. Therefore, the only way to change mentality would be violent revolution, a *coup* by a small group. Isn't that theoretically right? And then you are back to where Lenin started: "If people won't or can't do it, let's do it for them." But this led to an evil dictatorship, which is all too frequently the outcome of revolution. The people? Are they helped in all of this? Or hurt as much as they are helped?'

Jeanne flashed, impatiently, 'Useless questions! Think seriously about using some form of army to take over the television and radio stations before it's too late. (You may have noticed that this is where the 1989–90 Romanian Revolution began.) Don't delay! Fight while you can. You may live to regret waiting!'

Elizabeth Cady Stanton joined in, 'I'd like to see a revolution in thinking, but I don't like blood-baths. Even if it could lead to a change in mentality.... Isn't there another way?'

'About changing the ideology,' Athena broke in, 'I'll never forget how the Greeks used me as part of their ideological changeover from our ancient pre-history religion – in which women were equal or supreme – to their own patriarchal system. To work me in took them several centuries. I was originally listed in the early Greek pantheon as an independent goddess, then later they declared I had sprung out of Zeus's head! (Those men *do* have a problem giving birth.) And for centuries, they've been transforming Maria....'

Ariadne began thinking of what George – was it George? – had said about the mythical scenarios used by reporters.... Even in ancient Greece, then, the mythology was political, reality was consciously constructed through the stories with which the civilization identified itself. 'Reality' was created through repeating these stories over and over.

Now I understand why.... Whether 'news' stories will be accepted, and the twist they will be given, is fought over every day by news editors, media, critics, authors and publishers, Ariadne thought, remembering Earth.

Isis looked at Ariadne wisely. 'Convincing people involves the ritualistic telling and repetition of stories. To work, propaganda has to be almost pseudo-religious. It has to have indoctrination qualities. Christianity achieved this through constant repetition of scriptural stories, combined with mysterious ritual. But even Christianity eventually had to adopt the Mother Cult of Maria –

196

originally part of our "pagan" pantheon – before it could be accepted and survive.'

But Ariadne was feeling frustrated. 'Media, media, media! That's all I ever hear! Media and ideology!' And she pressed her hands to her head. 'Stop!' Was she having a nightmare? Reality always seemed to come back to the same point!

The night deepened and the debate intensified, some claiming to be for 'revolution', and others claiming to be for 'love' and 'understanding'. Defectors began hanging back and whispering, 'What kind of revolution is this going to be? I mean, will I have to give up my TV? What about my stereo and my air-conditioning?'

'What about my make-up?' another blurted out.

'Oh, stop worrying! You will not have to return to mud huts!' laughed Hypatia.

Hera's White Paper: The Eco-Feminist Programme for the Future of Earth

Hera asked for order: 'We conclude by endorsing a White Paper entitled "Women as Revolutionary Agents of Change".

'This paper – like White Papers everywhere – calls for more discussions (!) of the following eco-feminist goals for Earth:

1. Renourishment of the environment, both spiritual and physical;
2. A large-scale public debate about changing the aggressive ideology of Earth;
3. Re-empowerment of the animals;
4. Deconstructing and re-imagining the emotions of love;
5. Financial and quality-of-life re-organization between rich and poor;
6. Equal access to education and health care for all – those with money and those without;
7. A revision of the Ministry of Culture, that is, the TV empires; all news reporters to be elected; the founding of an international women's network;
8. An end to hazardous factory emissions and manufacturing

wastes, which cause environmental pollution, decay, an increase in acid rain, the death of the forests and ill-health in all living things;

9. A democratic global debate sponsored by television about the power of multinational corporations, the new 'states' which transcend the power of national governments; what this means for self-determination, individual rights and the 'democratic process';

10. Creation of a new spiritual culture.

As the meeting broke up, George Sand muttered to her companions, 'Ah, but what will we do after the revolution when we have established a perfect order? It will be boring!'

'Oh no,' Catharine the Great retorted, cynically. 'Then you'll have to fight the revolutionaries! There will be a CIA and an FBI and a KGB to establish, and then the disinformation system. You'll be busy. It will be no different than the old court intrigues.'

But Athena stepped forward to protest. 'No! We must steer beyond these hurdles, rise above these internecine rivalries! We have a vision of the future, and we must work to create it.'

'Yes,' a voice floated over Ariadne's shoulder. 'Our own vision can create a humane and joyous world – a peaceful world – if only we shall continue!' It was the great Ms Spender, grave and heroic woman of Planet Earth.

Ariadne's Dream-Vision

Ariadne decided she had to rest, and she lay back on the grass, gazing up at the vast, deep blue sky, while the voices continued around her. She began to feel a little distant. . . . It had been good to be here, this discussion did mean something, but still, another day-night was passing, and nothing had changed on Earth.

Just then – was she imagining it? – Ariadne thought she saw the planet Earth revolving before her eyes. . . . There were mysterious images of thousands of animals leaving, or at least their souls – a mass exodus, a mass vaporization of spirit matter wafting away from the planet, as it heaved in its death throes. . . .

Another scene took its place. Now Ariadne saw the animals marching across the galaxy, hundreds and hundreds of them. They marched across the galaxy, across the sky. . . . Where were they going? Were these animals of Heaven on their way to Earth? What would they do there?

As Ariadne was about to find out, the scene faded. . . .

Back at the Ball

Wearing Laphria's beautiful, pale yellow, wasp-waisted skirt, Ariadne found herself once again outside the Celestial Ballroom, where Jupiter was waiting for her.

It was almost dawn now, and inside, the few remaining people were lounging around on the comfortable old velvet couches. A small orchestra played café tunes from the 1920s and 1930s, á la Fritz Kreisler and Robert Stoltz, with a few czardas thrown in here and there. Jupiter took Ariadne to one corner, where Fala, Cleo and George were slouching around, playing charades.

'Where is Friedrich?' Ariadne asked, her hand on Jupiter's head.

Cleopatra pointed to the centre of the big ballroom, where Friedrich sat at a piano, talking intensely with three other musicians. Ariadne walked towards them, Jupiter trotting after her. She recognized Wanda Landowska, Clara Schumann, and Prokofiev, all hotly debating with Friedrich as to whether Russian music came out of the tradition of nineteenth-century German music. 'My dear fellow, if Shostakovich ever had anything to do with Brahms or Wagner. . . . You can't seriously be proposing this?'

Just then, Friedrich spotted Ariadne. 'Where on Earth have you been all this time? I was worried – and I missed you!'

Ariadne ran to put her arms round Friedrich. Delighted to see each other, they went for a quick spin around the floor to a spicy czarda that happened to be playing. Friedrich held Ariadne close, and she just managed to tell him, 'I went to a special meeting in the Matrilineal Seal Ring Kingdom, and I learned – '

'The what??!!' Friedrich stopped dancing to look at her. Heaven could be exotic, Friedrich thought, but a Seal Ring Kingdom?!

How many more Heavenly Galaxies were there going to be?

'Wow!' Cleopatra raced over, having heard the news. 'Were you there? That meeting was supposed to be one of the biggest confabs in Heaven history. You were lucky to be there! And – you must have heard about its Great History – the history, I mean *herstory*, that existed long before me! Before Egypt! Before patriarchy – we used to learn about it in our scrolls. I hear they still teach it to school children in Romania. . . .

'And Ariadne,' Cleopatra's flood of words continued, 'what was the ceremony like? Was Jeanne d'Arc there? Did they ask her why she was so military – and why she used her strength to save a king, a hierarchical power system? I advised Jeanne not to go, that they would just attack her for not promoting non-violence. But maybe she was right, maybe something productive can come out of it. Both sides might combine forces. . . . Ariadne, what did *you* think of it?'

Ariadne smiled at Cleopatra, so many things on her mind. . . . 'It was all deeply moving,' she said. 'I learned so much. I've got to think about everything a new way now. It's time to build a plan, a completely different way of seeing things, a way that will work. One that will last.' She looked at Friedrich, and feeling strengthened by Jupiter's warm fur rubbing against her legs, she added, 'And . . . don't laugh . . . I dreamed that the animals will make a great march across the galaxy.'

The Final Fragments of Swirling Conversation With People Who May Have Drunk Too Much Champagne

Just then, Beauvoir and Sartre, dancing together sleepily to an old fox-trot ballad, 'I Love Paris', passed nearby.

Ariadne had to ask just *one* more question – especially as women were very much on her mind at this moment – and she waved to Simone, who stopped dancing and came over for a chat.

'Tell me, Simone,' Ariadne pleaded, '*is* the Other transformed? Was I right? You must be able to see the Future – you who are permanently here – I can't! Tell me, *are* women changing who they are and what they think of men and of the society in a great cultural revolution? Will the world solve its problems? Will the animals be saved?'

These questions drew a rather large crowd. Especially as Beauvoir and Sartre started arguing. Engels whispered something to Rosa Luxemburg, who turned to him, saying loudly, 'Shut up. You never did understand women. That's why we lost the revolution!'

'You have to see the present as history,' Marx muttered cryptically. He turned to Beauvoir. 'I just want to say one thing to you. It's about the Other – as you call women. The irony of it all is that the Other *is* transforming – but into what? The yuppie pro-corporate model. A bunch of conformists, women in men's clothing (or are they men, in women's clothing?!) Is this the way the Other becomes the Seer? The great new actor on the historical stage Miss Rite has proclaimed?' And he glared at Simone triumphantly.

Cleopatra, Ariadne and Simone ignored him, thinking how ludicrous it was that he had to win the argument to be happy. They began laughing and chattering amongst themselves, trying on each other's jewellery, fixing one another's hair, and just generally having good time. Ariadne looked happy, terribly happy, and she leaned over to giggle about something with Cleopatra. . . .

More Absurdity

. . . Too happy, probably much too happy, because Tocqueville and some of the other Oracles spotted her and headed in her direction, saying things like, 'Ah . . . here is our favourite little idealist again! Tell us, this evening, do you still believe in the intelligent and wise thinking of the masses? How's the revolution coming?'

'Well,' said Ariadne, jarred back to another state of mind, 'all I know is, the women's movement on Earth has been outlining lack of equal pay for ages and it has not changed things. And when Jupiter and I tried to point out the problems for the animals . . . I'd like to tell myself that it's all changing, it's just slow, that

201

people's minds are changing, that children's lives will be different. ·
But will they be? And what about those alive now? Don't they
count for anything? Don't they need fairness, too? The animals,
the streams and rivers, they do not deserve to die. If things are
not changed. . .'

'But we *had* this conversation before!' Tocqueville lost his cool
and shouted at her.

'Yes, but we never reached any conclusion!' Ariadne shouted
back.

'I'm tired of you and your worries,' Wellington joined in rudely.
'What is the point of all this marching heroically into some supposed Utopian Future? All that people like you really want is
to feel how noble you are, the easy way – just by spouting
proverbs.'

'It's *you* who are being simplistic!' Ariadne stomped her foot
like Alice, now irritated herself.

Friedrich didn't know who these people were, but he did know
that he and Ariadne and Jupiter had done more than spout
proverbs. 'Look, fella,' he began, 'I don't know exactly who you
are, but you seem to be missing an essential part of your mind.
There are concrete conditions which need changing. You can't
just stick your head in the sand, and expect to survive. There
are people who are heroic, and others (maybe like you) who
either Do Nothing, or who Do Harmful Things to the world
around them.'

'Yes,' George Orwell turned to Tocqueville and the others
assembled. 'How would you say the Jews and gypsies should
have changed the German leadership in 1942, say?'

Faced with this United Front, Tocqueville became a little more
reasonable – for him. 'Ariadne, this is just a regular human
problem. People are not bright,' he remarked. 'Eliminate all the
stupid people, and things will take care of themselves!'

'But are they "stupid" for lack of education, or because they
refuse to learn?' Ariadne found him deeply prejudiced!

'If you could answer that, you woud have solved the riddle of
the universe,' Alexis laughed.

Since Ariadne had never seen him laugh before, she wondered
if he had been having lava cocktails too? If he would just loosen
up a little. . .

George read her mind. 'Ariadne, leave this guy and his pals in the dust! They're the past! The future battle is about something else. It's about the penetration of the psyche by unacceptable information.'

'Yes, but. . .' Ariadne just wanted to get away from Everything. Hadn't she already endured enough of this mind-torture the other day in the endless Whist Club Debate? She had already been polite until her hair stood on end to all these people, but now. . . . She began to tell Friedrich about the day of the big Heavenly Debate. 'I did learn a lot, it was sort of fun. . . . But now their ideas seem so limited to me! In the labyrinth, I have found other ideas, new ideas. . . . I want to go beyond all this, reformulate the questions. . . .'

Her face lit up. 'Yes! That's it! I want to reformulate the questions . . . and institute a parallel ideological universe.' She pulled a little white neon pencil out of her purse and began to take notes, 'And I will! In my Very Next Book! I'll figure it out, no matter how hard it is, no matter what it takes. . . .' (Another Scarlett O'Hara here? Has she seen *Gone with the Wind* too many times?)

'But first . . .' and she looked warmly, *very* warmly, at Friedrich, 'can you and I go off and take a long, long holiday somewhere together? For quite a while?'

Before Friedrich could answer, Ariadne spotted Voltaire coming in her direction, accompanied by a man with a briefcase – a lawyer? She turned round and rushed off in the other direction, running smack into one of the Super-Businessmen, who (glad of his chance) pompously declared, 'Ariadne! My dear! You are just suffering from the Great Mystery of Life. We *all* wonder if Power is somewhere else – it feels so elusive. . . . Women have got it, they just don't believe they've got it. As long as they don't realize it, it's fine with me!' And he tried to pinch her cheek rudely.

Ariadne felt Friedrich's hand in hers – wonderfully, he had caught up with her in her hasty flight – but he wasn't saying very much, in fact he had become strangely silent. She looked inquiringly into his eyes, 'How do you feel, darling? Are you all right? Anything wrong?'

'Well, I'd rather be somewhere alone with you – like in a little cabin far removed from civilization. Surrounded by ten feet of snow. We'd spend all day and night making love and playing house together.'

'I love you so much, my darling.' Ariadne pressed her body close to his.

Jupiter raced up, clutching the *Heaven Gazette* in his mouth. It featured a story about Ariadne and her constant questions: 'Why, Why, Why! That's All She Ever Asks! Who Does She Think She Is, Socrates?' This was their idea of a funny headline. They also reported that Groucho Marx had decided to write a comedy for Broadway about it all. Ariadne was tired and wondered if she was hallucinating. She begins to feel dizzy. . . .

She imagines a confessional scene with a priest who keeps saying, 'What's wrong with you? Don't you know your script? You're supposed to confess your scientific sins.' John Major, Margaret Thatcher and Ronald Reagan appear and agree. She is wearing a low-cut dress with a rhinestone cross on her heaving chest, her hair cascading over the front. (And it's sweeps week too!) The tension and excitement are palpable. Will she confess? She runs out of the studio and a spy chase scene ensues, in which an airplane tries to run her down. . . .

Jupiter is there too, in a basket on her arm, and someone is calling her Dorothy. As she looks down at her shoes, she thinks clearly just long enough to call out, 'There's no place like home!'

Then she hears Friedrich's voice as if from a great distance: 'I think one has been successful in life if one has found one other person to love. This is the most important thing. . . .'

She sees them all coming towards her – Tocqueville, Marx, Gertrude Stein, Wellington, and Pompadour – all with conflicting theories. Someone starts calling her a Silly Idealist again, and she calls them a cynical myopic selfish dope.

'We already had this conversation!'

'Yeah, but we didn't finish anything, we didn't solve it!'

'You are a bubble-headed idiot, you can't fix the universe!'

'Why not???'

'Because you can't! And who cares anyway! Can't we enjoy our drinks in peace???'

'Yeah! let's forget this – and have fun!'

204

Ariadne and Jupiter realize they are back at Square One; they remember their first TV talk show that day so long ago, when they sat naïvely in the studio audience and ended up chanting, 'More fun! More fun!'

They join in the chant again now, and soon everybody is chanting and singing, swaying back and forth, beating on the tables with their drinks and whatever else they can find: 'WE WANT MORE FUN! WE WANT MORE FUN!'

And it becomes a giant sound, a roar, rising to unimaginable heights of furious intensity, until the whole room is dissolving in her brain, twirling round and round, the singing ringing through it, creating a truly riotous Hollywood finish. The credits are about to scroll, when suddenly . . .

Alfred Hitchcock Changes the Script

Someone shouts, 'Cut!'

It's Hitch. 'No, no, no!' he screams. '*Cut*! This is not right, that ending is not working!' He can't stand it anymore, he knows he can do much better than this. 'There's only one way this story can come to a sensible end,' he says.

Ariadne is curious to see what the great movie director (who has as his first assistant, Andy Warhol) will do that is different. 'But first,' the master of suspense announces, 'a word from our sponsor. . . .'

During the commercial, frantic preparations for the next act are made, and suddenly Ariadne finds herself next to Friedrich, hanging from Mount Rushmore. They are dangling over the precipice, holding on by their fingertips, thousands of feet of free-fall below them. Elvis Trouble, the biggest and the baddest of the *Power Press* brothers, is dancing on their knuckles with a gleeful grin. . . .

Friedrich turns to Ariadne with a desperate look on his face. 'Is this part of one of his films? I haven't seen this one. Tell me, how does it end?'

'Well,' Ariadne pants, 'your part is played by Cary Grant. I am Eva Marie Saint. In the ending . . .'

205

But just then, they look up to see Cleopatra's luminescent white spaceship hovering above them, and Cleopatra's pet asp, Jennifer, coiling down to lift them up. The strains of *The Blue Danube* are emanating from the open door, where Cleopatra beckons, and Jupiter smiles radiantly at them from on high. . . .

'Hurry up, you two!' Cleopatra and Jupiter call out above the whirr of the spaceship. Cleopatra is wearing a lime-green stretch-satin pilot's suit, her hair slicked back under a moon-shaped diamond tiara. The lights of the ship are blinking (it's in 'Park') while the ship waits to take off. . . . 'By the way, this is not, I repeat, *not*, Hitchcock's idea. I can do better than that guy, any day. Say, are you two coming or not?'

Trouble begins to run around in circles, his hands pressed to his head, screaming that he has lost his mind. (And he can't even use this story, nobody would believe it. . . .)

Jennifer hovers over them, ready to wind round their waists and pull them up to Heaven. 'Did you know,' she whispers, 'that the snake is an ancient symbol of Eternal Life, of knowledge and wisdom?' And as she coils round both Ariadne and Friedrich, lifting them up, she tells them, 'You should read Elaine Pagels's and Marija Gimbutas's books, which tell the true early symbolism of us snakes.' Ariadne promises to read them as soon as she gets home. She's about to pull out a pad to jot down the titles when Friedrich tells her to cool it, at least wait until they get into the spaceship. . . .

Ariadne and Friedrich smile at each other as the asp lifts them up, up, up – through the bright blue sky, back to Paradise!

They climb on board. Jupiter is turning spectacular somersaults and shouting, 'Hip hip hooray! We're all together again! Together again!' And he jumps up to kiss Ariadne.

The door closes behind them.

Flying Away
in Cleopatra's Pearlescent Spaceship

As Cleopatra's pearlescent white Lucite spaceship with its golden crest takes off, it writes in fuchsia red lipstick across the glowing pink golden sky:

Ciao!!!
Love to Everybody!!!

Winking its lights, it disappears into the distance until it is nothing but a tiny speck, then . . . nothing.

Inside, Jupiter takes Ariadne aside. 'Ariadne, will things go on being the same between us?'

'Oh Jupiter, for us it will always and forever be the same! Let's go! Who knows what adventures lie ahead of us!' Then, turning to Friedrich, Ariadne holds out her arms. As they go into orbit, Ariadne and Friedrich kiss. And the Earth is moved.

THE END – or is it?